Shooting Stars
A Surah Stormsong Novel
~Book One~

H. D. Gordon

To Aisha
my BFF you always
H. D. Gordon

For the lovers and the fighters.

BOOKS BY H. D. GORDON

Blood Warrior
The Alexa Montgomery Saga: Book One

Half Black Soul
The Alexa Montgomery Saga: Book Two

The Rise
The Alexa Montgomery Saga: Book Three

Redemption
The Alexa Montgomery Saga: Book Four

Joe

"I know it's not much but it's the best I can do, my gift is my song, yeah, and this one's for you." —Elton John *Your Song*

"Anyway, the thing is, what I really mean, yours are the sweetest eyes I've ever seen." —Elton John *Your Song*

PART I: GIVE AN INCH
CHAPTER ONE

Charlie could tell there was something wrong with the old man as soon as he walked in the door. He couldn't pinpoint the source of the wrongness because it seemed to be everything and nothing at once. The way the old man dragged his left foot a little as he shuffled toward him. (Could be Charlie's imagination.) The way his creased eyelids seemed to be drooping a touch too much. (He could just be tired.) The way even the tattered cloak on the old man's back seemed not to ripple as he moved, but hang stiffly over boney, sagging shoulders. (Again, could be Charlie's imagination.)

The man pulled out a stool at the bar and took a seat, resting his elbows on the shiny bar top and his chin in his brown-spotted hands. His spoiled liver breath smacked Charlie in the face as he leaned forward. Charlie tucked the rag he'd been using to polish the bar into the waistband of his jeans and eyed the old man for a minute, the soft lights of the bar casting deep shadows in the crevasses of his face, making canyons there.

He was the last customer of the night. The bar would be closing in less than five minutes. Old Brad Milner had a habit of popping in at the last minute for one final nightcap, as if he had gone home just to dig around in his seat cushions for change, which he probably had.

"Hiya, Chuck," he said his voice the rasp of sandpaper on wood.

Charlie smiled. This greeting was normal. It set him at ease a bit. "How ya doin, Mr. Milner?"

The old man waved a hand. "Fine, Chuck. Just fine. Could use a nice shot of your finest whiskey." He winked and grinned. His teeth always made Charlie wish he wouldn't. They were stained with thousands of years' worth of booze and nicotine, the color of rotted wood. But Charlie grinned back. This was an inside joke. By *finest whiskey* Milner meant *cheapest whiskey*.

1

Charlie poured the drink and set it in front of the old man, feeling a tightness in his throat he couldn't explain. "Little late to be out, ain't it?" he asked, a question he posed most every night, and most every night received the same answer.

Milner waved his hand again, grinning now with his wiser-than-you grin, glassy faded blue eyes shining out of his sunken face. "And how many nights you suppose I got left to be staying out, Chuck?" He took a deep swig of his drink, the apple in his throat bobbing grotesquely, and set it down again. The glass thudded heavily on the bar, and a little whiskey sloshed up and spilled over the rim, running down the wrinkles in Milner's hand like dirty rivers. "I hope not too many." He laughed. More spoiled breath hit Charlie's face. He swallowed once and forced a grimace away before it could take stage.

Charlie watched as Milner's eyes went distant and glassy. "There's a storm comin'," the old man rasped, lifting the drink again and finishing off the whiskey in one final grotesque bob of his throat. Another *thunk!* on the bar as he set the glass down. "I can feel it."

Charlie's unease settled back over him in full force. He put his hands on the bar and leaned forward. "Hey, you okay, Mr. Milner?" he asked. "You seem a little…off."

Milner's head tilted in an oddly bird-like fashion, the movement almost too sudden for such an old neck. His creased lids blinked once. Now Charlie's stomach tightened. His hands were fists at his sides.

"Do I?" Milner asked, and let out a belch that made Charlie take an involuntary half-step back.

That was when Merin Nightborn walked through the door. Both Milner and Charlie turned their heads as she entered, and Charlie suppressed a sigh when the Sorceress fixed him with a wide red smile, white teeth gleaming out from behind. The cloak she wore was also red, the color of her family's crest, and her black hair fell down the back of it like a dark hood. She came over to the bar and took a seat two stools down from the old man, flicking her eyes to him once and wiping the disgusted twist of her lips away before it could really settle. Her gloved hands came up and rested on the bar as she leaned forward, pushing her cleavage up and out and smiling again at Charlie.

"Good morning, Mr. Redmine," she said, her speech that of a Highborn.

Charlie nodded, thinking this day might never end. "Lady Nightborn."

Merin's bottom lip pushed out. She had told him a hundred times before to call her by her first name, and he never did. Just as she never called him Chuck or Charlie. His reason for formality was because he didn't want to encourage her, not that she needed encouragement. Her reason was because a lady in her position should not be caught in public addressing him by his common name. Just speaking with him the way she did was slumming for someone like her.

"You don't look happy to see me," she said, her voice taking on that slight whine only a royal woman could affect so perfectly. It always made Charlie want to roll his eyes like a school girl. She was foolish to be talking to Charlie in such a way with Brad Milner present, even if he was just an old drunk.

But her constant hanging around could get him in trouble enough. To disrespect her would be even worse. He smiled his bartender smile. Nice, but just a bit too tight in the lips to be genuine. For a moment he forgot about the unease he'd been feeling because of the peculiarity of the old man, and a new unease took its place.

"Always a pleasure, Lady Nightborn," he said.

Merin ran her tongue out over her red lips, leaning forward over the bar even more, pushing up her breasts in hopes that Charlie might glance down at her low-cut shirt. He didn't. This woman was a bear trap waiting to be stepped on and snapped shut around his ankles. A married royal with a taste for a common country boy. That kind of situation always ended badly for one of them, and it wouldn't be the married royal. He had been careful with her. Very careful. Gently ignoring her advances without pushing hard enough for her to take offense. By the time the hour reached noon the next day, he would wonder if the snapping of the bear trap weren't inevitable.

The Sorceress sighed lightly, sending a puff of rose-scented breath his way. Somehow, he hated it almost as much as he hated Milner's. Almost. "I'm in town for the next week or so," she said, her lashes flapping like a hummingbird's wings.

That was when it happened. Had Charlie not been so distracted, he would have seen the old man begin to tremble under his old gray cloak. He would have seen the black redness flash behind his eyes. He would have seen him remove his wand from beneath his cloak and aim it at the young royal Sorceress. He would have been able to stop him, and maybe avoid everything that happened next. Maybe.

Milner didn't make a sound as he carried out the deed. No rebel yell or cry of fury. He just held the wand tightly in his old wrinkled hand and shot a bolt of what looked like lightening from the end of it, brightening the room with a flash. It struck the Sorceress right over her heart. Charlie had time enough to see her body jerk, her eyes go wide, to think *what the hell?* and then the Sorceress slumped in the barstool and fell to the floor with a thump.

His eyes snapped to the old man, whose face was twisted like that of a demon's from hell. Heat seemed to be pulsing from him, rolling off in noxious waves. Charlie acted without thinking. Again, it all happened so fast. Milner's eyes—not *Milner's* eyes, the eyes of a devil—lingered on the dead Sorceress for a minute, then they flipped to Charlie.

"*Rich bitch,*" the old man said, spitting the words out like acid. He gave Charlie a grin that made his stomach flip and his skin prickle. Then he aimed the cheap wand at him, that dark thing still lurking behind his glassy eyes.

The Stone that hung on a necklace around Charlie's neck grew hot and cold at the same time, burning him a little where it hung over his chest, tucked into his shirt, pulsing against his skin, where it had been since the day he'd received it. He looked at the old man and thought, *he's going to kill me*, and before the man could do so, Charlie's right hand came up and clenched into a fist.

And with his secretly gifted Magic, he crushed Brad Milner's windpipe without ever touching his throat. There had been no time to retrieve his wand. He really wished there had been, though it probably wouldn't have mattered anyway.

His heart did a standstill as he leaned over the bar, breathing harshly, his chest heaving up and down, staring at the two dead bodies lying on the shiny wood floor. A Highborn lady and an old drunk. Today was going to be even longer than he thought.

He was going to have some explaining to do.

CHAPTER TWO

The Sorceress crossed one leg over the other and folded her delicate hands in her lap. "I appreciate the offer, father, but I don't want the job."

Syrian Stormsong looked at his daughter with disapproval, only slightly overshadowed by the grief in his purple eyes. He was silent for a time before speaking, choosing his words slowly, as was his way. "You are the only one left," he said. "I have a kingdom to run. I would do it myself if I had the time."

Surah's face was impassive, her features relaxed and smooth. She wanted to tell her father that sitting in front of a fireplace in his office all day and mourning over the death of his son was not running a kingdom. It was not, in fact, productive at all. He was a man whose only talent was delegating responsibility to others, and she had been doing his bidding for nearly a thousand years without much protest. But things had changed. Surah couldn't say exactly what those things were, but she could feel the difference all the same. Her brother was gone now, and when she had come to her father, asking of him something for the first time ever, he had denied her any assistance. It didn't matter that her brother's murderer had met his end without her father lifting a hand. What mattered was that her father had been *unwilling* to lift a hand, and she would not allow him the guilt-trip he was attempting.

Surah tilted her chin up a fraction, looking at her father with the calm that had taken her centuries to master, despite the roiling black ocean raging inside her. A black ocean that was the accumulation of a long life and its losses. Yes, her brother's death had changed things. A final straw.

"This is no longer a place for me, father. I'm afraid I can't accept your proposal."

Syrian's emerald eyes flashed with anger, just as Surah had known they would. He may not be a particularly productive man, but he was very kingly in the sense that he was not someone who liked to be told no. "You would leave our people without a Keeper?" he asked, disapproval now bordering disgust dripping from the words. "I had thought better of you, Surah."

Surah's teeth clenched a little, but her tone was as sweet and soft and delicate as always, her eyes indifferent. "There are others with greater control of the Magic than I have," she said. "More knowledge and capability, even. I am not the only one who meets the requirements."

The snifter of brandy Syrian had been holding flew into the fireplace and shattered there with a loud crack, making the blaze flare, throwing licks of orange on the walls and making shadows dance in the dark room. Surah didn't flinch, though she felt the heat flash hot against her skin. Syrian hadn't thrown it with his hand, but rather with his Magic, and Surah was careful not to raise an eyebrow at what he would have called a "useless display of power." She loved her father, but that didn't mean her father was easy to love. Over the years his temper had been a constant headache for her, but over time she had come to understand it was only his nature, something that had to be expected if they were to maintain a relationship.

"I am not asking as your father. I am telling you as your king," he said, smoothing a hand through his dark, carefully styled hair, regaining his composure, like the flipping of a switch. "You will be Keeper, and assist the Hunters in their necessary and noble efforts. You should be ashamed that I have to demand this of you. Your brother fulfilled his duty with pride and without protest."

Now there was a hypocritical statement if she'd ever heard one, and though she knew her next words would set her father off like a fireworks display, she said them anyway. She was beyond the point of holding her tongue, which was a pretty distant point. Syrian was not the only one who was grieving, and she didn't need his attitude on top of everything else.

"*I* should be ashamed?" she asked, her calm delivery fueling the returning anger in her father's eyes. She knew she should just shut her mouth, but she didn't. She leaned forward in her chair, her posture straight and perfect, back rigid. "I'm not the one who calls myself a king and yet is too cowardly to seek justice for his son's death."

Harsh, she knew this, but also true. And he had started it.

Syrian's eyes bulged from their sockets and a blue vein pulsed on his pale forehead. His long, manicured fingers dug into the leather armrests of his chair. "How dare you speak to me like that," he said, spittle flying from his lips. "You ungrateful child. You think everything is about you. You have lived for hundreds of years and it has done nothing for your understanding of the world. Your mind is as youthful as your appearance. How is it you have become so selfish?"

Surah was a heartbeat away from saying that he had made her this way, but then a knock sounded on the oak doors of her father's study, and a silence fell over the large room. Surah watched the flames from the enormous stone fireplace flicker across her father's face as Syrian barked for the caller to enter. The double oak doors swung open simultaneously with smooth glides, and in walked Theodine Gray, the heels of his boots clicking softly over the polished wood. His black cloak rippled behind him with each smooth step he took, and his hard eyes spoke only of business. When they settled on Surah they softened a fraction and a crooked smile pulled up one side of his mouth.

Surah swallowed to keep signs of annoyance off her face. Theo was not her favorite person, as he seemed to be everyone else's.

"Princess," Theo said, coming to a stop in front of Surah. He held a black-gloved hand out to her, and she held her own gloved hand out for him, as she had done thousands of times for thousands of people over the years. Theo took it gently and bent at the waist to kiss the leather over the top of her hand, his gray eyes watching her the whole time. "Always a pleasure," he said, then turned to Syrian and offered another bow. "My Liege."

Syrian was not in the mood for interruptions, and though it was nearly painfully difficult for him, he wiped any emotion out of his expression and tone, his broad shoulders rigid. What went on between him and his daughter was solely their business. "Is it important, Theo?" Syrian asked shortly. "My daughter and I were having a discussion."

Surah could feel the Head Hunter's eyes on her, knew the crooked smile was on his face, and deliberately stared into the fire to avoid his gaze. She was a princess and had been for her entire life, so she was used to the eyes of others being on her and she was good at pretending as though they weren't even there. But Theodine Gray's gaze was different. She seemed to feel it slither over her skin, even when her head was turned. It always made her teeth clench for reasons she couldn't explain. Theo had never given her a reason not to like him, had always, in fact, been very formal and kind to her, but she couldn't help it. Reason or not, she didn't like him, and hundreds of years in this life had taught Surah to always trust her instincts.

But her father trusted Theo, so she kept her opinions to herself. Another thing she had learned was usually a wise choice.

"I'm afraid it *is* serious, my Liege," Theo said. His eyes and posture had gone back to all business. The seriousness in his voice made even Surah's head turn, and he looked at her when he said his next words. Surah found herself wanting to slap that crooked smile off his lips.

"We received word from the Dark Mountain. The Black Stone is missing. Someone has stolen it."

Surah's mouth fell open, a rare expression of involuntary surprise on her face. She picked her jaw up and smoothed out her face as soon as she realized she was doing it, but when she looked over at her father she could see it was too late. He had seen her horror, no doubt felt it, too. His violet eyes stared into her own, and she could see the victory there. His eyes said this was exactly what he was talking about, why she needed to be Keeper. Why she didn't have much choice.

What Theo said next sealed the deal like a licked envelope.

"Also, Merin Nightborn is dead. Looks like murder."

Surah sighed, sat back in her chair, and thought, *oh dear.*

CHAPTER THREE

"What do you mean someone has stolen the Black Stone?" Syrian said, his fingers digging deeper into the poor leather of his chair, the blaze from the fireplace reflecting in his eyes. Obviously the Stone was a bigger worry than the death of a royal woman. Which said something. "That's impossible."

Theodine nodded his agreement, then shook his head and spread his hands. "Apparently not," he said.

Surah sat silently, unmoving, even though both men kept glancing at her as though she should have some input. She didn't, at least not other than the same question her father just asked. The Black Stone wasn't supposed to be able to leave its place in the Dark Mountain. Everyone knew that. It *was* impossible. Also, she'd never much cared for Merin Nightborn.

Her father stood from his chair and began pacing the room, his thick brows furrowed and his head bent forward, thinking. His movements were not graceful or fluid like Theo's and Surah's, but he was a tall, bulky man who moved with deadly precision, and it was rare that he exhibited his anxiety through physical action in front of anyone other than Surah. This was not good. "How long has it been missing?" he asked, skipping over the disbelief to search for a solution.

"The word was sent as soon as the Hunters realized it was gone," Theo said. "They make hourly rounds to check on the Stone, as you know. The Hunter assigned to check on it at eleven p.m. reported it was still there. When the next man went to check at midnight, it was gone."

All three of them glanced up at the enormous black iron clock hanging above the fireplace. The hour read one-thirty.

"No one saw anything?" Syrian asked, the disbelief evident in his tone again.

Theo's jaw tightened and he shook his head. "No, my Liege. The

9

Hunters assured me no one was seen entering or leaving the mountain. They have no idea how it could have happened."

Syrian snorted. "Wonderful," he snapped. He stopped pacing the room and sat down again in his red winged-back chair, the cushions groaning under his weight, eyes settling on his daughter. Surah returned his stare with her usual indifference, but inside she was boiling with questions, and yes, more than a little fear. The Black Stone was one of the most powerful weapons in existence. In the wrong hands it could deliver catastrophe on an unimaginable scale. Syrian knew she wouldn't refuse his request now, and it made her clench her fists in her lap a little, because she knew it, too.

"These Hunters," Syrian said, addressing Theo but still looking at his daughter, "the two that were on watch over the Stone. You questioned them yourself?"

Theo nodded once. "Of course, my Liege."

"And you believe they're telling the truth?"

The Head Hunter considered for a moment, and a small smile came to his handsome face as his eyes fell on Surah once more. Surah's jaw clenched. "It would be wise to have the princess question them," Theo said, "since we have tragically lost Syris and that would have been his job. She would know better than I if they are lying. It's not my...forte."

No, Surah thought, *your forte is capture and kill.*

For just a moment, Surah fantasized about throwing a Lightning Bolt at the Head Hunter's midsection, watching him double over in pain, wiping that smirk off his officious face. Instead, she sat unmoving, said nothing.

Syrian nodded, giving his daughter a look that said *told you so.* Surah stood in one fluid movement, her long cloak rippling behind her, wanting all of a sudden very much to be out of this room, with the heat of the fireplace, where she had played many a nights as a child, with the eyes of her lost family watching her from the portraits hanging on the walls, with the dim lights that seemed to shadow pain.

"Take me to them," she said, and moved toward the doors without a backward glance at her father. She would do this task because it was *necessary,* and even though she may only look all of nineteen years old, she was not as young-minded and selfish as her father believed. She had lived well as a princess among her people, and she would not abandon them with the Stone missing. That didn't mean she intended to be Keeper, just that she could help in this matter and she would, and hopefully it would turn out to be a misunderstanding. Once it got straightened out she would take her leave, even though she had no idea where she'd even go. Just...*away.* Someplace without old fireplaces and portraits and shadows.

Theo bowed once more to his king and followed Surah out into the hallway, shutting the oak doors behind him with a small flick of his wrist.

"It's very generous for you to offer your assistance, Princess," he said, holding an elbow out to her.

Despite her unfounded dislike of him Surah laced her arm through his so he could lead her out of her father's quarters, where they would be able to teleport to their destination. For protection reasons one could not teleport into Syrian's dwellings, only out. And though Surah would rather not make physical contact with the Head Hunter, she knew well enough what was expected of her. Theodine was a Knight, and to disrespect him by refusing his arm would be plainly rude. It was one of the reasons she dreamed of leaving this place, even though she knew she could never live any more lavishly than she did in her father's kingdom. Too many appearances to hold up. Too many expectations. Too many secrets and shadowed sad times between these walls.

The hallway was dimly lit, no windows or points of entry save for the two arched doors at the end of the hall. Surah did not respond to Theo's comment about her generosity. She got the feeling that he knew as well as she did that he had not given her much choice with his charging in and saying how she was needed to question the Hunters, probably to help solve the murder, too. It was an understandable request. One of Surah's gifts, that both her lost sister and brother had shared, was being able to detect lies from most people, but that didn't mean she liked the way Theo had pulled her into this. She didn't like it at all.

Theo's wrist flicked again and the arched doors leading to the foyer swung open. The foyer was a large room, one of fourteen in the beast of a structure that was her father's castle. The ceiling towered thirty feet overhead, painted with a mural of a dark storm just rolling in. The bruised clouds seemed to sweep over the ceiling as if to swallow it, and the room was as poorly lit as the hallway they'd just emerged from. But the mural was no longer a comfort to Surah, just like the night black walls which held no windows were no longer, even though they used to be when she was a little girl. She could still remember when it had been painted, she'd been only a handful of years at the time. Syris and Syra had stood to either side of her, their necks craned back the same as hers.

"It looks like it could pour rain down on us at any second," Syris had said.

His sisters had nodded, wide purple eyes still glued to the ceiling. Syra had leaned in a little, pitching her voice low so that the artist still finishing the mural wouldn't hear her. "I don't like it," she'd said.

Surah had smiled at her older sister. "I do."

"May I inquire something, Princess?" Theo asked, pulling Surah out of her memories.

Surah restrained a sigh and nodded. People were always asking permission to "inquire" things, as though she weren't as accessible as any of them just because she was princess, the next and only person in line to the throne. No one just spoke freely to her like she was a real person. In her earlier youth, this had made her smug and conceited, made her think they should behave that way because she *wasn't* like them; she was *better* than them. But those feelings had long since faded, and her soul had grown humble and weary of the treatment. Now that Syris was gone, her father was the only one left who said whatever he felt to her. She wondered briefly if her life would always be that way. It was a surprisingly sad little thought.

Theo's eyes were on her. She could feel them. "Are you going to accept the position as Keeper?" he asked.

She lied without hesitation, smoothly. "I don't know."

Theo was silent for a moment, his hand resting on hers where she had her arm laced through his. This was one of the reasons she always wore gloves and long sleeves; so she wouldn't have to touch the skin of those who always wanted to escort her about, and she had reasons for this that were not as conceited as they may sound. She was a princess, not an old lady crossing the street. She was pretty sure she could walk without everyone's assistance.

"It would make me very happy if you did, my Lady," Theo said, his tone pitching low, his gray eyes lowering in a rare show of uncertainty.

When he said things like this, which he did a good portion of the time, Surah felt bad about her unexplained dislike of him. He was, after all, a Knight who had fought for her father and done his bidding for hundreds of years. She had known him since they were both children, and nearly every eligible woman in the kingdom would cut off a finger to be with him. Handsome, charming, intelligent, strong. It wasn't hard to see why, and Surah refused to believe her aversion to him was because of the small thing he'd done when they were children. When you lived as long as they did, everyone did questionable things at one point or other. She certainly had a fair share of her own. But, still…

Surah smiled her practiced smile. It wasn't difficult. "Thank you, Hunter Gray," she said. "I suppose we shall just have to see."

He had never, in all the years they'd known each other, asked her to call him Theo, but she knew he wished she would. She never did, not because she wanted to upset him, but because she felt as though he was just waiting for that kind of invitation, and she had no desire to encourage him.

Theo said nothing to this, only continued to look down at her from his taller position. Surah decided it would be best to get back to the business at hand. "Where are we going?" she asked.

It was a question she already knew the answer to, and Theo knew this, but he answered dutifully, letting the subject drop. "The Hunters who are stationed at Black Mountain are not allowed to leave their posts, my Lady, so the two that were on watch tonight are waiting for us there."

They were across the large foyer now, where five Hunters were guarding the Travel Room. They stood silent in their black cloaks, arms at their sides and faces unmoving. Two on each side of the door to the room, and one directly in front of it. Theo nodded to the one in the middle, and the Hunter twisted his wrist and the door slid open. Then he stepped to the side so Surah and Theo could enter, bowing as they passed.

It was just a small, square room, not much bigger than an elevator, the walls and ceiling all black, with a plush purple carpet on the floor. This was one of only five places in the castle where teleportation wasn't blocked, and it could only be used two at a time. Surah and her father were the only ones who were allowed to teleport freely in the castle.

In front of them, the door slid closed. Much later, Surah would wish she had never stepped into the room in the first place. Had she stuck to her guns, and refused a hand in all this, so much could have been avoided. Maybe.

Theodine held out a hand to the princess, a crooked smile on his face that made Surah sigh mentally. She didn't need the help teleporting any more than she needed the help walking, but there were those pesky expectations, *obligations*, really, so she placed her hand in his without hesitation, offering her royal smile as she did so.

Someday I will shed the mask, she thought. *Someday.*

CHAPTER FOUR

Teleporting would be a strange thing for a first-timer, and most people could never even do it, but Surah had learned and mastered the Magic when she had been just a child, so the feeling of vertigo and nausea no longer invaded her as they moved across space and time. She was here, and then she was there. Simple as that.

The night stars hung overhead, a thick glitter that was not visible in the part of her father's kingdom where she called home. Too many lights on the ground to see the lights in sky. But here was country, a land where only the farmers and their grasses, the Hunters and their mountain lived. Here was a land where the Beasts still roamed in the forests, where the night wind whispered the wishes of star-crossed lovers, where the Magic was still used for survival, not show or pride. Here was where the stars were allowed to shine.

She had only been here a handful of times, as her life demanded most of her time be spent in the city where her father's castle was. But sometimes she dreamed of this land, could see it through the eyes of a broken young girl, could see her sister's face as it had been so many years ago. Battles of the Great War had been fought here, back before the dividing of the Territories, and it was fair to say the land had acquired a haunted feel, as so many places where great death is wrought do. Surah knew this was the reason her father had built his city on the other large expanse of land that belonged to the Sorcerers, but even with the memories of Syra and her mother, she liked it here. Things were simpler here. You could see the stars.

Ahead was the Dark Mountain, living up to its name under the black glittered sky. The towering peaks seemed not to hold shadows, but rather to birth them, and a perpetual storm cloud seemed to hang not over the mountain, but around it. Jutting rocks the color of midnight scraped the air some twenty-thousand feet high, and a base for the Hunters who guarded the place was just a row of squat black buildings at the foot of it. A cast iron fence ringed the area, where admittance was only allowed to select few. The place was as impenetrable as a place could be, and for good reason. The Dark Mountain was where the Black Stone lived, or where it *had* lived, before it had gone missing, which Surah still hoped was some sort of stupid mistake. She couldn't even steal the Stone if she wanted to, and not only was she the princess, but she was more powerful than most when it came to the Magic.

If it was indeed gone, great trouble lay ahead. The Black Stone, unlike its brother, the White Stone, could be used only for Black Magic, for bad deeds. In nearly a thousand years, she had never even seen the thing, nor would she want to. Only the people who guarded it saw it, which was why this interrogation would not be a pleasant thing. Prolonged exposure to the Stone had a way of…shaping a person.

Theo still held her hand and he began walking her over the rich green grasses toward the mountain. She slipped her arm through his when he offered his elbow again, and ignored the tightening of her stomach the way she had learned to ignore most emotional impulses over the years.

"Don't be afraid, my Lady," Theodine said, looking down at her with his crooked grin.

Surah didn't respond to this. She stared straight ahead and clenched her teeth. The pride that she felt the need to assert when she was younger had faded away along with the rest of the things that fade away with time.

He led her toward the gates where two Hunters in their black cloaks stood to either side, their faces as stone as the mountain that loomed behind them. They recognized the Head Hunter and their princess immediately and bowed to first Surah, and then him. Theo inclined his head and the gates swung open, stirring the humid air that had caused a thin fog to sit over the land.

Surah's black hood was drawn up over her head, hiding her lavender hair from view and casting much of her smooth face in shadows. The Hunters here, all men, had not seen a woman in Gods knew how long. They made great sacrifices for their people, and she did not want to entice them unnecessarily.

The two of them, arm in arm, crossed the land that had gone barren under their feet, the grasses ending abruptly in dry brown dirt, and approached the foot of the Dark Mountain, which seemed to pulse something that made Surah's heart quicken, her breath fall short, like waves of tingling electricity that would eventually run you dry or run you completely.

Somehow, though the settings were as different as two settings could be, the feel of the place had the same as that of the Silver City that belonged to the Vampires and Wolves after she had watched their revolution take place there. The air here was warm, not frigid and cold, and the Mountain was dark like its name, not all white and silver with snow, as the Silver City had been, but yes, the *feel* was the same. Darkness. Pain. Death.

Surah nodded to all the Hunters they passed, who nodded in return and followed her with eyes that hung in the shadows of their hoods. As they reached an opening in the Mountain, five Hunters guarding the entrance stepped to the sides, allowing them to pass, allowing the Mountain to swallow them.

There were no shadows in here, for not even shadows could live in such complete darkness. Surah restrained herself from casting a Light Sphere in front of her, mostly because of Theo's comment about being scared. After a few moments in the void of blackness Theo snapped his fingers and a sphere of light, a baseball-sized thing that swirled perpetually like the eye of a hurricane, appeared in front of them, and it lit up that little crooked grin on his face, as if he knew she had not cast her own light just to prove a point.

This annoyed her a touch.

"Where are they?" she asked, deciding the silence between the two of them was too much in this small, dark space. Too *intimate*.

Still grinning, Theo nodded his head forward, sending the Light Sphere down the tunnel ahead of them. The shadows scuttled away from it like insects.

"Just around that bend, my Lady. They've prepared a room for us. The Hunters who last saw the Stone will be there."

Surah had already begun to move forward, and she wished that she could fling Theo's arm away and walk independently. She didn't.

When they reached room, which was no more than a small rounded cavern with three burning torches hanging on the wall, they found the two Hunters in question seated at a small, old table, which just barely fit in small room with its four chairs. The two chairs opposite the Hunters were empty, and Surah inclined her head, making one of them slide back from the table before Theo could pull it out for her. She took a seat. Theo stood a moment, then did the same.

Surah pushed her cloak off her head, revealing her lavender curls and partially shaved head. She raised her chin, her violet eyes settling on the Hunters. "I am Surah Stormsong," she said.

Both Hunters nodded in unison, obviously aware of who she was, and said, "My Lady."

"May I have your names, sirs?"

Both men were stocky and wide-shouldered. Their hair was cut close and their eyes were black, like midnight and ink, as were all the Hunters that were stationed at the Dark Mountain. Working so close to the Black Stone had its effects, but it was a necessary and honorable duty to uphold. Whether they were suspect or not they deserved their princess's respect.

The one on the left answered first. "Rand Fishwell," he said.

Surah nodded. Common name.

The one on the right said, "Brim Ironwater."

Another nod, slightly less common name, but still common.

"Can you tell me what happened Sir Fishwell, Sir Ironwater?" she asked.

"Wish there was more to tell, my Lady," said Fishwell. "I went in at eleven to check on the Stone and it was there." His black eyes flicked to the other Hunter. "When Ironwater went in at midnight it was gone."

Surah sat back in her chair, sure to keep the dread of what she had to do next off her face. She slid the glove off her right hand.

"May I ask you a question, my Lady?" said Ironwater.

Theo shot the Hunter a glare, and Surah decided she liked Ironwater for not flinching. She nodded, curious. "Of course."

"Are you going to be the new Keeper?"

Surah smiled. Her princess smile. On second thought, she should have declined his request. "That matter has not been decided, sir," she said, and placed her ungloved right hand on the table, palm up. Ironwater sighed and placed his rough hand in hers.

Surah took a deep, silent breath and let it out. She could already feel the darkness in the Hunter that was a result of years spent near the Black Stone. It was a feeling that quite simply sucked the light out of the world. "Now tell me again, please," she said.

Ironwater nodded. He repeated the story that Fishwell had told. Surah knew the way she always knew that he was telling the truth. She released her hold on his hand and patted it gently, then offered hers to Fishwell.

Same story. Same results. The two Hunters were telling the truth.

Surah sat back in her chair once more, giving Theo a nod that confirmed their stories. She bit the inside of her bottom lip a little as she wondered what she was supposed to do next, and wished for what seemed like the thousandth time in the past month that her brother were here. Keeper was Syris's job, and he had been good at it. She hadn't the slightest clue as to how to lead an investigation of this magnitude, or any magnitude, for that matter. She had a feeling it was going to be a very long day.

"The room that held the Stone," she said. "Has it been searched?"

Theo answered. "Of course, my Lady. I searched it myself before I came to King Syrian. There is nothing there."

The way he said this made Surah's back raise a little, as though this were a silly question, as if to point out that she didn't know what she was doing. Or maybe she was just defensive because she *didn't* know what she was doing. There had been no implication in the Head Hunter's tone. This was why she could never figure out if she disliked him for warranted reasons or not.

Surah stood from her seat, and the three men followed suit. "Thank you for your cooperation," she told the two Hunters. Then she turned and left the room, pulling her hood back over her head, the heels of her boots clicking on the hard earth and bouncing off the black walls of the tunnel. Theo followed right at her heels.

"What next, my Lady?" he asked, and Surah got the impression that he knew exactly what to do next, and was testing her. Seeing if she was up for the job.

She continued down the tunnel that led out of the Mountain, wanting to be free of its suppressing weight, willfully keeping the snap out of her tone. "Now we go see about Merin Nightborn," she said, and Theo smiled as if she were a toddler who'd just recited her ABC's.

The stone that hung around her neck, tucked into her shirt, pulsed against her skin as she thought again about casting a Lightning Bolt at the Head Hunter. Of course, she didn't. There were other matters to attend to, matters that seemed to be growing moldy and infected and more imminent by the second.

A Highborn was dead and the Black Stone was missing. It didn't sound like a coincidence to her. Not at all.

CHAPTER FIVE

Charlie called Jude Flyer first, only because he wasn't sure who else to call. Then he turned the sign on his door from Open to Closed, shutting down the lights at the front of the bar so hopefully any passerby would turn away without peering in too closely. He stared down at the two bodies lying on his floor, a drunken old man and a Highborn young lady. His throat felt tight. Today had started out like any other, and now he was waist deep in a mess he couldn't explain. It all carried a terrible sense of foreboding.

He'd hidden the stone though, the one that never left the place around his neck, even during sleep and showers. When the Hunters showed up they wouldn't find it.

When Jude tapped on the glass door to the outside Charlie jumped off his stool like a frightened rabbit, composing himself before he let his friend in. Composure would be key until this matter was cleared up.

He pulled the door open and Jude stepped through, his velvet cloak rippling behind his back, his soft shoulders ridged with self-importance. He was a short, pudgy man, with fingers that looked like they should be perpetually covered in grease, even though his little white hands were always clean and his fingernails manicured.

A lot of people in the town weren't fond of Jude, and some of this had to do with the cloak he wore and the way he spoke. Some of it had to do with his profession. He was just a step above a commoner, but he wore the cloak like the drapes of a king, spoke the language like a professor of the art, as though his step above them on the social scale was more a leap. But he was a decent man, conceited maybe, but decent, and Jude and Charlie had got on just fine over the years. Jude always paid for his booze, Charlie kept filling his glass. A fine relationship indeed.

"What in the name of the White Stone could be so important, Chuck?" Jude asked, skipping over a greeting. "I have a client due in my office in half an hour."

Charlie nodded. "Sorry bout that, Jude, but," he rubbed his hand over his jaw, "ah hell, I'll just show you."

He led Jude over to the bar, where the two bodies lay exactly how they had fallen, their skin as pale as paper, their chests unmoving. The Defender's expression did not show any alarm, and Charlie wondered how many times in his years he had been called to a scene like this in his line of work. Probably several.

When Jude pulled his wand from beneath his coat and began writing an invisible message in the air, his sausage fingers gripping it delicately, his pudgy, moisturized face smooth save for a crease between his thick brows, Charlie swallowed once and asked, "What are you doing?"

The Defender's expression didn't change, his wand didn't stop scribbling. "I'm canceling my appointments today," he said, signing his name in the air with the wand. The tip now glowed like the end of a cigarette, making the name hang in the air like the trail of a sparkler. His arm returned to his side. He looked over at Charlie now, his mouth a tight line. "This is serious, Chuck. If that's Merin Nightborn dead on your floor I'd say you're neck-deep in shit." He pulled a barstool out, the wooden legs scraping against the floor, and climbed up on it. "Now tell me what happened."

Charlie told the story as it had happened. Well, *almost* as it had happened.

***

He was being held prisoner in his own office. Jude Flyer sat beside him, his fat, jeweled fingers laced together over his stomach. Two Hunters stood on either side of the door to the office, and perhaps a dozen more were investigating the scene in front of the bar. They had asked him what happened, and he had given them the same story he'd given Jude. It hadn't been that hard. Charlie was good at lying. He just didn't like to do it.

The night dragged onward, and still Charlie and Jude were held in the small office. A Hunter brought them some dinner upon Jude's demand, and when Charlie had to use the bathroom a Hunter waited outside of the stall for him. The Hunters were cold people, Charlie knew that, knew that they *had* to be, but the hard way they looked at him made his stomach tighten nonetheless. He wasn't exactly worried yet. The Hunters were the protectors and enforcers of the law and they were just following procedure. They would investigate the matter fairly, and find that Charlie had not killed Lady Nightborn. He had faith in King Syrian. He was a fair king.

So no, he wasn't *exactly* worried just yet, but he did have two concerns. One was his use of the piece of White Stone he had no business having, the one he had taken from around his neck and hidden. The other was the question of who would be leading the investigation, seeing as how Syris

20

Stormsong, the former Keeper, was dead. He wondered if it would be Theodine Gray, and hoped not. Charlie had never liked the man, and Theodine had never liked him. They both had long memories.

Of course, there was a chance the new Keeper could be *her*, and he couldn't decide whether that would be a good thing or not, whether he *wanted* that or not.

When the princess walked into the office where Charlie and Jude still sat, the two men had been there for nearly five hours, having been questioned about the scene in the bar several times by several Hunters. When the door opened with a smooth glide, having been moved with Magic, Charlie looked up, his face wary but carefully composed.

And it was *her*.

She still looked exactly as he remembered her, only older, of course. Her hair was the same curly lavender, only it was cut short and shaved a little on the left side, where black jewels crept down her pierced ear. Charlie decided he liked the look immediately, even though it was not as he had so often imagined it, not the long flowing style she'd worn as a girl. It curled in and out around her chin, where her fine jawline made a nice frame for her full pink lips. She wore a cloak, black on the outside with what seemed like a million glittering stars sewn into the fabric, which shimmered as she moved. Her hands were gloved in black leather, her face a smooth expression of nothing.

Until her eyes settled on Charlie, and something flashed there that made him think she might know who he was, even though the two had not seen each other or spoken since that day when they were children, some nine-hundred years ago. But it was gone so quickly that Charlie chastised himself to even think the princess could've remembered him, let alone know who he was. They had only ever met that one time, and who was he to be remembered by someone like her?

And how young she still looked. Not a day over twenty. Charlie had stopped ageing around twenty-five, and had not had any children, which would cause the aging process to continue, if very, very slowly. Her youthful appearance told him the princess didn't have any children either, and this made a little guilty relief flood through him. It didn't matter. As far as birds went, Charlie Redmine and Surah Stormsong were not of a feather. Just his jeans, boots and flannel shirt said as much as that.

Charlie's heart seemed to be beating out of his chest, sinking when he saw that the princess would not even look back at him. Then his heart stopped completely, because following Surah, Theodine Gray walked into the room.

The Head Hunter no doubt remembered Charlie, just as Charlie remembered him, and a small sneer twisted Theo's lips as his eyes settled on him. He wiped it clean only a moment after, and that was the first time

Charlie realized that Jude had been right.
He was neck deep in shit indeed.

CHAPTER SIX

The scene of Merin Stormborn's death was just a small bar off the countryside, and soon as Surah saw it, she wondered what a lady like Merin would even have been doing in a place like this—though she had her suspicions, knowing Merin. Places like this existed solely in the country land, just a small wooden building, not like the trendy bars in the city. The road leading to it and the parking lot were a dusty brown, and two dozen Hunter's motorcycles were lined up in front like black and chrome wasps. The sign over the place read DRINKS, painted in a fire engine red that stood out on the wooden building. The night stars were the only illumination save for the soft light spilling through the glass door, the Black Mountain looming miles in the distance. It was kind of lovely in its simplicity, but Surah felt out of place here immediately in her black cloak and expensive black boots, which caught the dirt on the ground and held it as she walked.

"What could Merin have been doing here?" Surah asked, more to herself than to anyone else. The sight of the place had made her forget Theo was still at her side.

"That is an excellent question, my Lady," Theo said, giving her that crooked grin again.

Surah released his arm, ignoring his slightly insulted look, and took a deep breath of the fresh country air before stepping into the bar, where the aroma would surely be booze and cigarettes. The short heels of her motorcycle boots clicked on the wooden steps as she climbed up the porch. Flicking her wrist, the door to the place swung open and Surah stepped inside.

It wasn't as she had expected, not dirty and dusty, but instead clean and polished and warm. The lights were set intimately low, the walls a richer, darker wood than the exterior of the building, and paintings of the different scenes of the countryside hung on the walls. They were beautifully done oil works, the colors and strokes having captured perfect portraits of the land at perfect moments, as if the artist had sat out all day just to wait for the light to fall right. Wooden tables with soft chairs sat in the center of the room, and red booths lined the walls. To the right was the bar, a polished oak that gleamed under the soft lights. Rows and rows of liquor bottles lined the shelves behind it, standing like soldiers shoulder to glassy shoulder. Surah found herself taking another deep breath, and finding the smell not stale or unpleasant, but clean and inviting, like a grandmother's home.

There were no customers, of course, but Hunters were everywhere, standing around in their black cloaks, moving from here to there, writing things down with their wands. When they saw Surah and Theo, they all stopped what they were doing and bowed to their princess. Surah waved a hand, telling them to rise. One of the Hunters strode over to them, a tall man with a wiry build and nervous, flicking eyes.

The Hunter bowed again when he reached Surah and held out a hand to her. Surah placed her hand in his and waited while he kissed the top of her glove. "My Lady," he said.

Surah princess-smiled, pulling her hand gently from his. "Rise, sir," she said. "Are you the Chief in this jurisdiction?"

The Hunter nodded. "I am, my Lady. Hunter Sand. Very pleased to meet you."

"And I you, Sir Sand." Surah looked around at the Hunters, who were looking back at her. "Have your men moved anything?"

Sand shook his head, and Surah could tell he must have just recently been promoted and was uneasy about the job. She thought she could sympathize with that.

"No, my Lady. We were waiting for the Keeper."

Surah nodded, choosing to ignore the obvious question on his face asking if that would be her. "Show me, please," she said.

Sand led Theo and Surah over to the bar, where the Hunters there parted and lowered their heads respectfully. Her breath caught a little as she saw the old man dead on the floor, his milky eyes staring toward the ceiling. Then she saw Merin Nightborn sprawled on the floor as well, her fine cloak fanned out around her, her red lips parted but pulling no air. Also very dead.

Surah's stomach did not flip or twist at the sight, but something spiraled there. Maybe it was a little intuition, and it told her that this was in no way going to be an open and close case. Something serious was going on in her father's kingdom, and until it was settled she had an obligation to help. For the second time this day, she thought, *oh dear.*

"Who owns this establishment, Sand?" Theo asked, his eyes going hard at the sight of Lady Nightborn. Surah could tell he wanted justice. The playfulness he had been exhibiting with her was gone.

"We got the owner in the back, sitting in his office," said Sand. He paused, that nervousness back in his eyes. "He's got Jude Flyer with him."

Surah raised an eyebrow at that. Jude Flyer was a pretty well-known Defender. Not Highborn, but very good at what he did, nonetheless. Some of the Highborn Defenders used to laugh at the little man, but that had stopped after he'd won some pretty tough cases. He was uncommonly good at finding evidence that exonerated his clients, even when it looked like they were a step away from the chopping block, their hands all but painted red. The mention of him made Surah's unease grow, though she couldn't say why.

"Let's see them," Theo said, a smile coming to his handsome face that Surah didn't like one bit.

Theo allowed Surah to go first, as was the custom, and she flicked her wrist so that the door to the small office behind the bar swung open. Then she stepped inside.

And it was *him*.

She couldn't say how she knew it was him, just that *she knew*. He still looked the same as in her memories, even though he had grown older, of course. He had gone from a boy to a man, his body having filled out and grown hard with what she knew had to be years of actual labor, not the cultivated muscles that Theo wore, but harder somehow, as though they had been earned through callouses and sweat. Dark hair had grown in across his strong jawline, and his eyes were still the jade of topical ocean water that Surah remembered so clearly. He wore only a flannel shirt, faded jeans, and work boots on his feet. His position was relaxed, reclined in the chair behind the desk, fingers laced together over his chest, as though he had been sitting right there for hours.

Surah pulled her eyes away from him and they settled on Jude Flyer, who also looked as though he'd been sitting a while. He ran a hand through his thin, slicked-back hair and rose from his chair. After a moment, as though he had momentarily forgotten his manners, his client did the same. Both men bowed to their princess.

"My Lady," Jude said, offering a chubby-fingered hand. Surah sighed mentally as she held her own out to be kissed, glad once more that she always wore her gloves, especially since it was the same hand Jude had run through his greasy hair. "It is an honor," continued the Defender.

Surah nodded, pulled her hand from his and took a seat in one of the two chairs opposite the desk, all too aware that the other man's eyes followed her the whole time. Surah glanced over at him to see the smallest change of expression cross his face, just a slight movement that made her cock her head just a fraction.

From behind her, Theo said, "Good evening, gentlemen," and Surah thought maybe Charlie's expression had shifted—only momentarily, his face was back to blank already—because of the Head Hunter.

Charlie. That was his name. She remembered now. Just like that. *Charlie.* A good, simple name. She rolled it around in her head a little, thinking maybe rolling it off her tongue would be pleasant as well. It was hard to equate him with the boy from her memories. He had grown into such a...*man.*

Then she slapped those thoughts away. Those thoughts were no good. Those thoughts were futile.

Theo took a seat beside her, and Surah wished very much for no reason at all that the Head Hunter were not here with her, that she could do this on her own, even though she didn't even entirely know what she was doing. Surah's job in her father's kingdom over the past eight-hundred years had involved two things, helping the king make diplomatic decisions, and looking pretty and proper for the public. Most people just thought she did the latter, but many of the laws and assistance programs her father had passed over time were of Surah's creation, and the public was glad for them. They were happy under their king's rule. She never cared about getting credit for the work. She was just glad to be giving back.

But being a Keeper and being a politician were two different things. Work that involved hands-on action, not just power of the mind.

"What happened here?" Theo said, his words clipped. Surah restrained herself from shifting uneasily.

Jude Flyer answered, "Mr. Redmine was in the process of closing this establishment tonight when Brad Milner—an elderly gentleman who is a regular here—came in. Mr. Redmine poured Milner a drink. Lady Nightborn arrived next. She sat at the bar, ordered a drink, and when Charlie here turned around to retrieve the bottle of liquor, Milner removed his wand and sent a Light Strike at her heart. She died instantly. Then the old man killed himself by crushing his own throat."

The Head Hunter's eyes were locked on Charlie, and Surah had to stop herself from shifting uncomfortably again, though she had no idea why. Her mind was racing, going back to that day after the battle, back when she had been a broken little girl. A boy had been kind to her that day, and she had given him a gift she shouldn't have given him.

"Is that so, *Charlie?*" Theo asked, making the name sound like a dirty thing.

Charlie nodded, his jade eyes holding the Head Hunter's steadily, without fear. "Yes, sir," he said. "It happened fast. I don't know how he did it, or why he did it. Mr. Milner has never caused any trouble here."

"And you say he 'crushed his own throat?'" The incredulity was as thick as molasses in Theo's tone.

"I say he killed himself," Charlie said. "Don't know how he did it. But within a moment of killin the lady he was dead too."

Surah found herself staring at Charlie's lips, listening to the way the country land rode his words. It was so unlike the Highspeech she was used to, almost exotic. And then she pulled her eyes away and stopped those thoughts again. No good, those were.

"You realize," Theo said, "that something like that could not be accomplished with a simple wand. Crushing one's own throat and delivering a Light Strike that could kill is Stone Magic. How do you explain that, Mr. Redmine?"

Charlie shrugged, still holding the Head Hunter's gaze. "I can't explain it," he said. "Thought that was your job. I'm just telling you what happened."

Surah stiffened. The whole room seemed to stiffen. She couldn't blame Charlie for saying this. Theo's very tone was accusatory, but it took balls to talk to the Head Hunter in that way. Really big balls, especially from a common man, and Surah found herself admiring the Charlie Redmine's courage and wishing he would shut up at the same time.

"We intend to explain it," Theo said, his words clipped. "That's *exactly* what we intend to do."

Surah removed the glove from her right hand, wanting to stop this conversation for reasons she didn't really understand. She leaned forward and placed her hand on the desk, palm up. Looking straight at Charlie, her heart picked up a little in pace. She cursed it for doing so, and willed it to stop its girlish yammering. "Would you mind repeating the story for me, Mr. Redmine?" she asked, her sweet voice the exact opposite of Theo's tone.

Charlie's eyes met hers, and Surah felt something warm spiral in her stomach and she bit her tongue to try and force it away. His eyes seemed to really *look* at her, to almost *burn* through her, and she wondered if all women found his gaze so penetrating or if her hormones were just getting the best of her. This made her think of Lady Nightborn, and suddenly Surah thought she might have an explanation for what Merin had been doing here. She always had been a bit of a trollip, flocking around the boys at school like a bitch in heat. This made a terrible feeling of dread spiral in Surah's stomach.

Charlie's large hand came up and rested in hers, his palm rough and warm, his fingers engulfing her small hand. Her heart jumped again, and she told it sternly that that was quite enough out of it. She needed to concentrate. "Whenever you're ready, Mr. Redmine" she said, and swallowed when Charlie just sat staring at her.

She could feel rather than see Theo smirking beside her. She didn't like it.

"It's just like Mr. Flyer said," Charlie began, "Mr. Milner came in and ordered a drink. Lady Nightborn came in and ordered a drink. I turned around in time to see Milner aim his wand at the lady and shoot one helluva Light Strike at her heart. It struck her and she slumped to the floor. Milner smiled and squeezed his hand into a fist. Then he slumped over and fell to the floor, too." He paused. "There was somethin dark behind his eyes. I guess I should tell ya that. Something...*black*. Scared the Magic outta me."

Surah said nothing. Her tripping heart seemed to have stopped dead in her chest. That feeling of dread was back, and it was not just a spiral, it was a full-on hurricane raging inside her stomach. She seemed suspended for a moment, unable to decide what to do. It should have been a simple answer. Should have been, but wasn't.

Charlie was lying about something. And for some reason she knew that the piece of stone she had given him all those years ago, the stone that he had no business having, was involved.

Now, to lie for him or not to lie for him. That was the question.

It really should have been simple. And it wasn't. It just somehow wasn't.

CHAPTER SEVEN

Her touch was just as he'd always imagined it'd be. Warm, soft and surprisingly strong. He cursed his heart for what was probably the millionth time in his life as it hammered in his chest. On many a night he had forced thoughts of the princess away from him, knowing they would never do anything for him but cause pain and longing. He had even convinced himself that he had built her up in his mind, that she could not still be as beautiful as he remembered her from that day, when she had been crying by the lake after battle for her dead sister and mother. It was an imagined love that could never be requited. He was a common man, born and bred of a common family. She was a princess, the next in line now that her siblings were gone should her father pass on. It was an impossibility. Stars that crisscrossed like figure eights.

And now here she was, sitting right in front of him. *Looking* at him. *Speaking* to him. *Touching* him. And all the feelings he had cooked up over the years and flushed away came flooding back. They were so intense that sometimes he swore he hated her for making him feel this way. At the same time, looking at her now told him he could never hate her, not for anything. She was the girl who walked his dreams, who had walked them since he had just been a boy.

And now he had to lie to her. To protect both of them. He had to lie to her.

He told his story, wishing he had his stone with him so he might be able to stop her from detecting his lie, hoping she wouldn't slap cuffs on his wrists as soon as he was done speaking. Now his heart was practically vibrating in his chest, but years of practice had taught him how to keep his inner-goings invisible to the outside world.

His told his half-false story and waited.

The princess hesitated, then released his hand and sat back in her

29

chair. Charlie watched her closely with bated breath. The Head Hunter watched her, too, along with the Defender. Charlie felt bad for putting her in this position, even though none of it had really been his fault.

Surah pulled her glove back on her hand, her brows furrowing slightly in a way that made something warm circle in Charlie's stomach. She twisted her wrist sharply and the door to the office swung open. A second later, Chief Hunter Sand entered the room.

He bowed again to the princess. "You summoned, my Lady?"

Surah turned her head and addressed the Hunter. "Yes. Would you please search the old man, Sir Sand?"

The Hunter nodded once and left the room. The four of them sat silently and waited. Thirty seconds later, Sand returned. His face had gone sheet white and something dangled from his hand, which he held out in front of him as though it were poisonous. His voice was tight, and yes, a little afraid. "He had this in his pocket, my Lady," he said, holding his hand out to Surah.

She took the thing from him and heard Jude Flyer give a sharp gasp. "Is that…?" Flyer began, and didn't finish.

Surah nodded. "Yes, Mr. Flyer," she said, not at all feeling the calm she exhibited in her voice. "It's a piece of the Black Stone."

"How can that be?" Flyer asked.

Theo's face had gone hard and tight. He stared at the tiny piece of stone in Surah's hand, and then his cold eyes flipped to Charlie. "That's precisely what I'd like to know. Have any thoughts on the matter, Mr. Redmine?" Now the Head Hunter's gaze went to Surah, and he asked the question with his eyes that she had yet to answer.

Without allowing herself to think, but instead just making the decision before she could stop herself, Surah nodded. The Head Hunter's eyes seemed to flash with something Surah didn't like, didn't like *at all*. Her nod confirmed Charlie's story, and Theodine Gray, for whatever reason, did not want Charlie's story to be confirmed. Surah got a flash of a feeling that told her she had just opened a door which would lead to a world of trouble, a whole *universe* of it.

Her mind was flying, *jetting*, really. She needed to be out of this room, out of the lies that were floating thick in the air. She needed to see someone she could trust.

She sat back and in her calm, sweet voice said, "I've heard all I need to hear." She looked at Theo. "I'll report back."

With a snap of her fingers she was gone, flying instantly over space and time and landing in the hallway in her father's castle that led to her bedroom. Two Hunters stood guard outside her door and bowed to her when she burst onto the scene. These two were her personal protection, had been since she was just a little girl, so they could tell something was wrong with their princess as soon as they set eyes on her. She gave them a nod and a smile, and flicked her wrist so the arched doors to her room swung open. A moment later they slammed shut behind her.

CHAPTER EIGHT

Like that, she was gone. She disappeared from the room, taking with her the presence that had just filled it up, as though she had been exiting places in this fashion for hundreds of years. Charlie didn't gawk at the display of power, he wasn't a gawking sort of man, but he envied her freedom to just use the Magic without repercussions.

He also found himself missing her already.

That's how it was with her in his mind. She had just popped into his life the first time and changed it forever, then popped right back out again. Now, hundreds of years later, she'd done it again. The worst part was, she probably didn't even know who he was, probably hadn't spared him a thought over the years.

But she lied for you. She lied for you.

True, she had. There was no way the princess was fooled by the falsity of his story. Power flowed as strongly from her as it had from the last Keeper, her brother. Charlie had only met Syris Stormsong once, and his presence and Magic had filled the room same as hers. No, she hadn't been fooled, so why had she lied?

Charlie refused to allow himself to probe the matter with his mind. At least not yet.

Theodine Gray stood from his position, a terribly cold look behind his gray eyes. Like thunder clouds rolling in.

There's a storm comin. I can feel it.

"I'll be leaving two Hunters here to watch you," the Head Hunter said. "I would advise you to stay in close touch."

And of course, as if to prove a point, the Head Hunter disappeared in the same way Surah had, and Jude and Charlie were alone in the office.

Jude looked over at his client and offered a weary smile, his pudgy face greasy with the hours spent locked in the room. Charlie didn't like the smile. It was edged with just a little too much lawyer-sympathy.

"If there's something you're keeping from me, Chuck, I suggest you spill it right now," Jude said, "before this thing gets on any further."

Charlie shook his head and shrugged. He may have lied, but he wasn't *guilty* of anything. He hadn't killed Lady Nightborn, and he'd killed Milner out of self-defense. He wasn't the bad guy here. So why did he feel like one?

Because he shouldn't be in possession of the stone that was hidden in the floorboard right under his seat. He should have never taken the gift from the beautiful princess so long ago. It was a royal stone, having belonged to Surah's older sister, Syra. A common man like him had absolutely no business having it.

And that's when he realized she *did* know who he was. She knew who he was and that he had the stone and that's why she had lied. She could have told the truth and had him locked up, denied any allegations if Charlie tried to say she had given it to him. Not that Charlie would ever do that to her, he wouldn't. Instead she had lied because she wouldn't let him take the fall for the secret gift she had given him, or to save her own ass, he supposed.

Charlie had trouble wrapping his mind around this. He didn't like the pinpoint of hope that seemed to be blooming in his chest. Just owning that stone under the floorboards was a major crime. It was a quarter-sized piece of the White Stone that only princesses and princes received, but that's not why he had kept it over the years. In fact, he had never even once used it. Until this morning, that was.

He'd kept it because *she* had given it to him. He kept it because having it reminded him of her, and there had been plenty of times when he'd come close to tossing it into the jungles on the east side of the land, where it would eventually sink into the earth beneath the feet of the Beasts. He sort of wished he would have done that now, but of course if he had, he'd be dead.

Jude stood and stretched his legs, and outside of the bar the two men heard dozens of motorcycles thunder to life and go speeding down the road. After a few moments, the noise droned out. Most of the Hunters—all but two—were gone.

"Alright, Chuck, I need to be getting to the office," Jude said, clapping a meaty hand on Charlie's shoulder. "I'm going to put everything aside to work on this for you, because I have a feeling you're going to need me. You do need to stay close though, okay?"

Charlie nodded, the movement strangely robotic. "I 'preciate that, Jude. I have money. I can pay you."

Jude waved a hand. "We'll discuss that later, Chuck. I'm going to try and help you, because you've always been good to me. There's lots of folks out here who don't like me, who snicker behind my back and call me names, then come running with shit-eating grins on their faces when they get in trouble. Not you. You're fair. You're a good man." He clapped Charlie's shoulder again. "And unfortunately, it's always the good men who need the most help of all."

Charlie nodded again slowly, shook Jude Flyer's hand, and thought, *well…shit.*

CHAPTER NINE

Surah paced back and forth across the ancient Arkian rug that covered her bedroom floor. Samson watched her from his perch by the window, his enormous head resting between his paws, his ears perked and long tail tucked around him. He had been chuffing and sniffing around her since she entered, but now he just watched her, his golden tiger eyes following her back and forth.

"Dear Gods, Samson," she said, going over to him and running her hand through the soft fur on his neck. "What did I just do?"

Samson was a Great Tiger, about four times the size of those in the human world, his stripes black and blue rather than orange and black. Surah had saved him from a Great Serpent when he had been just a cub, and the Beast was loyal to her beyond all else. Her father's eyes had bugged out of his head when Surah had walked home with Samson one evening when she was just a girl, some eight-hundred years ago, and she had cried and cried until he finally agreed to let the tiger stay. It was impossible not to see how the tiger loved her, and eventually Syrian decided the Beast would be good protection for his daughter. He had already lost one child and his wife.

"I need to think," Surah whispered, wrapping her arms around Samson's neck and nuzzling her face against his warm, coarse fur. Samson let out a deep growl of a purr and licked his mistress's face with his rough tongue. He spoke in her head, an ability Surah had given him using Magic long ago. She was the only one who communicated with him this way, because he simply didn't care to communicate with anyone else.

His voice was deep and rumbling, like James Earl Jones'. *Is he the boy you gave Syra's stone to?*

"*Yes,*" she silently responded. "*And something tells me it plays a part here. Could be why he was lying.*"

Well, that's no good, Samson said.

"Yes, thank you. I got that."

Samson licked her hand to comfort her, and she rubbed his huge head as she thought. The tiger's eyes closed and he leaned into her hand. She was going to have to solve this problem, and the faster the better. She was a pragmatic person by nature, and made more so by time. She needed two things; to find the Black Stone, and to find the truth about Merin Nightborn's death. She was locked now into the position of Keeper for the time being, and she needed to do her job well.

Surah brought her right hand up, holding her fingers together as if clutching a pencil, and began to write in the air. The piece of White Stone tucked into her shirt grew warm against her chest. The words hung there before her eyes on an invisible sheet of paper, but Surah was the only one who could see them. It was a simple kind of Magic, like a mental filing system, much less risky than writing things down in a journal or with a wand, as common folks did, but most people never took the time to learn it. Syris had taught her this, had told her it was an important skill to have, and now she could really see why. She had to put the puzzle pieces together.

This was what she knew: The Black Stone was missing. Merin Nightborn and an old common Sorcerer named Milner were dead. The only witness to the deaths was a man who she'd met once as a girl. He was the boy she'd given her sister's stone to and pretended she didn't know what happened to it when the matter was questioned. It had been assumed to be stolen, and she'd let the assumption stay.

Now a Highborn was dead and the person she'd given the stone to was the main suspect. Both of the deaths had been caused by Stone Magic; that much was obvious. And the man had been lying. And she had lied *for* him. She needed to make sure that didn't blow up in her face.

Charlie. She wondered how she could have forgotten his name. He'd told it to her that day on the lake, when she'd been mourning lost her sister and mother, and she'd slowly lost the memory over time. Now it all came flooding back to her, and she realized if Charlie was guilty, and her sister's stone was involved, she could be in a spot of trouble here.

Well, she could lie, of course, if he accused her of having given it to him, and her word would certainly be taken over his, but the idea of this didn't sit right with her. That would be a nearly sinful thing to do, and Surah may be the most privileged person in the kingdom, but she didn't think she was a *sinful* person. No, she wouldn't deny his accusations if they came to light. But it would be a whole lot better for everyone if she could just solve this thing and place him in the clear before that could happen.

Assuming he *was* in the clear.

Surah sighed and stood, patting Samson on the head absently. The morning sun was just beginning to brighten the sky, filling the horizon with soft blues and pinks. She probably should have tried to get some sleep, but it was too late for that now. The next step was going to see her father, and she wondered what her report would be. Was she prepared to lie to him too? She didn't even the know the man she was protecting, or why the hell she was even protecting him, other than the guilt of having given him a gift that could get his head taken off. If she was going to set the record straight, now would be the time.

A moment later she was sweeping into her father's study, where Syrian sat in his chair in front of the fire. A table had been set up in front of him, and a breakfast of exotic fruits and meats and fresh bread was sprawled out there. He looked over at his daughter as she entered and smiled around a mouthful of food. "Surah," he said, "how were your travels?"

Surah took a seat in the chair across from her father, staring into the fireplace as if the answers to her questions burned there. She folded her gloved hands in her lap, her heart seeming to sink down into the chair with her. "Travels were fine, father," she said.

Syrian was silent for a moment. "Are you hungry?" he asked.

Surah gave her father a small, real smile, and nodded. The two of them could fight like cats and dogs, but they had an overall good relationship. They took care of each other. They loved each other, and they were the only immediate family either of them had left.

Silence hung between them, Syrian waiting patiently for Surah to speak, as he knew was best with her. A Hunter entered the room and delivered a table of food for her that matched her father's. The two of them sat eating for a time. Then Surah finally decided to just jump in.

"It doesn't look good, father," she said, fixing him with her purple eyes.

Syrian's hard jaw worked as he chewed, his face settling into that of a king doing business. Again, he waited for her to speak.

Surah told the story, leaving out the falsity of Charlie's recount. For now. When she was finished, Syrian sat back and released a slow breath, folding his large hands on his ample belly over the silver chain resting there that held his piece of White Stone, which was twice the size of hers. Surah knew what his first question would be.

"Was he lying?"

Yep. First question. Sometimes she hated that her father was so in-tuned to her. No one in the world could read her like him now that Syris was dead. She was careful not to avert her eyes. She hadn't known before if she would tell him the truth, but like always, she found it difficult to lie to him.

"I don't think the witness is guilty of murdering Merin Nightborn, or of stealing the Black Stone," she said. "It's...complicated."

Syrian raised an eyebrow at this. "Oh, I would say so, Surah. I would indeed say so. But my question is, why do *you* think it's complicated?"

Again, to lie or not to lie. Surah sat back and sighed. Not to lie, she decided. Lying only ever made things worse, and her father would be angry with her, but he wouldn't *hate* her. She had used some bad discretion when she was just a young girl, and now it had come back to bite her in the rear. It was time to come clean, and it would probably be a relief. Yes, he would be angry, but he would also understand. And he would help.

"Well, the Black Stone is missing and Lady Nightborn was indeed murdered," Surah began. "She was almost certainly murdered with Stone Magic, and I do think the two matters are connected."

Syrian said nothing, waited.

Surah reached into her cloak and pulled out the tiny piece of Black Stone attached to the necklace that the Hunter had found on Milner's body. She held it up. Her father's eyes first widened then narrowed as he realized what it was.

Now for the bombshell. Surah breathed deep. "I just don't believe Charlie Redmine has anything to do with missing stone, or the murder because—"

"What was that name?" Syrian snapped, cutting her off before she could tell him she'd given Charlie her sister's stone, and everything else. His face had gone hard, his mouth tight and fingers digging into the armrests of his chair. Surah's heart dropped, and she hadn't even known it'd been at risk of falling.

"Charlie Redmine?" she said, her voice just hardly above a whisper. She didn't like the look on her father's face.

Syrian spoke through clenched teeth. "I thought I remembered it from somewhere. Is Redmine still in custody?"

Surah swallowed, nodded. The blazing fireplace suddenly seemed very hot at her side.

Her father seemed to relax a little. "Good. Have him locked up immediately pending investigation," he said. Now his violet gaze fixed on her. "I bet he was lying, wasn't he? He didn't pass your test?"

Surah answered that with questions of her own. Her voice sounded somehow robotic to her own ears. "Who is he father? How do you know him?"

Syrian stared at her, and Surah's breath seemed to freeze in her chest. Whatever he was about to tell her, she probably didn't want to hear it. Just by his look she could tell it was going to seriously complicate matters.

"He's Black Heart's younger brother," Syrian said.

And Surah wasn't sure why, but for a moment, she couldn't breathe at all.

CHAPTER TEN

Charlie went home, which was just a small cabin behind his bar, and the two Hunters that had stayed to "watch him" followed and perched on his doorstep. He sighed as he slipped the key into the lock and opened the door to the cabin. "You fellas let me know if you need a sleepin' bag or something," he said, and then stepped inside and shut the door behind him before they could respond.

He stood for a moment in his living room, just looking around at the sparse contents of his home. It had been one helluva morning. Charlie ran his hand down his jaw and rolled his shoulders, trying to shake off the robotic feeling that had taken over him. He was in big trouble here. He could feel it, but he may as well try to relax.

He hid the stone first, underneath a loose brick in his fireplace, and felt a little better after having done so. Grabbing his guitar from the stand in the corner, he sat down on the couch with the instrument across his lap.

Music and painting had always been his comforts, and right now he didn't have the energy to sit at his easel. Later he was sure he would paint a portrait of the princess, one in which she was no longer a little girl. He had only allowed himself to paint her before once and had immediately destroyed the picture after, but now the image was new, and he eventually would have to get it out of his system, and be done with it. Especially now. Now that she was the Keeper on a case where he was the main suspect. He *had* to be done with it, once and for all.

Charlie settled back in his seat, intent on not thinking too much about the events of the morning. He strummed the guitar strings absently, the chords stringing together in a tune he had been playing for as long as he could remember, one that he never played for anyone but himself.

After a few moments, his exhaustion took over and he fell asleep with his fingers still on the strings. He was still asleep on his couch when the princess who walked his dreams popped into his living room twenty minutes later, not long after the sun had completely risen on this long day.

CHAPTER ELEVEN

As soon as she did it she wished she hadn't. In one hour Hunters would be here to haul Charlie Redmine to the cells, and she would be leading the arrest. She stood now in his living room, having just teleported from her father's chambers. She'd told Syrian she would report back to Theo and have him ready a team to arrest Charlie, but she'd come here instead.

She saw him first. He sat asleep on the couch, an old wood guitar perched on his lap, his handsome face peaceful. Surah tore her eyes away and glanced around nervously, taking his slumber as a sign from the Gods that she better just leave now before it was too late.

She was just about to snap her fingers and get the hell out of there when she stole one last look at the sleeping man to see that he was no longer sleeping.

His jade-colored eyes were open, staring at her in that penetrating way they had. Her fingers relaxed and her hand fell to her side, thoughts of leaving momentarily forgotten. Charlie said nothing, just sat up a little, straitening his flannel shirt, and slowly placed the guitar on the floor, his gaze never leaving Surah's.

She felt very much like a deer in the headlights. Couldn't think of a single thing to say. His face was carefully expressionless. "Princess," he said.

This snapped Surah out of her trance. "Do you still have it?" she asked, deciding to cut to the chase. The longer she stayed here, the worse it could be. For both of them.

Charlie nodded slowly, not having to ask what she meant.

Surah took a deep breath and a step toward him, and his head tilted back as he looked up at her from his place on the couch. She took the glove off her right hand and held her hand out to him. She thought she saw Charlie's jaw clench, but couldn't be sure. He placed his hand in hers.

41

"Did you use it to kill Merin Nightborn?" she asked.

"No."

Surah breathed a silent sigh of relief. True.

"Did you use the stone I gave you to kill Brad Milner?"

"Yes."

Surah sighed outwardly this time before she could stop herself. True.

"Was it self-defense?"

"Yes."

Her shoulders relaxed a little. True.

She took a deep breath. "Do you know anything about the disappearance of the Black Stone?"

Charlie's brows knitted together, a look of genuine confusion on his face. "No, ma'am," he said, momentarily forgetting the proper way to address her.

Surah dropped his hand and stepped back, relieved a little more than she probably should be. She pulled her glove back on her hand, still feeling the warmth of his touch on her fingers, ignoring it. Charlie's eyes watched her the whole time, and she found herself struggling to look right back at him.

But she managed it. "Is your brother Black Heart?" she asked.

Charlie swallowed, his face still carefully blank. "Yes, my Lady."

Surah waited for elaboration.

"I haven't spoken to him in years," Charlie said. His jaw was still just a little too tight, so hard it was to look at her. She had gotten even more beautiful and enchanting with age. And it was never pleasant talking about his brother. If the Black Stone was missing, he wouldn't put it past Michael.

Surah moved away from him, turning her back on his piercing gaze, and went over to the wall where more paintings like the ones in his bar hung. She looked over her shoulder at him. "Did you do these?" she asked, gesturing to the paintings.

Charlie nodded.

"They're beautiful," she said, wondering why in the hell she was making small talk with the clock ticking the way it was.

"Thank you, my Lady," Charlie said, his deep, country-accented voice matching the modest contents of his home, warm and clean.

It was so different from the way Surah lived, so simple and cozy, and it fascinated her. She wondered if all the common people in the country land lived so simply.

"You'll have to give me the stone," she said turning to face him again.

Charlie nodded and stood, and Surah had to stop herself from staring at his body as he did so. He seemed to be made of nothing but muscle and smooth skin. He walked over to the fireplace with lithe movements for such a big man, and removed the brick that hid the necklace she'd given him so long ago. Then he came over and stood in front of her.

Surah's breath caught little, and she chastised herself for doing so. He was much taller than her, probably a little over six feet, with wide shoulders clothed in flannel. She had an image of the two of them from the outside, standing next to each other, all of their differences so plainly evident, and it brought home the fact that she had no business being here, no business at all. She suddenly felt a little sympathy for Merin Nightborn, and was sure of the fact that the lady had gone to the bar to flirt with Charlie Redmine. This made sympathy for him pass through her as well. She wished it wouldn't.

He held the necklace with her sister's stone out to her on his open palm, his jade-colored eyes staring down at her. She reached up slowly, willing herself to look away from him, to break their eye contact, and not quite succeeding. Her gloved fingers brushed his as she took the necklace.

"Thank you," she said, and was aware only after that her voice had fallen to a husky whisper. And then, as if her tongue had a mind of its own, she added, "My father wants you arrested."

Charlie's expression didn't change, and Surah found herself admiring his self-control. He was almost better at it than she was. "I had a feelin'," he said, his voice also low and deep. "Because of my brother, right?"

Surah nodded, pulling her eyes away at last, and took a small step back from him. "I confirmed your story," she said, wondering why in the hell she was telling him this, why she was even still *here*.

"Thank you, my Lady."

Surah flicked her violet eyes up to his and away again. "I'll try to help you, but I'll be back here in an hour with Hunters to take you to the cells. King's orders."

Charlie released a slow breath. "Alright," he said.

Surah was just about to teleport out of there, to someplace where maybe her breathing could regulate, when Charlie stepped forward and put his hand over hers, halting her leave. Her heart kicked up in pace, and she was helpless to still it even with concentrated effort.

"Why, Surah?" the man from her past asked, his deep voice a pitch lower than it had been before. "Why're you here? Why you helpin me?"

Surah met Charlie's eyes, the same exotic ocean color as when he had been a dirty young boy of only fifteen beside a lake, and she a broken young girl, and he had comforted her. "I don't know," she answered truthfully, angry with herself for liking the way her name sounded from his lips. Her father was the only person who called her by name now, and she should have taken offense to it. Theo certainly would have.

But she didn't. "I don't know," she repeated, and snapped her fingers and got the hell out of there.

CHAPTER TWELVE

Jude Flyer arrived at Charlie's house thirty minutes after the princess left. He entered to find Charlie sitting on the couch, his guitar propped on his lap, his deep voice humming the rhythm to an old country tune, one Jude and all other common people learned early in childhood.

Charlie's fingers halted on the strings and he looked up at the Defender as he entered his living room. Jude flyer looked refreshed and ready to go, his pudgy cheeks holding roses and his hair slicked back to perfection again. He raised a thin eyebrow as he took a seat in the armchair across from Charlie, smoothing out his cloak with his fat fingers. "You look incredibly calm for a man who's thirty minutes away from being arrested by Hunters," Jude said.

Charlie took a deep breath, setting his guitar beside the couch. "Should I be flailin my hands and pacin 'round the room?" Charlie asked, a small sarcastic grin on his lips.

Jude shrugged and sat back in the chair. "You'd be surprised how many people actually do that."

Now Charlie shrugged. How could he worry about being arrested when all he could think about was *her*? She had been here, right here, in his living room. That thought alone was enough to occupy his mind for decades.

"We need to talk about your brother, Chuck," Jude said. "I know he's not your favorite subject, but we need to talk about him, and you *have to* be honest with me. You have to tell me everything you know."

"I will," Charlie said, "but it ain't much. I haven't seen Michael in over a hundred years."

Jude looked a little relieved at this. "So you have no idea what he's up to?"

44

Charlie shook his head. "Causin trouble, I s'ppose."

"Have you any theories about what happened in the bar? Any theories about all of this?"

Charlie was silent for a moment, wondering just what to tell the Defender. Certainly not about the princess, but Jude needed to know *some* things if he was going to help him. "The Black Stone is missin, Jude," Charlie said.

Jude's eyes widened and his mouth fell open, the fat fingers of his right hand coming up as if cover it, and then settling back to his side as though he'd realized this was a feminine gesture. "How do you know that?"

Charlie shrugged. "Been rumored," he said, avoiding the question. "And you saw that stone they pulled off Brad Milner. It was a fragment of the Black Stone. The princess said so herself, so it must be true."

Jude took a moment to take this all in. "How could that be possible?" he wondered aloud. "The Black Stone cannot leave the Dark Mountain, and that place is guarded better than the king's castle."

Again, Charlie shrugged and spread his hands. *Your guess is as good as mine.*

"Could your brother have anything to do with this?"

"I wouldn't put it past'em."

"Then you're in deep shit here, Chuck."

"Yeah, you told me that."

Jude stood from his seat and began pacing the room, his head lowered and fingers rubbing his chin as he thought. "Do we know when it went missing?"

"Recently, I would assume," Charlie said.

"Then we need alibis. Do you have anyone who can attest to your whereabouts for the past few days?"

Charlie considered. "I'm at the bar durin workin hours, other than that I spend most of my time alone."

Jude bit his bottom lip and stopped pacing, looking directly at Charlie with his sharp black eyes. "Is there anything else I should know, Chuck?"

Charlie shook his head without hesitation. Anything he should know? What, like how the princess had given him a royal stone nine hundred years ago, and how he had used it to kill Milner before Milner could kill him? Or how Lady Nightborn had come to the bar to hit on him? Or how he was in love with the highest born woman in the land, who also happened to be the Keeper on the case where he was obviously the prime suspect?

No, there wasn't anything else Jude Flyer should know. In fact, there wasn't anything else *anyone* should know.

45

CHAPTER THIRTEEN

Thirty minutes later there was a knock on the front door of Charlie's cabin, and he could tell by the demanding sound of it that it was Theodine Gray doing the knocking. Jude went over to the door and opened it, and sure enough there stood the Head Hunter, the princess standing quietly at his side. She entered first, her face an expressionless mask, as though she had not just been here an hour ago and warned Charlie of what was coming next. Charlie wondered how much more of her he could see without breaking his own blank face as staring at her outright.

She came to a stop in front of him, her eyes betraying nothing, her cloak flowing around her slim shoulders like black water. "Mr. Redmine," she said, "we are taking you into custody pending the investigation of Merin Nightborn's and Brad Milner's murder."

Charlie looked at the princess, said nothing. Surah felt a tiny ache in her chest and swallowed it away.

"We're taking you to the holding cells in King Syrian's castle," she continued, "You are not as yet charged with anything. This is merely a precaution. You may have your Defender present. Will you go willingly?"

As if he had a choice. Charlie said he would.

Theodine Gray stepped forward, a pleased grin on his face. He leaned in close to Charlie, who met his gaze unflinchingly. "Just doing our jobs, like you suggested," he said.

Charlie said nothing.

Surah stepped forward now, wanting to break up the two men, but not liking at all the feeling of being in between them. "Let's go, Mr. Redmine," she said. "Give me your hands."

Charlie pulled his eyes away from the Head Hunter and held his hands out to Surah. Her gloved fingers traced a figure-eight around his wrists, and handcuffs the color of white light appeared. "Are you ready, Mr. Redmine?" she asked, careful to keep her face smooth as she looked up at him.

Charlie nodded, then tilted his head. "Can I bring my guitar?" he asked.

Theo laughed deeply, as though this was an impossible request, and Surah couldn't keep her back from rising a little at this. If she was going to do this job, she was going to need his sub ordinance. He had to know she was running the show, that she was Keeper, at least until this was over.

"I don't see why not," she said, and ignored the look Theo shot her before he could stop himself.

Charlie gave a small bow. "Thank you, my Lady."

Surah twisted her wrist and the guitar propped against the couch rose into the air, the strap connected to it settling over Charlie's neck without the assistance of hands. Her hand fell to her side as the guitar came to rest against Charlie's back.

"Princess," Theo said, "I would be happy to escort the prisoner."

Surah suppressed what might have been a growl. She gave Theo her sweet princess smile. "Thank you, Sir Gray, but I believe that it is the Keeper's job to do such things, and he is not our prisoner until he's found guilty of something. I would appreciate it if you would escort Mr. Flyer instead."

Surah didn't like the look that passed behind Theo's eyes then, but a moment later it was gone, and she hoped she'd imagined it. "Of course, my Lady," Theo said, taking the Defender by the arm, who looked a little annoyed at the contact, but offered no protest.

Surah placed her hand on Charlie's hard shoulder, looking up at him under dark lashes, her purple eyes flashing an apology that he may have just imagined. "Just grit your teeth," she whispered, forcing herself not to let her fingers squeeze the corded muscles in his arm. "This can be unsettling the first time."

Charlie thought, *you're tellin me, honey. You're tellin me.*

CHAPTER FOURTEEN

The holding cells were not as bad as Charlie had imagined. In fact, they were more like sparse hotel rooms with round the clock guards instead of mints on the pillows. There was a twin bed, a table, and two chairs. No windows. No dressers or devices for entertainment. The bathroom was located out in the hall, and two Hunters escorted Charlie when he had to go.

After only two hours of waiting in the room with Jude Flyer Charlie was beyond grateful that the princess had allowed him to bring his guitar. Jude was a man who always seemed to have too many important things to say to allow him to shut up, and there might not be any bars in this room, but the four walls and one guarded door made it clear that he was trapped here until they decided to let him out.

If they decided to let him out. Charlie shoved that thought away as soon as it popped up.

At least he didn't have to be here alone, and once Charlie began strumming the strings of his old guitar, even Jude shut up. He had never been to the city, where most of the fast-talking and power-flashing Highborns made their home, and he felt out of place here, even though all he had seen of it was the hallway that led to this room and the room itself. It was almost as if he could feel the otherness that surrounded him outside these four walls, and he wanted nothing more than to be sitting back in his cabin where only open land neighbored him.

At lunchtime, Jude Flyer left the room to go get lunch for the two of them, leaving Charlie alone, leaning back against his chair and strumming his guitar quietly. As soon as Jude left the room, it happened.

The air in front of him grew warm, and out of it glowing golden letters began to appear, popping into sight like fireflies, coming together to form words and sentences. Charlie was only barely able to keep himself from glancing around as the message appeared in front of him, and could only hope that its sender had made it invisible to anyone other than him. No one was in the room with him, but he was being watched. He was certain.

He got only three words in before knowing who it was from, and his heart sank a little in his chest. It had been over a century, but only one person greeted him this way.

Hey Charlie Boy!

It was a message from his brother.

CHAPTER FIFTEEN

Samson walked alongside her as Surah crossed the courtyard that separated her father's quarters and her own. She could have just teleported into the foyer outside that led to his office, but she needed the time think.

Her tiger walked closely at her flank, his enormous head lowered, amber eyes seeing everything they passed, ears perked and tail swishing slowly. A large stone wall with hundreds of tiny waterfalls was to the left, and the other three walls crawled with green vines that sprouted thousands of violet flowers with blood red centers. The sky above was open for all to see, blue with puffs of white cloud drifting across, the air carrying a sweet floral scent. Hunters and Lords, Ladies and Knights met here, sipping caffeinated drinks and discussing political matters on the pathways and lawns, benches and fountains. It was a pretty place, but Surah avoided places like these. Too populated.

They all bowed as she passed by, and she nodded and princess-smiled as was her duty, wondering if any of them were aware of Merin Nightborn's death, thinking the answer was probably no. Not yet, at least. She was beyond grateful for this, but the peace wouldn't keep for long. Soon everyone would know, and being Keeper, they would look to her for justice.

Samson watched them all, could smell the small tang of fear that radiated from them as he moved by, could feel their eyes on his mistress. He was not a tame Beast, and the small increase in heart rate that befell those around him made his own blood pump hot, but he had been at Surah's side for centuries and had learned how to control himself. For her.

The tiger's head turned sharply to the side as Theodine Gray fell into step on the other side of Surah. Surah kept her princess smile on her face, but wished like hell he would just go away. Theo seemed to be buzzing around like a damn fly lately, and the urge to swat at him was getting stronger and stronger.

"My Lady," Theo said, holding an elbow out to Surah.

So much for time to think. She may as well have teleported. She laced her arm through his, giving him another fake smile. "Sir Gray," she said.

"On your way to see King Syrian?" he asked.

Surah nodded, her free hand reaching over to stroke Samson's side for comfort. She could feel the powerful muscles moving in his shoulders as he walked.

They reached the wall that held the entrance to her father's quarters, and two Hunters stepped aside to let them enter. Theo flicked his wrist, opening the doors for them. They stepped into the foyer with the storm mural hanging above, and two more Hunter's bowed to them in greeting.

Theo came to a stop at the center of the room, halting Surah's progress as well. They were alone here, save for the four Hunters that always occupied the room, as silent as the candelabras hanging on the walls. Surah looked up at the Head Hunter, her eyebrow cocked, her heart sinking a little for a reason she couldn't explain after seeing the look on his face.

"May I have a word with you, Princess?" Theo asked.

Surah swallowed. No, she thought, please don't. She nodded.

Theo rubbed his hands together, his handsome face apprehensive. It took Surah a moment to recognize that he was nervous, as she couldn't recall a time ever seeing him so. She found herself holding her breath.

"I would hope," Theo began, just barely above a whisper, "that you know how I feel about you." His gloved hands came up and took hers, and Surah had to use great effort not to take a step back. His gray eyes were all but burning. "I have loved you since we were children, Surah."

Theo paused, his handsome face dead serious, his jaw held in tight lines, watching for how she absorbed this information. Surah just looked at him, not sure what to say to this. The urge to hop on Samson's back and let him carry her out of here like she used to do when she was a little girl struck her, and she bit her tongue to keep back the laugh that mental image brought up.

"I hope," Theo continued, his voice low and deep, "that you will consider taking my hand in marriage."

At these words Surah's thoughts seemed to crash together and jam up, producing nothing intelligible and leaving only raw emotion. Her heart raced, her tongue going dry in her mouth. The urge to clench her fists struck and she fought it. The urge to laugh followed and she sent it away as well. Her feet wanted to shift beneath her and she didn't let them. Time seemed to lengthen into an endless tunnel, where silence and hanging words dwelled. Had she not been so practiced in the art of sophistication, she would have sputtered like a nervous child.

Then a thought came, and it was only one word, a name actually, but it was as clear as Sunday morning.

Charlie.

Her brow furrowed. Why was she thinking of Charlie? That was no good. She shoved the thought away. She opened her mouth to say something, not knowing what it would be until it came out. "You'll have to give me time to consider things," she said, and cleared her throat as the solution came to her, her voice taking back on the confidence that always carried in her sweet tone. "There is much to be done now, too much that requires my attention."

Theo's expression changed, not so much a hardening, as she was used to seeing from him, but more a poker mask sliding into place. Surah felt a pang of guilt. She had never seen this expression on Theo's face, and it was strangely disarming. She thought for just a moment that if he always wore this look, rather than the one he put on for all others, she might not dislike him so much. Her gloved hand reached up before she could stop it.

It rested against Theo's face, and his eyes softened as he leaned his chin into her touch. For a moment Surah could see why so many women were in love with him, and she had to work a little to hold his gaze. She gave him her gentlest princess smile, and he didn't know the difference. So few would. "I will consider it, Theo," she said, "and I am honored that you have asked." She swallowed. "But there are other matters at hand…you understand?" Her voice was sweet and low, the purr of a kitten. One of her more deceptive qualities.

Theo smiled a full smile of perfect teeth, dimples forming in his cheeks. He really was a handsome man, having stopped ageing at around twenty-seven, with fine lines to his face and dark lashes. He took Surah's hand into his now and kissed it, bowing his head. "Of course, my Lady," he said.

Surah was just breathing a sigh of relief when something nudged her hard in the back, making her stumble forward into Theo's arms. He caught her quickly and set her to rights, and Surah whipped her head around to see Samson staring at her, his amber eyes only inches from her own, his huge chest puffing as he chuffed and growled deeply. He sent her one word telepathically, then he shot off across the foyer in the direction of the king's quarters.

The one word was *trouble.*

Surah didn't think twice. She took to her heels and chased her tiger down the hallway to her father's study, her heart beating out of her chest, the stone at her throat growing alternately cold and hot. Samson had heard something. Something was wrong. She could feel it too now. *Big* trouble.

The tiger slammed head-first into the double doors to the study, crashing them open with cracks like thunder, and charged into the room.

Surah followed only moments after, with Theo right at her heels.

Her breath caught in her throat as she took in the scene. Her father stood off to the side, his thick hands raised and moving through the air in ceaseless motion as his lips recited spell after spell after spell. Lightening flew from his fingertips like snakes of silver. His face was all concentrated, sharp lines, and his hair stood up on end as if electricity were passing through him. Magic was so thick in here that it floated on the air like smoke and charged the room with heat like a divine furnace. King Syrian's two personal Hunters lay dead on the floor. Blood ran down the walls, pooled on the soft purple carpet. Screeches and screams of the damned bounced off the walls and floor and ceiling. The enormous fireplace in the west wall blazed like the infernos of hell.

And out of it poured demons.

Surah licked her lips and removed the two sais that she always kept crisscrossed at her back, thinking this was turning out to be one hell of a day.

CHAPTER SIXTEEN

Samson charged forward, his muscular body held low and his amber eyes flashing with battle lust. He leapt into the air and clamped his huge jaws around the black, rotted body of a demon, snatching it out of flight like a dazed fly. The demon shrieked, its cry of agony ripping through Surah's ears as the tiger and the thing came crashing to the ground, Samson's teeth ripping at the black skeletal figure and sending oily blood and body parts in all directions.

The smell in the room was awful. The smell was that of old death. Nearly choking.

Another demon swept down toward Surah, skeletal black wings blowing the heat of the fireplace against her face, lifting her short lavender hair from her shoulders, and her heart leapt as she spun around with her sais and skewered the thing right through the midsection, its long claws reaching and scraping, its red eyes widening and mouth gaping. Her lips trembled as she uttered a banishing spell. The thing disappeared in a thick cloud of black smoke, the smell that of burning flesh and spoiled fruit.

For a short moment that seemed incredibly long, all she could do was stand there and stare around the room. She had seen a demon or two before, on more than one occasion, and she even killed a few in her day, as the black slash-mark tattoos covering her left arm indicated. But she had never seen *so many* demons before. The sight was nearly paralyzing. Like watching a scene in hell.

It reminded her of the battle she'd witnessed a month ago in a place called the Silver City run by the Vampires and Wolves. In all her years she had never seen such a thing as she had that night, and she still wished she never had. She had watched the young Sun Warrior charge into battle, could still see so clearly the stark red that spilled into the white snow, the steamy breath that issued from the mouths of so many dying, visible last moments of life. She remembered the moment when the young Warrior lost her mind, the battle lust overcoming her and the destruction that followed. The look in the girl's eyes—Alexa, her name had been—was the same look that now rode behind the glowing red eyes of the demons in the room. The eyes were dark abysses. You stared into them, and they stared back.

And the smell. That awful, awful smell.

It was nearly paralyzing indeed, but when another demon whipped its head toward her, fiery eyes flashing and sharp claws raised, its throat issuing that ear-clenching screech, she snapped out of her reverie and slid into battle mode. It was not difficult. Death was the only thing in life Surah knew to be a certainty, and as much as she had faced it, she also dealt it. If not for the worry of her father, who was currently fighting off a demon of his own, and moving not quite as fast as he used to, she thought she might enjoy this. Killing demons was not something she'd had the opportunity to do for ages.

She gripped her weapons, the ends of which were black with rotted blood, dripping ropes of it. Her cloak fluttered with her movements, dancing around her as she moved through the room and battled the demons, like an angel dancing on storm clouds. Beside her Theodine Gray danced with his sword as well, and slid its blade across the throat of another demon, its shrieks of anger and agony filling the room.

But Syrian was moving too slowly. Just her glimpses of him, his movement stiff, his eyes bulging and the vein in his forehead standing out, told her they were in serious trouble here. They were too far outnumbered.

And more were coming out of the hearth. Ugly, black creatures with glowing red eyes, their bodies nothing but bone and rotted muscle. Their hands were claws and their feet hooves. Horns protruded from their skulls, beneath which sat faces from nightmares. Bat-like wings flapped at their backs, stirring the hot air and pushing the scent of decay and death around the room in rank waves. Surah had to close the portal they were coming through, or at least try. Gods only knew how long they could hold the demons off.

"Samson," she said, her voice sounding strange in the unintelligible chaos of the room. Small somehow. Out of place.

The tiger's huge head whipped toward her. He moved to her side immediately, leaping into the air again and severing the body of a demon with his powerful jaws in mid-flight. He landed on his paws in front of her, black blood marring his fur and teeth, and shook his head, whipping a piece of rotted demon flesh against the wall where it splattered like a bug on a windshield and slid down to the floor in a nasty pool.

Surah clutched the stone at her throat and closed her eyes, knowing

Samson would protect her while she did this. She ran through the spell Syris had taught her for closing portals, hoping she would get it right. She had only ever performed it once in training with her brother, and he'd had to help a good deal.

She recited the words, her brow furrowing in concentration, doing her best to ignore the growls of her tiger and the cries of the damned, the pure *wrongness* in the room. Sweat trickled down her back as she clenched her hands into fists and recited faster, the stone squeezed in the palm of her hand burning now. Her head grew light with the effort, the power washing through her and sweeping her away. She planted her feet and continued, her breath coming short and heart pounding like a death toll.

She felt it when it worked, like a puzzle piece snapping into place, and all sound seemed momentarily sucked out of the room. The wonderful feeling that accompanied successful Magic swept through her, and her eyes snapped open and propelled her back to the scene. She looked first to the stone fireplace, and breathed a huge breath as no more demons came out of it. A screech issued to her left and her head whipped around to see Theo removing the head of one of the remaining demons, his left hand gripping the demon's large horn as he ran his blade across the thing's throat, his lips moving swiftly in a banishing spell, the small Head Hunter's stone around his neck glowing red. Then to her right, where her father was sending two more demons away in noxious clouds of black smoke, his big chest heaving in a way that made more worry spiral in Surah's stomach. Samson sat at her side, licking black blood from his paws and teeth, his eyes narrowed to slits and powerful shoulders relaxed, as though he'd just finished dinner rather than killing demons.

At last it was done.

Four Hunters came rushing through the double doors of the study, way too late to the party, and stood staring at the scene in the room with slightly wide eyes, the only indication of their alarm. Surah looked down at herself, eyeing the rank black demon blood that marred her cloak and gloves. She felt a trickle of something roll down her neck and reached up to wipe at it, repressing a gag when she saw that it was more of the nasty blood.

She ran her hands down the air in front of her, reciting a spell to clean away the mess, and allowed herself to just breathe after she'd set herself to rights. Her father and Theo cleaned themselves off as well, and the three stood looking at each other not knowing at all what to say.

It was Theo who broke the silence. He slid his sword into the back of his cloak and his jaw clenched. "I better go check on the prisoner," he said.

CHAPTER SEVENTEEN

When Charlie's brother entered the room, Jude Flyer happened to be in the bathroom. Something in the lunch he bought must not have sat right with him, because he'd been gone for almost twenty minutes. Charlie sat on the bed, thinking about the message he'd received an hour earlier.

And then out of nowhere, Black Heart appeared.

Charlie didn't start out of his reclined position, didn't cringe as so many would in Black Heart's presence. He only sat staring at him, his hands folded in his lap, and his brother stared back.

Michael looked different now, so different than Charlie remembered. It was a wonder what a century could do, how much it could change a person. Michael had aged, and not just a little, but a lot, looking to be in his forties rather than his twenties like Charlie even though he was only a couple of years older. His dark hair was long and pulled back into a severe ponytail, his skin pallid and white. The lines of his face were harder, all angry angles and slashes. He wore a fine black cloak made of velvet, the hood pulled up and hands tucked underneath. His eyes, the same jade color as Charlie's, floated inside of it, but those too were colder than Charlie remembered.

"Brother," Black Heart said, his arms opening beneath his cloak.

Charlie stood from the bed and embraced his brother, a mixture of love and disappointment washing over him. No matter what Michael had become, Charlie could not find it in his heart not to love him. Michael had taken care of him when their parents died, had raised him, taught him how to hunt and use Magic. Despite what most people thought, Charlie knew there was good in his big brother, it just had been slowly buried over time.

"It is so good to see you, Charlie Boy."

Charlie stepped back and ran a hand over his jaw. "S'good to see you

57

too, Mikey."

Black Heart laughed heartily, and Charlie found that different too. Almost sinister. He clapped Charlie on the shoulder. "No one has called me that in over a century little brother," he said, a wide grin revealing very white teeth. He squeezed Charlie's shoulder, the way he used to do when they were boys. "I have missed you."

I've missed you too, Charlie thought. *The* real *you.* He nodded at his brother, his stomach twisting. "Been a long time," he said.

Black Heart's smile widened, but fell into a deep frown as he looked around the small room. "How long have they been holding you here, brother?"

Charlie's heart began to beat a little faster as the surprise of seeing his brother gave way to the possibilities of the consequences of his brother being here. "You must be crazy comin here," he said. "You know what they'll do to you if they catch you?"

Black Heart put a finger to his chin. "Oh, I can imagine," he said, "but that's *if* they could catch me, little brother, which they can't. Did you read my message? Will you come with me?"

Charlie never had time to consider the answer, because at that moment, Theodine Gray and Surah Stormsong popped into the room. Charlie had only time to see the princess's eyes widen a little and to feel the sharp dread circle his chest once before Black Heart took his hand and teleported them out of there.

Charlie had been wrong. He hadn't been neck-deep in shit before.

But he was now.

CHAPTER EIGHTEEN

Her heart didn't sink. She didn't know him well enough for her heart to sink, but it tilted. She examined the emotion as they stood there in silence, staring at the spot where Charlie Redmine and Black Heart had been just a moment ago. It was just a beat of time, but in it she acknowledged that she felt a little disappointed at this new development, at what she'd just seen. It was then she realized she'd really wanted Charlie to be innocent, to come out of this unscathed.

But the moment passed on a single bated breath, and she wiped the thoughts away as one might chalk from a blackboard. Why should she be disappointed? They had only met once before, when they had just barely been teenagers, and she had been a grieving, scared young girl. She wished now she could go back to that moment beside the lake, when she'd given her sister's stone to the common boy with the dark hair and jade-colored eyes. But it was far too late to be worrying about such things now.

Theo broke the silence, which he seemed to be doing a lot lately. His voice was hard and deep. "Can you perform a Tracker spell, my Lady?" he asked.

Surah nodded, her head curiously light on her shoulders. She kept trying to shove thoughts of Charlie away, and found the name kept coming back, along with the tropical ocean color of his eyes, the calmness and control that radiated from them. His eyes were the only things that were the same as she remembered, but she couldn't remember having this reaction to him before. Surely she was too old to be as vain as to be spellbound by just his appearance, though she had to admit said appearance had become rather spellbinding. There was no denying that; he was a good-looking man. A quite, reserved, good-looking man. But so what? If you asked most people, so was Theodine Gray. It meant nothing. Nothing to her, or at

59

least, it shouldn't.

"How long will it take you to prepare?" Theo asked yanking her out of her troublesome thoughts.

Surah's mouth felt a little dry. She licked her lips. "Half an hour," she said, "and I'll need to consult with Bassil first."

Theo nodded and opened the door that led out into the hallway. Surah stepped through and he followed, shutting the door behind him. "I'll have the Shaman sent to your quarters."

Surah forced herself to look up into Theo's gray eyes and smile. She may not be too fond of him, but at least he wasn't a traitor. She refused to recognize the twist of her stomach that came with that thought. "Thank you," she said. Then she snapped her fingers and teleported back to her chambers to prepare the spell that might track down Charlie Redmine and his brother.

She couldn't say for certain if she hoped it would work or not.

***

Bottles clanked together and flew from the shelf inside the cabinet, floating on the air and settling on the counter in a neat row. Surah walked in front of them and read the labels, her posture stiff and rigid, placing the ones she needed in a pile off to the side without even touching them. Her father would have thought it a useless application of Magic, but Surah was on edge and she didn't particularly care what her father would say right now. He'd forced this work on her, shoving her into being Keeper, and she would complete the tasks in the manner she pleased, because backing out now was not an option.

Bassil stood behind her, motionless, watching. His hands were tucked into the sleeves of his cloak where he crossed his huge arms over his chest. Surah turned her head to the side, looking up at him from the corner of her eye. "Quit staring at me like that, Bassil." She smiled a little. "It's creepy."

Bassil laughed, a deep, rich laugh that seemed to match the dark tone of his skin. His white teeth glinted behind a wide smile. His voice was slightly accented by the Northlands, even after all these years. He turned on his heel, making his multi-colored patchwork cloak flip around his legs, and went over to the window to sit by Samson. He stroked the tiger's head. Samson lay unmoving, his huge head resting on his paws, amber eyes watching his mistress. He didn't lean into the touch. He would let Bassil and a select few others pet him, but he only responded to Surah's hands.

"As you wish, my Lady," Bassil said. "You just go on and keep flinging bottles off the shelf like a worried housewife."

Surah spun around on her heel, the smile gone from her face, her voice flat. Her princess-etiquette momentarily discarded. "The Black Stone is missing, Shaman. A Highborn lady is dead. Demons just flew out of my father's fireplace and tried to kill him. How is it you think I should be acting?"

Bassil clasped his hands together in front of him and smiled humbly. "Ah, a real reaction from the princess. You are getting better at showing your emotions, my Lady."

Surah's head tilted back, a mischievous glint in her eye, and she flung a bottle of purple potion at the Shaman with her Magic. Bassil laughed and his hand shot up, halting the bottle mid-flight. He moved his hand to the side and the vial settled on Surah's dresser. Surah relaxed a little, taking comfort in the interaction. She had grown up with Bassil. He had been her mentor since she was a little girl, and this was a normal exchange between them.

"You still throw like a princess, I see," he said.

Surah rolled her eyes and continued picking out bottles for the spell. "I thought you were here to help me," she said. "Isn't there something you should be setting up? What do we pay you for?"

Bassil laughed again. "My wise council, of course, and you seem to be doing a fair job of it yourself, my Lady."

Surah inventoried her selections so far, turning her back to Bassil and replacing the unneeded bottles. "Maybe I should tell Samson to bite you," she said. Her head turned to the side again. "He likes dark meat, you know."

Bassil looked down to see the tiger looking at him with those golden eyes, and took a step away from the window where Samson was perched. He knew Surah wasn't serious, but the tiger had been listening, and now he could practically see the idea playing out in the Beast's head. "Very funny, my Lady," he said.

Surah smiled and gathered the bottles, moving over to the table by the window and placing them on top before taking a seat in the chair there. Bassil took a seat across from her, eyeing the ingredients. "This would work better with eagle's blood," he said.

Surah's purple eyes lifted to the Shaman's face, her hands pausing over the small bowl she was arranging at the center of the table. "Perhaps," she said, "but that's Black Magic. You know this, Bassil."

The Shaman nodded once. "True, but you're *searching* for darkness. It lays on the horizon, princess, rolling toward the land as we speak. Black Magic killed Merin Nightborn and allowed demons to enter your father's chamber. Black Magic may be the only way to face the things ahead."

Surah's teeth clenched a little. A terribly cold shiver had walked its way up her spine. Bassil's voice had taken on that haunting tone she'd learned to both trust and fear over the years. She gave him a level stare, restraining a reaction that would give away her unease, retaining her manners. "I'll try this way first," she said.

The Shaman spread his hands. "Of course, my Lady."

She spent the next thirty minutes attempting the spell, staring into the mixture of potions in the bowl, concentrating until sweat rolled down her neck, saying the incantations over and over again, until finally, she sat back and blew out a heavy breath. She brought her gloved hands up and rubbed her forehead, squeezing her eyes shut.

Bassil raised an eyebrow. "No luck?"

Surah opened her eyes and gave him a droll look.

The Shaman smiled. "I see."

Just then, there was a knock at the door to her room. Silence fell over them as they stared at each other, unmoving. A second knock sounded, and Surah dragged her eyes over to the door. Samson had lifted his head from his paws, his ears swiveling and perking. Surah took a deep breath and flicked her wrist, opening the door.

Theodine Gray stood there. Of course he did.

His appearances were routine lately. And by the look on his face, Surah could tell he did not have good news to share. Why would he? Things were on that kind of track lately, and she knew from experience that bad times had a way of proceeding worse, like sliding down a slope slicked with oil. Black oil. The ball of life just rolled that way, right on forward through the messes, through the rough skies, and she felt the truth of the Shaman's prediction in that moment, all the way done to her bones, as the Head Hunter delivered the word.

Another Highborn woman was dead.

Yes, darkness was indeed coming, rolling in like storm clouds.

CHAPTER NINETEEN

The first thing he heard was the call of the birds. Charlie blinked, a little dazed from the trip. He was not used to teleporting places, as most common people weren't, and his stomach jumped up to his throat. He bent over, clutching his knees, his hands gripping the faded denim of his jeans, rasping in breath. The air here was warm, thick and humid. He stared down at the jungle green vines that snaked around his boots, wondering where he was. A hand fell on his back.

"Sorry about that, little brother," Black Heart said, patting Charlie's back, making him start a little in surprise. "Traveling that quickly can unsettle your stomach. It'll pass."

Charlie straightened, taking in the scene around him slowly, bit by bit. They stood beneath a canopy of trees so thick and green that the sky was scarcely visible, and only fragments of sunshine penetrated. Red flowers with black centers crawled up enormous brown tree trunks, and leaves rustled and branches swayed where unseen creatures crept through them. He drew in a sharp breath. "Where did you bring me?"

Black Heart smiled widely, his hands spreading out at his sides. "We are in a jungle in the Southlands. Untamed lands. Beautiful, isn't it?"

Charlie chose his words carefully, eyeing his brother with uncertainty. It had been a long time since the two of them had last seen each other, and who knew how much Michael could have changed. If some of the stories he'd heard were true, the answer was a lot.

"You gotta take me back, Michael."

Black Heart had begun walking through the trees, but he stopped now and turned back to his brother. His eyebrows rose slightly at the same time his eyes narrowed. "I'm afraid I can't do that, Charlie Boy."

Charlie met his brother's stare levelly. "I'm 'spected of murder. This won't look good."

Black Heart nodded slowly, stepping forward and placing his hands on Charlie's shoulders. "Did you commit a murder?"

Charlie almost said no, but then he thought about Brad Milner, about how he had crushed the old man's throat in his fist. It had been self-defense, but Charlie wasn't sure that didn't constitute as murder. He said nothing.

Black Heart smiled. "That won't look good either, little brother."

Charlie took a cautious step backward. "Did you set me up for this, Michael? What've you done?"

For the first time Charlie could remember anger flashed behind his brother's eyes as he looked at him, and it was such a cold thing that Charlie felt a shiver race up his spine despite the warm air. He swallowed once, seeing now the man who called himself Black Heart rather than the sibling who'd raised him, taken care of him. Charlie's heart broke a little realizing that at least some of the rumors had to be true about his brother, and if they were, Charlie needed to tread carefully. Michael had always had a temper. Who knew how time had fueled it?

"What have *I* done?" Black Heart said, his voice as sharp as a blade. "I have done nothing." His hands clenched into fists as he took a step toward Charlie. "It is *them* who have forced such actions from me. *They* are guilty of the crimes they accuse me of. Now they're just getting what they paid for."

Charlie held very still, watching his brother the way one might watch a pacing lion. "And what's that, brother? What do you plan to do with the Black Stone? Kill all the Highborn women?"

Black Heart laughed. It was an ugly sound. It made Charlie's teeth clench. "And why not? What do I care for their precious ladies? Did they care for us during the Great War? Did they care for you or me when our parents died?"

Charlie felt a twist in his heart, a small burning of a scar that had mostly healed long ago. Apparently Michael's hadn't healed so well. "That was long ago, brother. Lotta people died. Highborns too."

Black Heart slammed his fist into his hand, a vein pulsing in his pale neck as he leaned into Charlie's face. "Why do you think that is?" he asked, spittle flying from his lips. "Why do you think we were so unable to defend ourselves against the other races? I'll tell you why, because the royals keep all the powerful Magic to themselves. They locked away the Black Stone and refused to use it to protect their people. They put laws on certain Magic, deciding amongst themselves what is appropriate for use, forbidding others to use it and in turn using it as they see fit." He paused, rubbed his temples the way he used to do when they were just boys and Charlie was being particularly exasperating. "I am disappointed in you, Charlie Boy. Are you so easily fooled? Do you not question the decisions made for you?"

Charlie thought that made two of them for the disappointment, but he said nothing, something he knew was usually best in most situations. His brother had obviously fallen off the deep end, become a fanatic. Things in the kingdom were not that bad. No one was suffering, and for the most part the people could do as they pleased, live and work and make a life for themselves. His brother's desires weren't about getting justice, they were about revenge. And that made him more dangerous. In fact, Charlie thought he was growing more dangerous by the minute. He had to tread *very* carefully. He seemed to be doing that a lot lately.

He looked around, his stomach tightening as the gravity of his situation settled over him. He was not standing in a jungle arguing with his brother. He was in the middle of nowhere—*untamed lands*—arguing with a madman. And surely suspected of murder by the woman who walked his dreams at night. Let's not forget that.

He chose his words slowly, his deep voice soft and low. "You would force me into this, Mikey?"

Black Heart waved a hand, having regained his composure, looking more like Michael than Charlie thought was safe to believe. "I am opening your eyes, Charlie Boy." His wide smile returned. "You will thank me in the future. Come, let me explain things to you. There is much you don't know."

Black Heart turned to go. Charlie didn't follow. "The Hunters will come lookin for me."

Black Heart turned to face his brother once more, still smiling. "Yes, Charlie Boy, that's the plan. That is the plan indeed." He wrapped his arm around Charlie's shoulders. "I hear there's a new Keeper. King Syrian's last living child. I do hope she is as good at finding things as her older brother was. I've always wanted to make Princess Surah's acquaintance. I hear she's quite lovely."

Charlie looked up and saw the murderous gleam in his brother's eyes, and his heart did a dead standstill.

The shit just kept getting deeper.

CHAPTER TWENTY

Surah patted Samson's head before entering the Grand Room, where she knew dozens of royals would be waiting. The tiger leaned into her touch, his amber eyes sympathetic.

Remember, he told her silently, *don't mention the Black Stone. Your father doesn't want them to panic.* He paused. *I don't want them to panic, either. It makes them smell like roasting meat.*

Surah nodded once, gave her tiger a quick hug, and took a deep breath. She squared her shoulders and tilted up her chin, slipping on the royal posture and mask that she'd learned from her mother as a child. This was certain to be an unpleasant experience, but in her life she'd dealt with thousands of those, and her mother always said that composure was key. Surah agreed. She rolled her neck and went into the room, Samson at her heels.

As soon as she entered, dozens of faces turned toward her and conversation stopped. The lords and ladies bowed to her, and Surah nodded to them, her heart twisting to see that many of them had tears streaked down their faces. Merin Nightborn's family stood off to the side in a cluster, mother and father clutching each other, cloaks all black to represent their mourning. Everyone in the room was wearing black actually, and for a moment Surah's mind flashed back to the demons that had flown out of her father's fireplace, with their shrieks of anger and agony and their dead, rotted faces.

King Syrian sat at the head of the room on his throne, an enormous thing made of metal and polished wood the color of violet, where a similarly violet runner led up to his feet over the marble floor. Around him stood his two new personal guards, since his previous ones had died in the demon attack, which was another thing Surah was not supposed to mention. She walked gracefully up to her father's side, taking the hands of those she passed and offering condolences to those who had lost someone in a sort of macabre dance train. Merin Nightborn's mother had smeared mascara under her puffy red eyes, and her hands shook as she kissed the back of Surah's hand. Surah pulled her into a hug and held her for a moment, earning a collective sigh from the room. This was why she was so loved in the kingdom, and she knew it. Not because she went around smiling and greeting her people, but because she actually cared when they were hurting, and she hurt with them. Maybe even more so than her father.

And now they would turn to her not just for comfort but for answers and justice. Her respect for her lost brother grew in that moment. Being Keeper was not a pleasant job.

When she reached the head of the room she turned and faced her people, bowing to her father as she stood beside his throne, waiting for him to start the dialogue, but someone in the crowd spoke first.

It was Merin Nightborn's father. "My Liege," he said, "what is being done about my daughter?" His voice broke on that last word, and Surah's chest tightened. She had just last month lost her own brother, and she understood his heartache. She understood it too well.

King Syrian spoke gently, his composure as solid as Surah's, though she knew he didn't like any of this as much as she didn't. "We are doing everything we can to bring light the situation regarding Merin's untimely death, Lord Nightborn," he said, "and we will bring to justice those responsible."

Gregert Lancer spoke next, his voice as unsteady as Lord Nightborn's. He was the father of Cynthian Lancer, the second Highborn lady who had been killed in the past two days. A death a day. No wonder the tension in the room was thick. If this kept up, if Surah couldn't find a way to stop it, soon the whole kingdom would be crying out for answers and justice.

In fact, Samson could smell the fear and anxiety on them already, but he didn't tell his mistress this.

Lord Lancer seemed to speak Surah's thoughts. "My daughter makes the second murder in two days," he said. "Something very serious is going on here, and we need answers."

Surah didn't miss the fact that his eyes flicked to her as he said this. There were nods of approval and mumbles of agreement. She cleared her throat. "We offer our sincere condolences for your losses, my Lords and Ladies." She looked to her father and put a hand on his shoulder, which he reached up and covered with his own. "We have all suffered too much death lately." She looked back to the crowd, swallowing back just enough of her grief to keep the tears out of her eyes and still show her empathy. "And I intend to see the loss stop here."

"This is Black Heart's work," Lady Nightborn called out, swiping at the black smudges under her eyes. Her voice was clear and strong but laced with pain. Surah's respect for the lady grew at this. Most Highborn ladies held their tongues in such meetings.

"We all know he's behind this," Lady Nightborn continued, "and he has gone too far. He must be brought to justice." Her small, gloved fists clenched at her sides.

Now there were outright shouts of approval, and Samson swished his tail around him as he sat by Surah's side. His eyes watched them all as he breathed in the smell of the emotions in the room that had kicked up a notch at the mention of Black Heart. Surah placed her free hand on his back for comfort.

She took another deep breath, her mind flashing back to an hour ago when she had seen Black Heart standing beside Charlie. When Charlie had escaped with him. When things had gone from not good to worse. Now her people were calling for blood, and she couldn't blame them. Hadn't she gone off to kill the man who murdered Syris just a month ago against her father's orders? No, she couldn't blame them, but she still wasn't sure *who* to blame, and now it was her job to find out.

She was also not supposed to mention Charlie's escape. As of right now, three people knew about Black Heart's acquisition of his brother, and she wanted to keep it that way. She opened her mouth, not sure what to say, but knowing it was her turn.

"I will find him," she said, her soft voice carrying sweetly and strongly through the room, "and if he is responsible for this, he will pay."

And she could see by the looks on their faces that they were going to hold her to that.

CHAPTER TWENTY-ONE

"Surah, sweetheart, may I have a word with you?" King Syrian asked, after all the people had left the room.

Theo gave a low bow and left too, leaving her alone with her father and Samson, who spoke up in her head.

Run for it, love. I've got a feeling this isn't a conversation you want to have.

Surah ignored him, rather than snapping at him about how that was not in the least helpful. "Of course," she told her father, taking a seat on the arm of his throne, smoothing her cloak out delicately beneath her. Syrian looked a little peaked, his cheeks slightly red and complexion very pale. She could tell he was thinking about her brother, one of those moments when the grief just seemed to slam into you harder. She was well acquainted with it. She took her glove off her right hand and touched his forehead. He was a touch feverish. Her heart seemed to skip a beat.

"It's going to be all right, father," she said, giving him a small smile, which he returned. "I'll figure this out."

He took her hand and kissed it, looking up at his last remaining child with gentle love. "I know that, Surah. I know." He coughed into his hand, a deep hack that shook in his chest. Surah's brow creased, heart skipping once more.

"You should lie down," she said. "You don't sound well."

Syrian waved a hand. "There is no time to rest now, dear. Too much to be done. There is a matter I want to discuss with you."

He coughed again, and Surah couldn't say why, but her gut twisted at the sound of it. Syrian's next words shocked her out of whatever she was going to say about it.

"I want you to consider accepting Theodine Gray's proposal for marriage."

Surah stood up involuntarily, the movement less graceful than was her custom, and paced over to Samson, who had a look on his face that said *told you so*. Surah resisted the urge to thump him on the head. Now her heart wasn't skipping, but racing.

For a moment she couldn't think of a single thing to say. Then she said, "Surely you don't expect me to consider this while the Black Stone is missing and Highborn women are being murdered." Her tone just bordered accusatory, and when her father coughed again she felt bad for this, but it was better than voicing the *Gods no!* that was bouncing around in her head.

Now Syrian removed a handkerchief from beneath his cloak and coughed into it. Surah saw there were spots of red on it when he removed it from his mouth at the same time he did. He tried to hide it from her sight, but she stepped forward quickly and snatched the white cloth from his hand. Her heart dropped as she looked down at the smattering of blood there.

Her breath came short, her voice falling to just above a whisper. "What is this, father?" she asked, holding the handkerchief up for him to see. "What is ailing you?"

Syrian eyed the cloth with distaste, and Surah could tell by his face that he had been keeping this from her. He seemed to be unable to find his words. Samson crept forward and sniffed at the blood on the cloth, his amber eyes were regretful as they flicked to her.

I smell demon poison in his blood, Samson told her. *He must have been scratched or bitten.*

Even in her own head Surah's voice sounded far away as she stared at her tiger. *"Are you sure, Sam?"*

Quite sure, love.

Surah's heart clenched and seemed to slide down low in her chest as she looked at her father. Her voice sounded robotic and far away to her. "Where is it?" she asked.

Syrian released a heavy sigh, as if he would really rather not show her, then pulled the collar of his cloak aside, exposing his shoulder. Four long, ugly scratches were raked across the skin there, an angry red color puckering the edges. The centers of the gashes were black, giving a visual of the poison inside his body. Surah's hand came up and covered her mouth, her breath catching in her throat. She gave no effort to try and repress her reaction. She didn't even think to.

She stripped her glove from her other hand and gripped his arm, leaning in close to get a better look. "You've tried healing it?" Her voice still sounded funny, as if she could hear it outside of herself. Stress seemed to keep mounting and mounting in the past two days.

"Of course I've tried healing it," Syrian said, gently removing Surah's hold and replacing the collar of his cloak, hiding the ugly marks.

Surah's heart hurt, actually *hurt,* as she looked at her father, into the violet of his eyes which were the same color as her own. He was all she had left as far as family went, and her heart knew those scratches were death marks. Unless she could find the Black Stone. Black Magic was the only thing that could heal a demon poisoning, and Surah could see on her father's face that he had already thought of this.

"You used the piece of Black Stone that was removed from Brad Milner?"

Syrian smiled as if this were a silly question, and she felt the urge to snap at him, but didn't. "Yes," he said. "It's not big enough to perform the kind of healing I require."

Surah had figured this, but she still had hoped. Her mouth fell open, wanting to ask him why he hadn't told her, why he hadn't mentioned the urgency of her success in the mission ahead of her. Instead she leaned forward and kissed her father's brow, which was warm and clammy under her lips. Syrian gave a small smile and patted her hand. Surah straightened her back, taking a deep breath, trying for her composure. "I will find it, father," she said, and swallowed. "I promise."

Syrian smiled again. "I know you will, Surah. I know." The trust in his eyes made her heart hurt more still. He coughed into his hand, using his Magic to summon another kerchief, which went to his mouth a clean white and returned splattered with red. He eyed the mess and crumpled it in his fist, regarding his daughter with gentle eyes. "Think about what I said. Please."

Surah nodded, but instead of thinking about Theo, what she thought was, *I'm coming to find you Charlie Redmine, and Gods help us both when I do.*

Samson heard the thought, so clearly it had been projected, and he turned his amber eyes up to his mistress, studying the expression on her face. She hid her emotions well, but she couldn't hide them from him, and what he saw there made him think *Oh. Oh, dear.*

CHAPTER TWENTY-TWO

The fire in front of him blazed orange and blue, and Charlie stared into it, listening to its crackle and the silent night around him. His brother sat next to him, also silent, letting his words sink in. Charlie knew Michael was waiting for some sort of response, but he didn't have one to give. He couldn't think of a single damn thing to say, not with the emotions that were roiling around inside him.

What an incredibly shitty situation. How had things unraveled so quickly? Worse, he had a feeling they had just *begun* unraveling.

Black Heart sighed, wrapping an arm around his brother, who used great effort not to cringe at his touch. "It's a lot to take in," Black Heart said. "I know that, but I'll need all the help I can get here, brother. It's a...big task."

Charlie swallowed. His mouth felt dry. "There must be some other way," he said. "This can't be the only way to go about it."

Black Heart sighed again. "I wish there was, brother. How I wish there was. But consider this, how will you feel when another war between the races erupts, and your beloved royals are unwilling to use Black Magic to protect you?"

"What makes you so certain another Great War is on the horizon?"

Black Heart smiled now, that wide, white grin that was foreign and unpleasant to Charlie on his brother's face. "I bet you didn't know the King of Wolves and Vampires murdered the Keeper just last month, did you?"

Charlie watched his brother closely, but he could tell he was telling the truth. "The Vampire king killed Syrian Stormsong? They told us it was an accident."

Black Heart laughed. "Of course they did, brother. Why wouldn't they? They lie about everything else. They know there's trouble brewing between the races, but they don't want us common folk to know that. Afraid we might start getting ideas, questioning things."

Charlie wasn't sure what he thought about that, but he knew murdering innocent women was not the way to go about. It was a wonder to him how his brother couldn't see how fanatical he sounded. He found himself wondering just what had happened in the past century that had made Michael so angry, because while he laughed and smiled, Charlie could see now that it was anger that laced his brother's tone, what made it so sharp and hostile.

Charlie stared into Michael's eyes, wishing he could take from him whatever pain had made him this way, because he had not *always* been this way. "What did they do to you, Mikey?" he asked, his voice low and cautious. "What has made you hate them so?"

The anger that flashed across Black Heart's face was so abrupt that Charlie found himself leaning back, his heart jumping up in his throat. It was like watching a demon possess Michael's features, twisting his thin lips into a snarl and drawing his eyes down to slits. "This isn't about me," he snarled, and Charlie could see that for the lie it was even if his brother couldn't. "This is about protecting our people, about making sure there is equality among our kind. Can't you see that? Or do they have you so brainwashed that you are blind?"

Charlie swallowed. Chose his words carefully. "What is it you plan to do, Mikey? Kill them all so you can allow Black Magic to be performed without monitoring? Give common men like Brad Milner a piece of the Black Stone so they can murder Highborn women, or anyone else you see fit? *That's* a better life for the people?"

Black Heart rubbed his head, exasperated, regaining his composure. Charlie relaxed, but only a little. Then his brother looked back up at him, the grin on his face once more, and the tension flooded back into Charlie as though it had never left. "I have their attention now, Charlie Boy. That's all I needed, and I don't have to kill them all," Black Heart said, and waited. He knew what Charlie would say next.

"Why is that?"

The grin grew, stretching across Black Heart's face and revealing every one of his flat, white teeth. "Because King Syrian is sick and dying as we speak, and there is only one other person in line for the throne, and she's going to walk right into our arms." He reached into his cloak and pulled out the Black Stone, which was as big as a baseball and as shiny as a black diamond. It made Charlie's stomach clench while looking at it. Goosebumps popped up on his skin, even though the night was warm. The thing just radiated darkness, glimmering with its black power.

"She will come for this," Black Heart said, gazing at the stone with a fondness that made Charlie's teeth clench. When his brother looked up at him his face was smooth, but Charlie could still see the monster hidden behind his eyes, the one that had grown there. "Because she loves her father," he continued, "and royals see no problem with using Black Magic to save one of their own. You'll see. Bunch of fucking hypocrites, don't you think?"

Charlie swallowed, nodded. "Yeah," he said, "Buncha fuckin hypocrites."

Charlie knew he had to tread carefully here. Whatever happened next, he had to tread very, very carefully here.

CHAPTER TWENTY-THREE

There was a knock on her door. Samson raised his head from his paws. Surah shot him a look telling him to relax, then flicked her wrist and opened the door. Theodine Gray stood there. Her heart picked up in pace at the sight of him, but it wasn't a pleasant feeling.

And you tell me to relax, Samson said in her head, the smirk clear in his tone.

Surah bit back a response and offered the Head Hunter her best princess-smile. "Are you ready?" she asked.

Theo bowed to her, then nodded. "Yes, my Lady. Whenever you are."

Next Surah called her two personal guards into the room. Noelani entered first, her sharp, pretty face set into Hunter mode, making her look older than usual. She wore a black cloak, the hood covering aqua-colored hair that was cut short and close on both sides of her head. She bowed to Surah, offering a small smile. Lyonell followed on her heels, his expression as serious as his wife's, his large shoulders just a little too tight, his mouth set into a grim line. Surah had already filled both of them in, and they were determined to protect her in her mission, though she thought she could move faster on this if she could work alone. But they were having none of that, not after the thing she had pulled when she went to avenge Syris, and after nearly a thousand years of having them as her protectors, she knew arguing would be futile.

Lyonell bowed to his princess as well. "We are ready when you are, my Lady," he said.

Surah nodded, wishing again that she could just take Samson and do this by herself. But her father's life was on the line, and she wasn't stupid enough to refuse the help. She took a deep breath and looked up at Bassil, who was standing next to her. "I need eagle's blood to find the Black

Stone," she said, and the Shaman nodded at the others to confirm this. "I am normally opposed to the use of Black Magic," she continued, "as it stands against the beliefs of our people, but certain circumstances call for certain actions. I do not *want* to find the Black Stone, I *have* to find it," she paused, "and I will do whatever it takes."

Everyone in the room nodded their agreement, as she knew they would. She didn't like talking to them this way, could hear the challenge in her voice, but she was a princess after all, and she was used to giving orders. They needed to speak now or forever hold their peace, and no one was going to dare speak now.

She gave another nod, this one somehow more final, as if the show were just really about to begin. "All right, good," she said. "Step one is acquiring some blood from a Great Eagle, because I will need it to perform a spell to locate the Black Stone." Surah's face was set hard as she looked at them. "You all understand what sort of task this is?"

Nods all around.

"Good. You also understand how *urgent* this task is?"

Immediate agreement. Surah offered her best smile. She brought her hands out of her robe and held them out to Noelani and Lyonell, who gripped her hands with thousands of years' worth of trust. Theo stood independently in front of her, gray eyes staring deep into hers.

Bassil touched her shoulder. She turned her head to look at him. Once again the look on the Shaman's face made a chill walk down her spine. "You need at least a pint, Princess," Bassil said, his deep rumbling voice as grave as the dead.

Surah nodded, silently steeling herself for what lie ahead. Samson unfolded himself from his relaxed position by the window and moved lithely over to where his mistress stood, his head held low, amber eyes surveying the room. He slid in between Surah and Lyonell, forcing the two of them to reach to maintain hold of each other's hands.

The tiger's huge head turned as he looked over at her, brushing against her side with his enormous body. *Let's go, love,* he said. *I am born of the Wildlands. Do not fear what waits there. I am the greatest when it comes to Great Beasts. The eagle's blood will be yours.*

Surah could barely hear him over the sound of her heart beating out of her chest, and the silent confession she gave just before zipping them out of the room surprised even her when it sounded in her head.

But I am scared, Sam. I am.

Samson brushed his head against the hood of her cloak, his warm breath caressing her face, coarse whiskers scratching her skin. *I know, my love. I know.*

***

It had been so long since she'd been here, a few centuries at least, but as soon as she felt the warm air against her skin, all the memories of the place came rushing back to her. The smell here was incredibly green, like flowers and thick grass and fresh rain. The jungle trees loomed overhead, casting millions of shadows around every curve, giving the place a late day hue, even though the sun wouldn't set for another six hours. Tree branches rustled and birds called and water rushed somewhere in the distance. The Wildlands was a beautiful place, untouched by people and left to flourish under its own rules, but it was also a dangerous place, where the Beasts also lived under their own rules.

Noelani and Lyonell already had their swords at the ready, their stances relaxed but alert as they took in the scene all around them. Theo's weapon was still concealed beneath his cloak, but Surah could see the tension in his shoulders no matter how much he tried to hide it. She could feel the tension in her own.

Samson moved forward first, his head raised as he tested the air. Surah moved right alongside him, gesturing the others behind her, where they would watch her back. They would need to move as a unit if they hoped to pass through the jungle without loss. The place held everything from Great Serpents to Great Primates, and wild didn't even begin to explain some of their temperaments. They were called Beasts for a reason. Samson was the only one Surah knew of that lived peacefully outside of the jungles, and it would be a mistake to think that even he was tame.

The nests are too high to get a scent, Samson told her. *You'll have to perform the spell.*

Surah knew this would probably be the case, though she was loathe to do such a thing. The spell would bring an eagle for sure, but it would also be pissed off when it arrived and found it to be a trap. She hadn't done something like this since she rescued Samson as a cub, and that had been just pure luck. Then again she had been just a young girl then, and she was well seasoned with the Magic this time. She took a deep breath.

Gripping the stone around her neck in her right hand, her left resting on Samson's back, where the powerful muscles in his shoulders were bunched and ready, Surah recited a Thread Spell to show them the way. A golden light as small as a pinprick appeared in front of her, and then it shot out ahead in a string of light that looked very much like the golden thread it was named for, revealing the location of the nearest eagle nest. Surah let go of a breath she hadn't realized she'd been holding and looked around at the others.

"Stay together," she said, and began to follow the thread, which slowly laced up and up through the canopy of green.

A tree branch cracked and rustled off to their right, much too loud to be a small creature's movement, and all five of their heads whipped in that direction. They stopped for a moment, their bodies tense, blood flowing hot and hairs standing up on the backs of their necks. Samson let out a low growl that almost made Surah shiver. She swallowed, listened. When nothing else moved or sounded, she slowly pushed her group onward.

Her voice came out just above a whisper. "Move quickly," she said, and was met with four looks that said, rather plainly, *no shit*. Oddly, she had to suppress the urge to laugh at this vulgar thought.

They followed the thread, moving as quickly and quietly as they could manage, the thick growth of the jungle floor a maze of vines and roots. Several times someone tripped, but they were standing so close that someone else always caught them before they fell. Finally, they reached a point where the thread angled directly up to the treetops, and Surah craned her head back, searching for the nest, though she knew it was too high to see from the ground—even if it was probably the size of large bedroom. Surah swallowed at the image, hoping this was the home of a young eagle that hadn't fully grown into its size.

Surah removed her sais from beneath her cloak, her heart thundering against her ribs. She looked at her companions, her eyes falling on Samson last and settling there. "Ready?" she whispered.

She took their silence as answer enough. Her fists were tight around her weapons. She licked her lips and began another spell. In front of her, the enormous pine, its trunk the width of a pitcher's mound, began to shake and sway, its branches making a sound like pouring rain, thousands of green needles falling from the tree and showering over them in a storm of green. A minute later, they heard it, the outraged cry of a Great Eagle from hundreds of feet above their heads. The sound was a screech and caw that was so loud they had to resist the urge to cover their ears. Surah, though she knew this had to be done, immediately found herself wishing she hadn't done it.

She pushed the thought away. There was her father's health to consider. She had no choice here. She wondered briefly if she had ever had a choice.

The bird seemed to crash through the trees as if descending from heaven, its wide wings spread out to ease its fall. Its enormous talons were outstretched and snapping branches like twigs as it made its way toward earth to investigate who had disturbed its home. The eagle was even bigger than Surah had been expecting, its wingspan spreading some forty feet, its razor sharp talons terrifyingly large. Its eyes were huge golden orbs, its beak as menacing as Samson's fangs. Surah had only time to breathe one short breath, see the eagle cock its head in that birdlike manner, hear it issue one more enraged screech into the air, and then the Beast attacked.

Surah's group scattered like field mice, breaking apart just in time to avoid being plucked from the ground by the bird's enormous claws. The jungle around them seemed to grow quiet, very quiet, as the Beast took to the air again. Surah knew she had to act fast. She had but seconds before the eagle swooped again. She wrapped her hand around the stone at her throat, closing her eyes and hoping like hell Samson would watch out for her.

I'm here, love. I'm here. Samson's voice was hardly more than a growl in her head, the sound of his pumping blood almost audible in it. *I will take the eagle's blood. I will take it take it take it.*

Surah tried to ignore the eagerness in her tiger's tone and concentrate on the Holding Spell. It would take a lot of energy to subdue a creature of this size. And she could hear it coming now, couldn't she? Sweeping through the air in another strike. Coming and coming.

Breathe deep. Just breathe deep and concentra—

She was ripped from the thought when something wrapped around her body in a vice grip. Her eyes flew open as her feet left the ground, and a moment of pure, hot panic seized her as she realized she had been seized by the eagle. For a split second she could think of nothing to do, of no way to save herself as awful panic took control of her mind and made the blood seem to rush in her head. Then she gained control of herself, as her years had taught her to do, and managed to snap her fingers, which were pinned to her side, and teleport herself back to the ground and out of the bird's death grip.

It was a clumsy transition, and she found herself tucking rolling as she hit the ground, losing the sai still clutched in her left hand along with the other one that hand flown free when the bird snatched her. Her shoulder ached where it struck the ground, but she found her feet swiftly, glad to be back on the earth, even if it was a rough landing. Her mind was clear and focused now, and she called her weapons back to her with her Magic. She caught them out of the air and spun around just in time to avoid being grabbed again by the bird. The eagle let out an enormous cry of rage, but this time, it didn't take off again fast enough. Not fast enough to escape Samson, anyway.

The tiger leapt through the air and tackled the eagle to the ground, the two of them rolling in a heap of feathers and fur and talons and fangs. The bird tore at his back with its sharp beak, making sounds like that of an oversized, angry rooster, somehow much scarier than one would think. Samson snapped and ripped and clamped with his powerful jaws, roaring out at the injuries he was sustaining under the eagle's strikes. Surah's heart seemed to stop dead in her chest as she watched chunks of fur and huge feathers and red blood spray through the air. She gripped her stone, her concentration strong now for the worry over her tiger. When Samson hurt, she hurt.

She saw it when the spell worked, they all did, and her companions uttered a collective sigh as the eagle's body went stiff, trapped in the

Holding Spell. It seemed to take Samson a minute to realize the bird had stopped fighting—or maybe he just wasn't done tasting its blood yet—and for a moment Surah felt fear for the bird. She was sure Samson was going to kill it.

He wanted to. She could read that as easily from him as if the desire were her own. The muscles in the tiger's chest heaved and contracted as he stared down at the motionless bird, scarlet dripping from his formidable incisors. For a long moment the world seemed to pause, as if the earth itself were holding its breath; a moment where everything present was as unmoving as the eagle. Then Samson's long tongue flicked out and licked the blood ringed the fur around his mouth, the sound wet and thick.

His eyes didn't leave the great bird, but his head tilted in Surah's direction, and she knew the moment was over, that the eagle would more than likely live through this.

But she needed to move quickly. The jungle was silent around them, eerily so, even though the battle had surely ruffled some feathers. She found herself swallowing a laugh around this dry joke.

She slid her sais into the back of her cloak and removed a pint-sized vial from a pocket hidden inside the velvet folds. Surah approached the bird, her boots snapping twigs and crunching pine needles like egg shells, moving slower than she would have liked but unable to help it. She knew her spell was working, but she couldn't deny the caution that was pulsing in her body. She suddenly understood why everyone except her always tensed when Samson entered the room. The Great Beasts were just so damn *big*.

Samson didn't leave his position over the eagle, but his eyes flicked to her as she approached. His tongue snaked out and ran over the red on his face again. *I told you I would take his blood for you, love. I don't know why you even worry.*

Surah raised an eyebrow at the tiger, glad that her back was to the others, because she could feel the worry creeping onto her face, though she fought to keep expressionless.

"Looks like he took some blood from you too, Sam," she replied silently. *"You're hurt."*

Samson's eyes went down to her arms, where deep gashes had been cut by the eagle's talons. *Looks like I'm not the only one. Finish this up so that we can go home and lick your wounds.*

Surah smiled as she placed the vial underneath a deep laceration on the bird's underbelly, pushing her hand into her his warm feathers to make the blood flow faster. The bottle would fill quickly, and that was good, but it also made her feel bad. The eagle was seriously hurt.

"You mean lick your *wounds,"* she told Samson.

He gave what could have been a toothy grin. *That too.*

"Princess," Theo said, making Surah jump a little before she could stop herself, spilling some of the blood in the nearly full vial and stopping a curse just short in her throat. The others had been so quiet she had nearly forgotten they were even there.

Surah raised her eyebrows at Theo, asking why he was interrupting her, but he was glancing all around cautiously, his sword still held at the ready. "It's time to go," he said, his voice just above a whisper.

Surah heard what was causing the urgency in Theo's tone just as he spoke, and her head whipped to the south. What she saw there made her heart stop dead in her chest, her eyes going wide as the scene took on a sharp focus.

A group of five Great Primates were smashing through the trees, barreling toward them like monster trucks. Their huge fists pounded the earth and shook the ground under their feet. Grunts and roars issued from their huge mouths. Surah capped off the vial with quick hands and shoved it back into the pocket inside her cloak, unaware that her jaw was unhinged.

"Yeah," she said, her voice incredibly small beneath the sound of the Beasts thundering toward them. "I'd say so."

Noelani and Lyonell were at Surah's sides, gripping her hands, and Samson moved next to her in the same heartbeat. Theo was tense and ready to leave as soon as she made the move, but Surah spared one more look for the eagle, whose huge golden eyes seemed to be accusing her from their halted position, where its head lay cocked toward her. Her heart hurt a little seeing the bird so badly injured, knowing she did not have time to heal it, knowing she was leaving it at a terrible position with the primates approaching.

But the decision was clear and easy. The eagle would have to handle its own. Her father was counting on her. Hell, a whole *kingdom* was counting on her.

She broke the Holding Spell, releasing the bird, and snapped her fingers, transporting her companions out of the Wildlands just seconds before the group of Beasts reached them, wishing she could have waited long enough to make sure the eagle got away, hoping it would, and thinking it was probably the least of her worries.

It still sucked, made her feel not very good about herself, but it was the least of worries indeed.

CHAPTER TWENTY-FOUR

The tiger's rough tongue ran over the cuts on Surah's arms, making her clench her teeth to bite back a wince. Samson had been literally licking her wounds since she was a child, and though she knew other people would be nervous about having a tiger do this, she wasn't. She knew Samson would never hurt her, not even if he did like the taste of her blood, which he must.

She pulled her arm back and stood from her bed. Samson gave her an annoyed look. "Okay," she said, "I've had my bath. Now let me heal you. I have business that needs attending."

Samson sat back on his haunches and slid to the floor, licking his paws. *I'm perfectly fine. The bird didn't hurt me.*

Surah coughed into her hand. "Bullshit."

He raised his head. *You really shouldn't mumble and curse, dear. It doesn't become you.*

Surah rolled her eyes. "You sound like the etiquette teachers of my youth. Now, stop your nonsense and hold still."

She wrapped her hand around the Stone at her throat and ran her free hand over Samson's wounds, saying the Healing Spell over and over until the torn skin repaired itself, weaving together slowly like stitch work. The tiger narrowed his eyes to slits and let out low growls as the pain slowly left him.

When it was done, he rubbed his big soft head against Surah's side, knocking her over a bit with his weight. *Thank you,* he said.

Surah ran her fingers through his fur, performing a spell to clean away some of the blood clumped there. Samson caught her hand in between his massive jaws, but gently, the tips of his long teeth just barely pressing into her skin. She raised an eyebrow at him, and he opened his mouth to release her.

You have work to do. That's more than enough fussing over me.

Surah said nothing for a moment, thinking of the bird she had left so wounded in the jungle, wondering if it had been able to fly away before the gorillas reached it. Samson nudged her with his nose, as if to knock the thoughts away.

No time for that, he said softly.

"Do you think it got away?" she asked, cringing at the hope in her voice, as if Samson held the definite answer to this.

He licked at some leftover blood on his blue and black paw. *It put up a hell of a fight.*

Surah released a big breath, nodded. "I suppose it did," she said, and then she spoke to him silently, her next words too revealing to be spoken aloud.

"I don't know what to do, Sam. I'm scared. Not even sure if I should be, but I am. I can't seem to organize my mind. I don't even know what I'm supposed to be doing. Things are moving too fast."

Samson rose to his feet, his amber eyes watching Surah closely. He leaned in and ran his warm, sandpaper tongue slowly up her cheek. Surah wrapped her arms around his neck and held him tight, burying her face in his warm fur. She was beyond grateful to the universe for allowing her to keep such a great friend. At least it had left her that.

You know what to do, love. Just one step at a time. Step one, find the Black Stone. Two, save your father. Three, see that whoever is responsible for the murders meets justice. See? Easy as one-two-three.

Surah pulled back from him and gave a dry little laugh. She ran a hand though her hair and smoothed out her cloak. "That easy, huh?" she said. "What would I do without your wise guidance?"

Samson's lips pulled up in what Surah knew to be his version of a smile. *Oh, I don't know. Maybe get fed to baby eagles at the top of a tree in the jungle. That sounds about right.*

Surah laughed in earnest now. "I love you, Sam," she said.

Right back at you, honey. Now summon the Shaman and let's take that first step.

Surah nodded, but had a strong feeling that the first steps had already been taken, and that it was all downhill from here.

CHAPTER TWENTY-FIVE

It took Surah and Bassil three hours to prepare everything. By that time the sun was finally setting on what seemed to her to have been an incredibly long day. She stared out the window in her chambers, beneath which Samson had recalled his position. The lights of the city were just beginning to flicker on out there, the people of her father's kingdom leaving work and heading home for dinner with their families. Down on Side Street the bands would be striking up and beer would be flowing in the taverns. On the east side of town mothers would be walking their children home from school. Fathers would be kicking off work boots. At times like this Surah couldn't help but envy these common people, though she understood well that the grass was always greener.

Bassil eyed her from across the small table where the ingredients to the Tracking Spell were spread out. He tilted his head as he looked at her. Surah's face was as emotionless as ever. "Ready, Princess?" he asked.

Surah snapped out of her thoughts and rolled her shoulders, nodded and pulled the hood of her cloak over her head. Even if her face gave nothing away, her heart was thumping. Black Magic was something she didn't have much familiarity with. Her teachers over the years, which included her brother, had all been unmovable in their positions regarding the Dark Arts. This was the common feeling among most of the people— or at least she so assumed—something that was regarded as taboo, not to mention illegal.

She reached out and began pouring the various liquids on the small round table into a clay bowl at the center, forcing the thoughts of her brother away gently. Wondering what Syris would think of her actions were he still alive would do her no good right now. *Something* needed to be done, and she was doing it. There would be plenty of time for contemplations later, like when her father wasn't slowly dying of demon poisoning and a murderer wasn't on the loose.

The mixture in the bowl let off a pungent scent, filling the room with the smells of burned things and wet dogs and spoiled sugar, almost to a choking capacity. Surah breathed shortly through her mouth and held her hands out to Bassil over the table after adding the last ingredient, the stolen eagle's blood. The Shaman placed his hand in hers and began the spell, chanting low in the tongue of the ancients, his deep voice but a rumble in his chest. Surah looked down at the paper beside her and read along with the words, echoing Bassil in her sweet, soft voice, creating a juxtaposition that sounded eerie to her own ears.

Samson watched from beneath the window, his ears perked and muscles tense.

Their chanting seemed to carry on into oblivion, and after a while Surah was at the point where she felt like giving up. Nothing but that terrible smell had been produced by the spell thus far, and she was beginning to think she just couldn't do it. But she carried on a little longer. If this failed, it was back to the drawing board, and she didn't have time for that. Her father didn't have time for that.

In a matter of forty-eight hours the demon poison could be fatal. And that was a highball.

She shoved the doubt away, as she seemed to have been doing with a whole range of emotions lately, trying her hardest to concentrate on the spell and the words, trying hard to settle the roiling in her soul. Salty sweat rolled down her back, the weight of the cloak somehow heavy there. She ran her tongue out over her lips, feeling sudden tears of frustration threaten. She swallowed them away.

Then at last, when she was just thinking she couldn't do this any longer, it happened. Bassil felt it at the same time she did, his large hands tightening around hers to an almost crushing proportion. Surah's heart went from sinking to pounding like a racehorse out of the gate. She stared into the smoke drifting up from the clay bowl, unaware that she was biting down on her lip hard enough to draw blood. The room was darkly silent now, both of them having stopped the chanting on the same syllable.

An image began to form in the smoke, the scene moving like an eagle's eye over the land. Surah swallowed back more tears as the thought reminded her of the bird she had all but left to die. She stared into the smoke and got the feeling of vertigo as the lens passed over the city, where people were walking the streets and store windows were going dark and the neon lights of the taverns were blinking to life. It soared over the buildings, over the alleys and backyards of private homes. Then out further still, over the grassland and forests and small towns and further still and still.

The Black Stone was in the jungles of the Southlands then, because nothing else was out this far. Surah's throat went tight as the smoke scene proved her right, and now she felt the perspiration roll down the side of her face as well. The jungles of the Southlands were even more dangerous than the ones to the north where she had obtained the eagle blood. The things that lived there were more monsters than beasts.

The scene halted over its destination, still high above the green canopy, where only the shadows penetrated. She could only imagine what could be waiting, hidden there. Then the picture vanished and was replaced by numbers, which Surah knew were longitude and latitude. She committed them to memory instantly, letting out a long breath and finally releasing Bassil's hands. He looked as peaked as she probably did, his dark skin having taken on an ashy tone. Surah could tell by the expression on his face that his stomach was as queasy as hers. Black Magic had a way of doing that to the user.

But she had what she needed. She knew where she had to go. And time was ticking.

She stood from her chair and ignored the lightheadedness that rushed over her in a wave, blinking back a few spots that appeared before her eyes. She ran her hands down her cloak, composing herself, clenching her teeth against the complaining of her stomach.

"Where are you going?" Bassil asked, wiping some sweat from his brow with the back of his hand and settling back in his chair.

Surah raised an eyebrow at the stupid question.

Bassil chuckled. "You are not going into the Southland jungle at eleven o'clock at night, especially not if you're feeling at nauseated as I am."

Surah tilted her head, her lips quirked in a small half-smile. She leaned forward, gripping the chair in front of her more for support than effect. Not that she would admit it. "You're giving me orders now, Shaman?"

Bassil gave her a droll look. "Oh, no, dear Princess," he said. "Wouldn't dream of it." He spread his hands. "Go on and get yourself killed if you like. I'll do my best to help your father in your stead."

Surah got the urge to stomp her foot like a toddler and ignored it. She spoke through her teeth, not really angry with Bassil so much as frustrated and tired and nauseated. "You know I don't have much time. The Black Stone could be moved and then we would be back at square one. This is imminent."

Bassil nodded. "And so is being able to get out of the jungle alive. You really want to walk into that place in the middle of night? Like I said, be my guest. Ignore my council. Gods know you've never had trouble doing that."

Surah knew he was probably right, that she would need to prepare for this mission, and yes, she needed to rest and probably eat, since she couldn't remember the last time she'd done so, but that didn't stop a little impatient anger from spiraling in her belly. You wouldn't know it from her face, though.

"Well," she said, taking a seat on her bed. Samson jumped down from the window sill and hopped on the bed beside her, making her dip to the side. "You don't have to be such a dick about it."

This made them both laugh, relieving some of the tension that seemed to have been brewing in the air for the last couple days. Bassil stood and bowed to her before taking his leave. "Sleep, Princess," he said, "I will let the Head Hunter know you want to leave at first light." He checked the pocket watch that hung from a chain inside his cloak. "That'll give you a little over six hours to rest. I think you should sleep longer, but I know you won't."

Surah looked at him, letting her mask slip for just a moment because she couldn't help it. "I don't think I can sleep at all, Bassil," she said, and hated that her voice sounded small.

The Shaman gave her a gentle smile and opened the door to leave. "Try, Princess. Just try," he said. Then the door clicked shut behind him.

After he left, Surah kicked off her boots and slung her cloak over the chair by the window, crawling into her big bed beside Samson, who took up most of it, and snuggled into his warm fur. She felt very alone right then, as she had for a good portion of her long life, very alone and very tired, but she was right about not being able to sleep despite her exhaustion. How could she? Things seemed to be getting worse and worse with every passing moment, drifting further up the creek and losing paddles.

She clenched her jaw and closed her eyes, trying not to think about all the people she had lost over the years, her brother, her sister, her mother. Trying not to think about the possibility of losing her father as well. Trying—and this was somehow the most disturbing of all—not to think about the boy she had given Syra's Stone to beside the lake that day so long ago, the one that had turned into the mysterious country man, with his stilted words and controlling eyes. Trying not to think about the man named Charlie Redmine. The man with the criminal brother who seemed hell-bent on causing trouble.

No, she should not be thinking about those things at all.

CHAPTER TWENTY-SIX

At some point after mid-night sleep finally found her, and she dreamed about that day beside the lake. It was such a vivid dream, so much so that all five senses were immersed, not just sight or sound. She could feel the warm sunshine on her skin, could smell the earth and wildflowers covering the land. The lake shimmered in front of her, where Pixies skimmed over the surface trailing light behind their wings and shooting ripples across the glimmering water. A soft breeze lifted her hair from her face, which was wet and warm with ceaseless tears. The pain she felt was also present in full force, her gut wrenched and her soul aching in sharp agony. *Fresh* agony.

It seemed endless. It had to be.

She was only thirteen years old, and her mother and her sister were dead, and no matter how long Surah lived, they would never be coming back. The thought was too much to bear, one that stabbed a corkscrew in her chest and twisted and twisted. Her hands, covered in gloves of purple velvet, came up and shielded her face, and she pulled her knees up to her chest—her terribly, awfully twisting chest—and she rested her head on them and cried and cried and thought she would never be able to stop, that even if she lived to be ten-thousand, the tears would never stop.

She wished she could wake from this nightmare, but felt somehow certain that the truth of it would carry into reality anyway.

It was impossible to accept that two days ago she had shared tea with her sister and mother in the parlor of the castle, eating light pastries and gossiping about the events taking place in their world. Trouble was outside their door, the supernatural world at a state of great unrest, but being a privileged girl of thirteen, Surah didn't even consider the possibility that the battle could reach her. She was a princess, and bad things weren't supposed to happen to princesses.

How wrong that had turned out to be.

Bad things happened to everyone. People died, people grieved. She was young, but she knew this now. The Great War was reaping the blood that is sowed with all wars, and she was a fool to have thought it could not touch her, not her and her family. But it had. It hadn't only touched her, but ripped out her soul by the feel of it.

She heard the boy before she saw him, just a rustle in the grasses that surrounded the lake, and she jumped up from her seated position on the ground and removed the sais that were strapped across her back under her cloak in one swift motion. She had been given the weapons as a tenth birthday present, and already she was quite lethal with them, but her broken heart jumped into her throat anyhow as she spun on her heel and sought the source of the noise. She hoped it was just Syris or her father looking for her. Big trouble was still raining down on everyone, and she, the last Sorceress princess alive, had no business being out here alone. There were plenty of people who would see her death as a great victory.

But it wasn't Syris or Syrian, it was a boy who looked to be a couple of years older than her, maybe fifteen or so. If his clothes were any indication, he was of common blood. He was barefoot and dirty and dried blood stained his tattered shirt, which was probably two sizes too small for him, making his wiry muscles stand out in sharp contrast. His eyes were the jade of tropical ocean water, and they stared out on his pale face like gems in a dark cave.

The two of them stared at each other in silence for a long time, Surah feeling a little bad about the richness of her cloak and jewelry, knowing just from the look on the boy's face that he was hurting the same way she was, grieving someone—or maybe more than one someone—who had surely been stolen by this terrible war. She knew the look well. It had been on the faces of everyone she passed for the past week. Needless to say, times were bad, but by the looks of him, they were worse for some.

How naïve she felt.

He spoke first, and Surah found herself listening carefully to the way a slight twang rode his words, she had never heard such an accent before. "You plannin on skewerin sumthin with those?" he asked, eyeing the silver sais still clutched in her hands.

Surah watched him closely, wishing she had mastered teleportation for what seemed like the billionth time, so that she could just take herself out of here. She didn't think the boy meant her any harm, he was obviously just a common Sorcerer, not a spy for the Vampires or Fairies or any of the other races currently feuding over the Territories, but in the past two days the young princess had learned a very important lesson, one that she would carry with her for hundreds and hundreds of years.

You couldn't really trust anyone.

She gave a slight shrug, held his gaze, which was somehow very penetrating. "I was thinking about it," she said, hastily brushing the tears from her face that she just remembered were there.

The boy approached the lake slowly, giving Surah a wide berth, his dirty hands raised at his sides, dark hair falling into his face. Then he plopped down on the shore of the lake and stared out over it. He settled his arms on his knees and put a hand over his chest were his heart was. "Alright," he said, "right here, then. Put er right here." He looked at her now, his eyes burning with the same amount of grief Surah felt burning in her own soul. A piece of her broken heart went out to him then, even though she tried with all her might to call it back. She felt broken, but he *looked* broken.

"And don't miss," he added.

She should have left him then, she knew very well she should have just left. Walked away. Instead she found herself replacing her weapons in the back of her cloak and taking a seat beside him on the ground, smoothing the expensive material out beneath her.

"That's a crazy answer," she said, staring out at the lake along with him, seeming to drown in the pain that floated in the air.

The boy laughed, a deep laugh for someone so young, but there was no humor in it. "Been a crazy week."

Surah nodded. She didn't know this boy from Adam, but some feelings were just universal, and she found herself relating to him even though she knew she shouldn't. Just by the looks of the two of them it was obvious she had no business talking to this boy. What would her father say? She just couldn't find it in herself to care right now.

"No shit," she said, knowing her mother would have scolded her for such foul language, cringing a little as she always did when she let an inappropriate word slip.

The boy tilted his head and looked at her. Surah stopped short the thought that despite the obvious sorrow painted there, he had a pleasant face. What did it matter if he had a pleasant face? It didn't.

The boy held a hand out to her, and Surah chastised herself for hesitating to shake it. Her gloves were a rich material that stained easily, and his hands were crusted with dirt, and what looked like dried blood was caked under his fingernails. She swallowed back her distaste and offered her hand, thinking it wasn't his fault that he was not as fortunate as her, and to deny his touch would be just plain snobby.

"Charlie," he said.

Surah gave him the best smile she could muster, which probably looked more like a grimace. She rolled the name around in her head, thinking that it had a nice, simple way to it. *Charlie*. Yeah, nice. Not that that mattered, either.

"Surah," she replied.

Charlie looked at her from the corner of his eye now, studying her in a way that made her shift uneasily, struggling for that *composure* her mother was always talking about. *Had*, she corrected, what her mother *had* always talked about. Her throat tightened. "What?" she asked.

"Surah...Stormsong?"

For a second she couldn't decide how to respond. Then she let out a heavy breath. What did it matter? "The one and only," she said.

He looked all around him now, no doubt searching for her escort. This annoyed Surah a little. She didn't need a damn babysitter everywhere she went, no matter what her father thought. His next words annoyed her more.

"You prob'ly shouldn't be out here alone. It's not safe."

Surah pushed out her chin, wishing he hadn't seen her with the tears still on her face, not sure why she should care. "And you probably shouldn't give me orders," she said, and felt bad about it as soon as the words left her mouth.

He smirked without humor. "Suit yourself."

Surah looked down at her gloves. She should have just left if she was going to be rude to him. She shouldn't be taking out her emotions on this boy who was obviously in a bad position, a worse position than her even, and right now, her position sucked. It was too close to kicking a dog when it's down. She felt bad about *that* mental comparison as well.

She decided to drop the act, the mask she had been wearing over her face for the last week, and would wear for a very long time, though she didn't know it yet. It felt like a weight sliding off her shoulders. She knew why she hadn't left already, why she was still sitting beside this dirty common boy with the ocean-colored eyes and too-small clothes. Because he was feeling the same as she was, no matter how different their attires and social statuses were, and it was oddly comforting to see up close that she was not the only one hurting, even if the comfort did come with a good dose of guilt.

"What happened?" she asked her voice soft and low, somehow almost conspiratorial. "Who did you lose?"

The boy plucked a long grass from the earth beside him and stuck it between his teeth, still staring out over the lake as if the cure to what was ailing them and so many others hid there. His words came out in a choked whisper. "My mother and father," he said.

Surah was silent for a moment, staring at him and seeing her pain reflected on his face. She had to look away, and found herself staring off the way that he was, not seeing a single thing in front of her. She thought about her mother and sister and her eyes began to burn, the heartache seizing her in an iron fist.

"I'm sorry," she said, swiping at the single tear that managed to escape her eye and roll down her cheek. Then more were coming, hot and wet and awful, and then there was nothing she could do to stop the sobs that were wracking her chest.

Charlie said nothing, just sat there watching the beautiful, heartbroken princess, feeling even more helpless as if such a thing were even possible now. He wanted to comfort her but didn't know how when all he had left in this world was his brother, who was hardly old enough to be a man. She obviously still had her money and rich food and warm showers. He, on the other hand, had his mother's blood on his shirt and his father's wand tucked into his back pocket. But he wanted to comfort her all the same. It was somehow too tragically beautiful to watch her cry.

He scooted over to her, moving cautiously, glancing all around to make sure they were alone. He stopped when he only a foot away and awkwardly put a hand on her shoulder. "Hey," he said, "It's…uh…it's going to be okay."

Surah uttered one last sob and peaked out between her fingers, looking at him. Then her hands dropped into her lap, revealing her pretty, tear streaked face, and she fell into an abrupt fit of giggles, her violet eyes glittering with moisture. Charlie looked at her like she was crazy for a long moment before bursting in laughter himself. And for what seemed like a long time, they both laughed. They laughed until their stomachs ached. It was painful laughter, but it was marginally better than just the pain.

When Surah pulled her hood over her head and lay back in the grass, Charlie did the same, and they lay that way for a while, the giggles finally ceasing, staring up at the blue sky. Charlie broke the silence after quite a long time, as if he had been mustering the courage to speak again.

"I'm sorry about Queen Suri and Lady Syra," he said, hesitantly.

Surah had to swallow twice before she could speak. Hearing the names cut at her heart like razors. "You heard about it," she said.

It was not a question, but he answered, "Course I did. Pretty sure the whole kingdom heard. Those that're left, anyway."

Surah turned her head toward him, admiring his profile because she couldn't help it. He really did have a nice face underneath all that dirt and grime. "Is it so bad out there?" she asked, not sure if she wanted to hear the answer to this question. Her father had been adamant about keeping the conditions of his kingdom out of Surah's ears so as not to worry her and instead had just stowed her away in a "safe place", as if she could be more worried than she already was. No one would speak to her of what was really going on, and all that told her was that it had to be bad. Really bad. She supposed this was why she snuck out in the first place, why she was here, because she needed to see for herself.

Charlie turned to look at her now, his gaze seeming to burn into hers stronger than the warm sun over their heads. "So many are dead," he said, and then his eyes turned skyward again, as if that was all the explaining it needed.

She supposed maybe it was.

"Do you have other family?" she asked him, hoping his answer would be yes, and knowing she shouldn't care either way.

When he nodded, her heart rose a fraction, but his answer made it sink again. "A brother."

A moment or two passed in silence. Then she asked, "Is he old enough to look after you?"

Charlie shrugged. "Guess he'll have to be. Shit, guess we'll both have to be."

Surah hid her amazement at his language. No one ever said such words around her. "Do you have somewhere to live?" she asked.

Another shrug. "They burned our house down."

Surah's hand came up to her mouth and she gasped before she could stop herself. She stared at him, composure vanished, if it had ever been there in the first place. "What will you do then? How will you...*survive?*"

His eyes flicked to her, and Surah felt her cheeks heating up and found she couldn't look at him. When she realized she was blushing, she couldn't even begin to imagine why. It was highly inappropriate for multiple reasons.

Charlie lifted his hands and propped them behind his head. "However I have to," he answered.

Surah couldn't even begin to guess at what that meant. "Do you have money?" she asked.

His chin tilted down as he looked at his attire. Then he quirked an eyebrow at her. "What do you think, Princess?"

Surah nodded, feeling stupid for asking, feeling her cheeks go red again at his formal address. Her voice was hardly above a whisper when she spoke. "You can call me Surah," she said, knowing she shouldn't, and cursed in her head when more fresh tears began to burn her eyes. She was certain this pain would never leave.

Charlie looked over at her. "Okay," he said slowly, drawing the word out. "You gonna be okay, Surah?"

She swiped at the tears on her face and gave a short, humorless laugh. "What do *you* think, Charlie?"

He smiled then, and Surah thought that it was the first real smile she'd seen in days. It made her throat tight, and of course, more tears followed.

Charlie scooted closer, careful not to touch her. "Please don't cry," he whispered.

Surah's words came out hitched and broken. "Why not?" she asked. "You said it yourself, so many are dead. Why shouldn't I cry?"

He was silent for so long that Surah thought he wasn't going to

93

answer, probably because there *was* no answer for this.

Then he said, "Because I don't think I can bear it."

Surah pulled herself into seated position and stared down at him, searching his face for something and finding it there though she didn't even know what it was she was looking for. All of a sudden she felt very much like she shouldn't be here, though she didn't really want to leave.

"I should go," she said.

He nodded once. "Okay."

She hesitated, telling herself very sternly to get up and walk away. Lingering. "Are you and your brother going to be all right?"

Another nod. "Sure."

Surah looked around, anxious to be out of there and yet still there. She lowered her voice back into the conspiratorial whisper. "Are you practiced in the Magics?"

"I know what they taught me in school." He smiled again. It was a sad smile, but somehow Surah thought it was sad for her, as if there was no much about life she would never know or understand, simply for who she was. Rather than making her take offense, it made her feel sad for her, too. Sad for them both.

"Us common folk do go to school, by the way."

Surah stopped herself from rolling her eyes. Now there was composure for you. "Sure you do," she said, earning a small chuckle from him. "What I mean is, are you equipped to take care of yourselves?"

He raised his brows. "Sure. I'm plenty equipped. No need to worry bout me. Though I'm touched by yer concern."

The idea struck her out of nowhere, and though it raised a bright red flag with it, she reached into her cloak and pulled out her sister's necklace, which held a piece of the White Stone. The words came out of her mouth before she could stop them, and she found herself holding the necklace out to him. It was an identical match to the one she was wearing, a powerful thing that only very high ranking royals were given.

Charlie sat up now, looking at her like she was crazy again.

"Take it," she said.

He said nothing, just looked at the Stone and shook his head, his dark hair, which could use a cut, swishing on his forehead.

She grabbed his hand and closed his fingers around the necklace, feeling the warmth of his touch even through her gloves. "It can help you. You can use it to get food and clothes and hide if you need to. Please. Just take it."

He still looked reluctant, but he slid the chain around his neck after a few moments' debate, tucking it under his shirt. "This could get me in big trouble if I'm caught, Surah," he said.

One side of her mouth lifted. "Then don't get caught, Charlie."

"Will it make you feel better?"

She thought about this a moment, then nodded. "Yeah, I guess it will."

He nodded once, his jade-colored eyes staring into the violet of hers. "Alright, then. I'll take it."

They both stood then, preparing to go their separate ways, knowing that whatever strange moment they had stolen was over. It was time to go.

And that was when she snapped out of the dream, waking with sharp gasps as she sucked in air around the lump that seemed to be lodged in her throat. Sweat matted her hair to her forehead and her heart skipped a little when she came to the slow realization that she had been dreaming. She was still caught up in the emotions of that long ago day, feeling for several long moments as though it had all just happened, reliving the grief over again.

Then a little panic seized her as she felt around on the bed for Samson, who was always there when she woke up, and who wasn't there now. It was too dark in the room to see, so she cast a Light Sphere in the air and blinked as her eyes adjusted to the glare. Her mouth opened to call out for her tiger, but his name jammed up in her mouth when she saw where he was.

Well, it wasn't so much where he was as what he was doing and who he was doing it to.

The tiger stood over by the window, his head lowered and teeth bared in a silent growl, amber eyes glowing the dark room. And pinned between him and wall, holding himself impressively still, was Charlie Redmine.

Surah's first coherent thought was, *Speak of the devil.*

CHAPTER TWENTY-SEVEN

Would you like me to kill him for you, love? I will gladly kill him for you.

For a few moments, Surah couldn't seem to form another thought, she just sat on the bed staring wide-eyed at the scene in front of her, her mouth hanging open as she sucked in air. There was no thought for composure. Samson was staring at Charlie, but Charlie was staring at her, his hands raised in surrender, his back pushed up against the wall, only his wide chest moving with his deep breaths. It was somehow paralyzing to wake from that dream, where the jade color of his eyes had been so crystal, and coming back into reality and seeing them with even more clarity there. To go from looking at him as that boy beside the lake to the man—*very, very much a man*—standing within her bedroom.

About to be eaten by her tiger.

She opened her mouth to say something, but instead spoke to Samson in her head, practically tripping over the words to get them across. *"No, don't kill him."*

The tiger's only response was a small grumble, but he held his position between Charlie and his mistress.

Surah climbed out of bed and grabbed her cloak from the chair beside it, wrapping it around her shoulders and feeling a little better with the weight of her sais on her back. She used her Magic to return her boots to her feet. Then she just stood there like an idiot. Now what?

When Charlie spoke, his voice was deep and low, cautious. "I come in peace, my Lady."

Surah still didn't know what to say, so when she opened her mouth, even she was surprised by what came out. "Are you insane, Charlie?"

Whoops. She hadn't meant to call him that.

One side of his mouth quirked at this, but his hands were still raised at his sides, and Samson was practically breathing in his face. "It's nice to see you again too, Surah."

This seemed to snap her out of whatever trance she'd been in. She stalked forward, removing one of the sais from her back and clutching it in her right hand. "Do not speak to me like that," she said, all her anger over the events of the past two days rushing back to her. "I am your princess. You will address me as such."

Charlie said nothing to this, just stared at her in that annoyingly mysterious way he had, and Surah ignored the fact that she felt a little guilty at the harshness of her tone. Why the hell should she feel guilty? Highborn ladies were being murdered, her father was dying, and she knew his brother and him had something to do with it. She just *knew* it.

"Where is the Black Stone?" she asked, fully expecting him to evade the question.

He didn't. "My brother has it."

Surah's brow furrowed as she was taken aback, not sure what to think of this blatantly honest answer. She found herself fumbling again for her words. "And why are you here?"

His next answer sounded as honest as the first, but Surah wasn't young enough to let that make her think it couldn't be a lie. She happened to be a master at deceit as well. "I've come to help you stop him."

Her voice came out smaller than she would have liked, even though both of their tones had yet to reach above a whisper. "Why?"

She got the feeling his next answer was not the one that was flashing in his head, but still may have been a half-truth. "I don't know," he said.

Surah raised her eyebrows, still holding the sai in her right hand. "Well, that's rather reassuring."

"Your father's sick, right?" he asked, and Surah's eyes narrowed. He continued on before she could say anything. "You want my help or not?"

Her teeth clenched, and she raised her weapon for the first time and pointed it at him, her violet eyes as hard as stones. No one spoke to her so plainly. Except maybe her father. "What makes you think I need your cooperation? I could kill you right now. You obviously have a hand in all this."

Charlie shrugged, as if it didn't matter either way. "You could."

They were silent for a moment, and Samson spoke in her head. *You going to invite him to tea, my love, or do you want me to tear his throat out.*

"I don't know yet."

You're oddly indecisive with this one.

"I know."

A pause.

Be careful.

"I'm trying."

Charlie spoke in that slow way of his. "I'm sorry bout everything that's happenin, my Lady, but I'm here to help you. If you wanna have me locked up," his eyes flicked to Samson, "or kill me, that's your choice."

Surah found herself looking at his lips and forced herself to stop. "You just want me to trust you?"

His eyes seemed to pin her, even though he was the one who was pinned, his voice as calm as if they were just sharing tea. "That'd be nice."

"You think I'm a fool."

He shook his head once, slowly. "Not at all, Princess."

Surah looked out her window, trying to make a decision—any damn decision—and saw with a drop of her heart that the sun was making an appearance over the horizon, the first light of the new day. Bassil or Theo would be here soon, expecting her to be ready to set off to the jungles of the Southlands, where the eagle's blood had traced the Black Stone.

She approached him now, feeling the urgency in her movements. If she didn't make a decision here soon, the decision would be made for her. She stepped up beside Samson and held her hand out to Charlie, her face grave and beautiful. He gave her his hand, his inscrutable gaze locked on hers.

"Are you planning to betray me?" she asked, hoping he would pass her lie detector test and also hoping he wouldn't. Somehow she knew that his answer would seal an envelope, though she had no idea what was tucked inside it.

"No," he said.

Just then there was a knock at her door, and all three of their heads whipped in that direction.

Time's up, Samson told her. *What do you want to do?*

Charlie watched her closely, said nothing, but his heart was beating out of his chest. He could not even begin to fathom what her answer might be. She really had no reason to trust him.

In the end, it was Samson who made the decision.

Oh, for Gods' sake, let's see what he has to say. You obviously want to. If he tries to betray you, I'll kill him. But you better take us out of here now, love. Whoever is calling won't wait much longer.

Before she could question her tiger's council or her own warring thoughts, Surah gripped Charlie's hand, which still held hers, and placed her other one on Samson's shoulder.

The door swung open and Theodine Gray entered just a split second after Surah squeezed her eyes shut and teleported the three of them out of the room, feeling like she was falling over a ledge into a gorge that would be impossible to climb out of rather than flying through space and time.

Yes, it felt very much like falling indeed.

CHAPTER TWENTY-EIGHT

They landed in the small forest that lay just outside the city, where only the woodland creatures and the occasional hunter roamed. The sun was slowly making its ascent in the sky, filtering through the trees in streams of golden light. The forest was quiet this morning, with only the sound of squirrels jumping from branches and birds calling from their nests. Charlie stumbled a little when Surah released his hand, bending over and clutching his knees at the feeling of vertigo that came with the sudden departure. Samson stood very close to her side, watching Charlie with a slightly amused expression behind his eyes.

Charlie straightened up, boldly giving Samson a look that said he knew the tiger was enjoying this. Surah couldn't help but be a little impressed at his bravery. People didn't just look at Samson any way they wanted. Only she did that. It made her wonder just who Charlie Redmine really was. She couldn't get a read on the man.

She crossed her arms over her chest. "Start talking," she said.

Charlie stared at her for a moment, and she didn't like the fact that she had to plant her feet to keep from shifting under his gaze. "My brother has the Black Stone, and he wants you and your father dead."

For a moment, she was lost for words again. She wondered if his blunt way of delivering information had that effect on everyone. She was usually quicker on her feet. "Wonderful," she said, "and you escaped his clutches to come tell me this? How did you get into my room?"

Charlie reached up and pulled out a necklace that had been tucked under his shirt. On the end of the chain was a small piece of the Black Stone, not enough to cure her father, but enough to teleport somewhere, like right outside her bedroom window, even with all the spells around the castle blocking the travel. Her eyes narrowed. "How'd you get that?"

"Michael gave it to me."

"Michael?"

"My brother…Black Heart, I guess."

"Why would he do that?"

"Because I told him I would help him."

She raised an eyebrow at this. "And instead you've come to help me."

"That's bout the short of it."

"Well, forgive me, Mr. Redmine, but the 'short of it' sounds like drivel."

"It ain't."

Surah threw up her hands, looking at Samson for an answer. The tiger gave her a look that conveyed his amusement. *Do you want me to decide everything, love? I can, but at some point I might decide to just eat him, and something tells me you wouldn't like that.*

"Who says I would care? I never said that," she snapped silently.

Samson gave his version of a grin. *You don't have to.*

Charlie was watching them as if he could hear their silent conversation. As if he was the only one with mysteries. "We gonna stand here all day, or do you want get goin on saving your father?"

Surah sighed, trying not to look at Charlie too closely, seriously afraid that she was making a huge mistake here. She shouldn't be doing this, and she knew it. But no one had talked to her this way since Syris died, and his blunt, certain way of speaking had a way of making her listen. It had absolutely nothing to do with his wide shoulders and muscled arms and mysterious jade eyes and perpetually calm manner. Nothing at all. He just dealt differently than she was used to. That's all.

"I suppose you have a plan on how to do that?" she asked.

"To help you save your father? Yeah, you could say that."

"And then what?"

Charlie was silent for a moment, his handsome face carefully expressionless. "I can't help you catch and kill my brother, if that's what you're askin," he said. "I'll help you, but I can't do that."

Surah swallowed and licked her lips. "Alright," she said, "Help me save my father, and I won't ask you to."

She wasn't sure if this was a lie or not, but it sounded true, so that was good. She had come this far, and the clock was still ticking. Step one was curing her father. She could decide on step two when the time came.

Charlie nodded. "Okay." He took a step toward her, a slow one, his eyes flicking to Samson, and held out his hand to Surah. "Let's go, then."

Surah just looked at him for a moment, studying the dark, trimmed facial hair that covered his strong chin and surrounded his soft-looking mouth. The unwarranted thought that came next scared her more than anything else that had happened in the last two days. The thought was she wondered what that course hair would feel like against her skin, how his lips would feel against it too.

The realization that he wasn't just a handsome man, but a rather *gorgeous* one was even worse. Her eyes wandered down Charlie's body before she could help it, and that was probably the very first time that she knew she was in serious trouble here.

Samson's head tilted toward her, and she cursed silently as she realized the tiger knew what she was thinking. She must have been projecting the thoughts pretty clear. She had to watch it. "Where are we going?" she asked, using great effort to sound as sure and strong as she didn't at all feel.

Charlie reached down and took her hand, the movement as sure and unhesitant as his words. Samson shocked the Magic out of her for letting Charlie do this. People didn't just reach out and touch their princess without permission.

She shocked herself even more when she didn't protest.

"Shoppin," he said, and when he smiled, perfect white teeth peeking out behind those lips, Surah's heart flipped. There was nothing she could do to stop it. "You like to go shoppin, Princess?"

Surah knew he was trying to lighten the mood, but her mood was anything but light at the moment. The expression on her face was as blank as a fresh sheet of paper. She said nothing. But she didn't pull her hand away from him, either. And when the thought came to her that she wished she weren't wearing her gloves, so that she could feel his touch again, she chastised herself in her own mind like an angry mother.

Her silence seemed to have no effect on him. "We gotta be careful, though," he continued.

Surah gave him a droll look, ignoring the hammering of her heart.

His small smile returned. "We'll need some things if we hope to pass through the Southlands and get what we need for your father. This means we gotta go see some folks, and those folks will recognize you in a second."

Surah nodded and snapped the fingers of her free hand. Charlie watched with wide eyes as her hair went from the short lavender to a long, pale blond, the violet leaking out of her eyes and leaving them a dull brown color. Her facial features shifted slightly, making her look ten years older and not like herself at all. Even her attire changed; her rich cloak faded into an old, used black. She couldn't help a small smile at the amazement on his face.

Samson seemed to be grinning, too.

"Well, I'll be damned," Charlie said.

Surah said nothing, but as she stared into those deep eyes of his, a strange feeling of fluttering and tightening in her gut, her breath catching in her throat, what she thought was, *we both may be.*

CHAPTER TWENTY-NINE

Theo knocked once more on the princess's chamber door, the sound of his knuckles rapping on the wood echoing down the windowless hallway, thinking that she was probably just rousing from her sleep. When still he heard no movement or response from beyond the door, his lips pinched together a little as he let out a sigh and looked at Lyonell, who stood guard to the right, Noelani to the left.

Lyonell shrugged. "Probably sleeping," he said.

Theo gave him an impatient look and reached for the door, but Noelani stepped in front of him, ignoring the plain anger that passed behind the Head Hunter's eyes. She met his glare evenly. "I'll check on the princess," she said. "She may not be descent."

Theo still looked unhappy about being interrupted, his face smooth but hard-lined, and he waved a hand to tell her to get on with it then. Noelani opened the door to Surah's room and pushed her way inside, closing the door behind her with a soft click. Her eyes went first to the bed, where the lavender silk seats and large comforter were rumpled, the blanket kicked to the foot and one purple pillow spilled onto the floor. Empty. She looked then to the spot in the window sill, where Samson was usually perched. Also empty. Noelani's heart skipped a beat then as her gaze flicked toward the bathroom, whose door was open and insides were dark. She didn't even bother to call out the princess's name. She just let out a deep sigh, turned and opened the door, and looked right at the Head Hunter, knowing that Theodine Gray was going to be very pissed off about this.

"She's gone," Noelani said, and had to jump out of the way so as not to be knocked over when Theo charged into the room.

The Head Hunter's eyes followed the same route hers had. The empty ruffled bed, the window, the bathroom. As they flicked from place to place a darkness seemed to pass over his expression, his lips pulling down and his eyes narrowing in his masculine face. For a moment, he said nothing, but both Noelani and Lyonell could see this was in great effort of controlling himself. Noelani had been right, Theo was madder than a rattled rattlesnake.

When he spoke, it was between clenched teeth. "Where did she go?" he asked.

At that moment, Bassil entered the room, moving in that eerily silent way the big Shaman seemed to have perfected, his patchwork cloak rippling with his movements. His deep voice sounded almost amused when he spoke. Almost, but not quite. "To save her father, I would assume," he said.

Theo's head whipped toward him, and Bassil could see the Head Hunter's dislike for him clearly, though he was sure he had never done anything to Theo to deserve it. "That's what we were scheduled to do this morning." Theo said his voice almost a growl now. "She's not supposed to go alone".

The Shaman lifted his wide shoulders once and dropped them. "Maybe she got tired of waiting."

Noelani spoke up now, ignoring Lyonell's look that asked her to stay silent. "And the princess is not a prisoner here. She can leave whenever she likes."

When Theo looked at her, Noelani could see that he wanted to slap her, the way that every women can tell when a man wants to do so. She felt a little fear spiral in her belly as she watched the thought form behind his cool gray eyes, and wondered at how she could have found him attractive all those years ago, wondered at how anyone could find him attractive with eyes like his. He was well built with fine features, yes, but his eyes betrayed uglier demons inside.

Surah was the only one who seemed to agree with her on this point, however. And Surah obviously wasn't here right now.

But Theo didn't strike out at her, of course, because whatever Noelani may have thought, he would not sink so low as to hit a woman. Instead, he regarded Bassil again, which almost enraged Noelani more than if he'd hit her, and something told her he knew this. He wouldn't hit a woman, but he was very good at dismissing them.

"You said the Tracking Spell worked, correct?" Theo asked.

The Shaman nodded.

"And you have the coordinates?"

Bassil nodded again.

Theo was silent a moment, trying to think of his next move. Ordinarily, as Head Hunter he was to await orders from the Keeper before making any decisions or pursuits, but this was not an *ordinary* situation. Syris—who'd been the best Keeper Theo had ever known, even better than his father before him—was no longer here. And while he may have been in love with Surah, he was not the type of man who completely trusted a woman to these kinds of matters. These kinds of matters were between life and death. Highborn ladies were being murdered. King Syrian was poisoned with demon blood. The Black Stone was missing. No, this was no job for a woman. Women had soft hearts. Theo didn't think this was a bad thing, an insult to females, rather just the way it was and was supposed to be. A natural balance. He would need to lead this case. Besides, the princess could end up getting hurt.

Then there was Charlie Redmine. Fucking Charlie Redmine. How long had it been since he'd seen that country, common scum? Long time, he supposed. But not long enough. He knew that son of a bitch had something to do with this, had known it right off the bat, even before he and the princess had witnessed Redmine escape with Black Heart. Yes, he would need to put a stop to all of this, punish those who were responsible.

Not only that, but he hated the way that common shithead had looked at Surah. He *hated* it.

But there was protocol to follow, or at least appear to follow as long as he could stand to. He would wait for the princess to show back up for a few hours, and then he would take the coordinates that Basil knew and go searching for the Stone.

"She could just be in with King Syrian," Lyonell said, cutting into the Head Hunter's thoughts.

Theo's teeth clenched, but his tone was composed, his face smooth, even amicable. It was a wonder how much control one could gain from a thousand-year lifetime, but there was nothing he could do to stop the dark emotions from storming through his head. "I just left King Syrian," he said.

Noelani chimed in. "I'm sure she'll return shortly."

Now Theo very much wanted to tell her to shut up, but being a woman, she would probably run back to the princess and tattle-tell on him. And that surely wasn't the best way to convince her to be his wife. He nodded, giving a small smile that struck Noelani as indulgent. "Of course," he said. "We'll wait for her then."

Then he swept out of the room, his heavy cloak swaying behind his swift, sure steps, leaving the two Hunters and the Shaman standing in the princess's chambers and staring silently at each other as the early morning light coming through the arched windows strengthened with the growing of the new day.

Theo walked down the hallway that led back to the foyer, listening to only the click of his boot heels on the polished hardwood floor and the blood that seemed to be pulsing in his ears. He would wait for the princess, all right. He would wait for exactly three hours.

And then he would go looking for her.

CHAPTER THIRTY

Surah stood staring at the small stone cottage, her heart thumping nervously in her chest. The silence of the place is what struck her first, surrounding her so completely in an instant. Green vines sporting yellow flowers crawled up the front of the little house, framing the door and two square windows. The path leading up to the porch was collaged stone, red and gray and black that fit together in a sort of mosaic. The only sound was the wind rustling through the long grasses all around them.

The sunlight was beginning to strengthen, reminding Surah that the clock on her father's life was still ticking. She took one more moment to take in her surroundings, looking all around in every direction and seeing no other civilization in sight, just miles and miles of green and yellow grasslands.

"Where did you bring me?" she asked, avoiding Charlie's eyes, wishing she didn't feel like she had to. She gestured to the cottage with one gloved hand, the glamour she was wearing making her expensive glove look old and tattered. "This doesn't look like any shop I've ever seen."

Charlie began striding up the stone path to the cottage in that slow, sure way of his, and Surah found that she had no problem looking at him when he wasn't looking back. She decided against her will that she liked the way the denim of his jeans sat below his waist, how she had never known that such common attire could be attractive. She personally had never donned a pair of jeans in her life, and she wondered if her rear end would look as good in them.

When she looked over and saw Samson staring at her, she shut those thoughts off like a faucet.

Eyes on the prize, the tiger told her silently. *Don't trust this man, Princess.*

"*I know what I'm doing and I don't trust him.*"

Good.

Charlie climbed the steps of the cottage and turned to look at her. "You comin?" he asked.

Surah remained where she was, her hand resting on the tiger's shoulder. "Not until you tell me what I'm walking into. You still haven't told me anything about this plan of yours, Mr. Redmine. I'd like to hear it."

Charlie moved back down the steps and stopped in front of her, and Surah had to swallow twice to hold his gaze. His deep, low voice seemed to fill up the world in the emptiness around them, those jade-colored eyes burning. Maybe always burning. "This is a friend's house, my Lady," he said. "I've known Carolyn for over five-hundred years. She deals in the kinds of items we'll be needin."

Surah just looked at him, her face carefully expressionless. "What kinds of items would that be?"

Charlie was silent for a moment. "I think you know."

"The use of Black Magic is forbidden in my father's kingdom, Mr. Redmine. I would have assumed you knew this."

Charlie nodded once, either completely ignoring her incredulity or not hearing it. She couldn't tell. She just couldn't get a read on this man. "Sure," he said, "but I would assume that you know Michael is usin' Black Magic to stay hidden and to keep…unwanted folks away. How do you propose we get anywhere near the Stone without using it too? I s'pose I just assumed that you wouldn't be opposed to it with your father's life on the line."

Surah's teeth clenched. How dare he speak to her in such a way? Charlie Redmine clearly had no manners or concern for social status, and she found the thought flying out of her mouth before she could stop it. "You've got some nerve, Mr. Redmine, speaking to me the way you do."

Charlie said nothing to this, just sighed and rubbed a hand down his slightly scruffy jaw. He looked as exasperated as she felt. She found herself growing defensive. Meanwhile Samson looked slightly bored and amused at the whole thing.

Charlie looked at her now, his eyebrows raised. "Make up your mind, Princess," he said. "You gonna trust me or not?"

Surah tilted her chin up a fraction. "Not," she said, and began striding up to the cottage with her perfect posture and sure steps. Samson followed at her side. She was just about to knock on the door when Charlie spoke from behind her.

"He should stay out here," he said, and Surah glanced over her shoulder to see he was talking about Samson. "If Carolyn sees him, she'll know who you are, even with all that glamour. No one else in the kingdom owns a Beast like that."

"I do not *own* Samson," she said, taking defense of her tiger. Charlie Redmine seemed to have a knack for pissing her off, even with all her long gained composure.

Samson surprised her by chuckling in her head, the sound just a deep, growling rumble. *Sure you do, love. Sure you do.*

"He shouldn't be speaking to me this way," she told him silently, her tone more of a snap than she intended. *"No one speaks to me this way."*

Surah thought if Samson could have shrugged, he would have. He hopped off the porch and began walking to the back of the house, his head held low as he sniffed at the green and yellow grasses. *Isn't that what you're always complaining about?* He asked her as he slipped into the field to the east of the cottage, the amusement clear in his tone. *I thought you wanted to be treated like everyone else. Sometimes you just have to give an inch, princess. I'm not saying trust him, just give an inch.*

Surah sighed and looked at Charlie, who was silent, which seemed to be his way. Looking at her as if he were the one having some secret, internal conversation. She wished he wouldn't look at her. She seemed to be able to feel his gaze on her skin, something that stroked rather than just saw, and her returning thought to Samson surprised even her. She regretted it as soon as it was born.

I know that's what I wanted, and that's why I wish he wouldn't do it.

The tiger stopped in his tracks, the long grasses brushing against his powerful legs, the strengthening daylight casting a heavenly light around his blue and black stripped body. His head turned, ears swiveling gracefully, and Surah thought the look Samson gave her when his amber eyes met hers was sort of painful, then he turned and slunk into the grasses, body held low. A bit of real fear spiraled in her gut. She refused to examine the question *of what?*

Surah turned back to Charlie, her chin held slightly raised. When he just stood there unmoving, she waved her hand impatiently to tell him to get on with it. Just because she didn't trust him didn't mean she didn't intend to see where he led her. As of right now, he seemed to be the most direct path to the Stone she needed to save her father, and she was fully prepared to kill him if worst came to worst. At least, she thought she was.

Charlie climbed the porch steps once more, flashing Surah that small smile of his when she moved away before his shoulder could brush hers. He reached up and knocked on the wooden door, which thumped hollowly. Surah had to stop herself from shifting her feet as they waited, despite the fact that she was not a shifty person.

A minute passed, then two, and another, and Surah was a split second away from telling Charlie to knock again when the door swung open, the hinges creaking in way that would have been comical if not for the uneasy feeling in her stomach. It was an oddly gripping sound.

The smell that wafted out of the cottage and bombarded Surah's senses was that of rich flowers and thick herbs, stale smoke and spoiled milk. It rolled out toward her on a wave that made her eyes water and her throat itch, and no amount of etiquette training could keep her nose from wrinkling. She covered her mouth on the shoulder of her cloak just in time to catch the three sneezes that forced their way out.

She almost summoned a handkerchief before she thought better of it. She was in disguise, and common people didn't just use the Magic in such frivolous ways, and if she did summon one she wasn't sure she would be able to keep from covering her mouth and nose with it anyway. And that sort of delicate, royal behavior was not going to cut it here. She loosened her shoulders, adding a slight slump to her back, breaking her perfect posture. Maintaining the Magic that held her false appearance in place was not the hard part—though it wasn't *easy* by anyone's standards. The hard part would be not conducting herself like a princess.

A voice issued from the darkness of the cottage, where the only light was from the two dusty square windows that shed dirty streams of sunlight into the room. The voice was soft and low, a woman's voice, that of deep trolling bells. The sound of it making an unexplained chill crawl up Surah's spine, but she didn't allow herself to shiver.

"Charlie?" the voice said. "That you, Charlie Redmine?"

The room filled with light then, the overhead bulb in the ceiling coming to life and illuminating the contents of the place. Surah's eyes flicked around the room, settling on the stacks of old books, the jars and vials set on the shelves that held various substances, the old leather couch and armchair, and finally on the carved table in the corner, where the owner of that deep bell voice sat.

Surah's first thought upon seeing Carolyn was that she was an extreme juxtaposition to her home. Her hair was a long, yellow blond, hanging in soft waves over shoulders that sported a rich black cloak. Her face was fine lines and delicate curves, with plush pink lips and big crystal blue eyes. Her makeup was styled perfectly, her hands ungloved but clean with blood-red fingernails. The woman stood in one smooth movement, her back held straight and her cloak flowing around her gracefully, a smile lit up her face as her eyes settled on Charlie.

She held her arms out to him the way a mother might do a long lost child. *Or the way a lover might a long lost flame,* Surah thought, then shoved the whole matter out of her mind. Focus was key here. Eyes on the prize.

"Charlie Redmine," the woman said, coming forward, arms still outstretched. "I'll be damned. It is you."

Surah resisted raising an eyebrow. This woman was a whole bucket of juxtaposition, it seemed. Her foul, common way of speaking matched her house but not her appearance. Charlie stepped into the cottage, his face giving away no indication that he could even smell the foul mixture of scents that invaded the room. He went over Carolyn and pulled her into a hug that Surah thought lasted too long, knowing she had no business feeling that way at all, averting her eyes from the two of them and standing outside the open door in awkward silence.

"S'good to see you, too, Carolyn," Charlie said, stepping back from her and offering her a small smile. "You look good."

The way Carolyn smiled and fluttered her eyelashes in return answered one of Surah's earlier questions. So Charlie Redmine did have an effect on other women. Apparently, she wasn't the only one who found him attractive. She wasn't sure if she was happy about this or not.

Carolyn slapped playfully at his shoulder. "Still a charmer, I see," she said, and then her crystal blue eyes flipped to Surah, and the smile fell from her face like melted snow, the smooth lines of her jaw that Surah thought were pretty upon first sight sharpening and becoming harsh. "And who is this you've brought with you?" she asked, her gaze traveling up from Surah's feet and to her face and back again.

Surah found herself clenching her teeth, but she smiled, and it looked real. She was very good at that. Then she realized that she and Charlie hadn't discussed the false identity that went with her false appearance, and she floundered in her mind, searching for a common name to spit out.

She needn't have worried. Charlie answered for her, his slow draw as sure and true as ever. Surah realized that he was an even better liar than she gave him credit for, and had she listened to her gut right then, and transported out of there, she might have been able to save herself a lot of trouble.

Give an inch, Samson had told her. Sure. She had no idea that she would be plenty sorry for ignoring her instincts and taking this advice later.

"This is Sarah Whittle. She's an acquaintance of mine," Charlie said, and looked back at Carolyn. "She needs to make some purchases."

Surah stepped into the house, careful to keep her smile in place and her nose from wrinkling. "Good to meet you," she said, hoping that her fake common accent didn't *sound* fake.

Carolyn inclined her head, making Surah's hackles raise, if they weren't raised already. "Sarah Whittle, huh? Never heard of you."

"She's from the Westlands," Charlie answered, stepping to the side a little and drawing Carolyn's attention back to him. That suggestive smile found her face again as her blue eyes travelled up Charlie's body.

Surah decided rather instantly that she didn't like this Carolyn.

"The Westlands you say?" Carolyn leaned her head around Charlie, looking at Surah again, and Surah finally came to the realization of what this woman was. The word sounded in her head in a distinct tone of disgust.

Witch.

"What part of the Westlands?"

Surah's smile remained in place, her shoulders relaxed, her composure held carefully intact. A geography test was nothing to her. She knew the lands and cities of her father's kingdom as well as anyone, and Charlie Redmine wasn't the only one who was a good liar. "Mountain Home," she said, "It's a small town about an hour outside of Raven City."

Carolyn gave no indication of whether or not she knew the place, and really, Surah couldn't care less if she did or didn't. She could check a map if she wanted. Mountain Home would be there. Surah just wanted to get what they needed and get out of here, preferably to some place where she could breathe through her nose again.

Carolyn turned back to Charlie. "What're you lookin for?" she asked.

Charlie rubbed a hand over his strong jaw. "A Stone Vial and a Shading Spell."

One of Carolyn's sharp eyebrows arched, and her eyes flicked back to Surah, who got the feeling that the Witch could see her through the Glamour as surely as Surah could see what she was through hers. Not a common Sorceress, but a Witch who dealt in the Black Trade. Had circumstances not been what they were, Surah would have had Carolyn arrested. In fact, she made a mental note to do just that after this was all settled. It would be her final act as Keeper. She hoped.

"That's goin to run you a pretty penny," Carolyn said, flashing teeth that were too white and too straight. "You got that kinda money? This ain't a charity house I'm runnin."

Surah nodded once. "I can pay."

"Of course you can," Carolyn said, and Surah didn't know at all what to think of that.

Charlie didn't shift his feet or adopt an uneasy look, but Surah got the impression that this made him tense nonetheless, or maybe it was because it made *her* tense.

"How much you want?" Charlie asked.

The Witch waved her hand, long fingers with the tips painted that blood-red stirring the unpleasant air, and glided over to the wall, where a shelf holding empty glass vials hung. She scanned the items and selected one. Then she moved to the shelf beside it and selected another vial containing a dark purple mixture. Her back still to them, she said, "Not too high a price for a princess, I suspect."

Surah's heart stopped in her chest. Carolyn turned her head and looked at her over her shoulder, a small smirk pulling up one corner of her pink-painted lips, crystal blue eyes glittering with mischief. Surah dropped her Glamour, her hair going lavender and her cloak reverting back to the black that shimmered when it caught the light. She raised her chin a fraction, almost relieved to shed the pretense. "You know of me, then, Witch," she said, it was not a question, or a compliment.

Carolyn laughed now, the sound crawling up Surah's spine rather than ringing in her ears. "Everyone knows of you, *Princess*," she replied, making the address sound as dirty as Surah's had.

Surah looked at Charlie, hoping her undeniable disappointment didn't show on her face. But he looked as surprised at this revelation as she felt, and that one moment of her furrowing her eyebrows in confusion was the last moment that she couldn't have possibly made her escape. And maybe escaped her fate as well.

The voice came from the open doorway, which Surah had left ajar to vent some of the putrid smell in the dark cottage. She heard it at the same moment that the dark power washed over her, at the same moment as she felt the necklace holding her royal Stone snap and fly free of her neck. Her hand reached up to catch it, her breath catching in her throat as well, but she missed, the chain just narrowly evading her fingers, and it was too late.

She spun on her heel, cloak fluttering around her in a quiet swish, and there stood Black Heart.

Her royal Stone rested in the palm of his black gloved hand. Surah considered trying to make a grab for it, but Black Heart closed his fingers around the Stone and smiled the way one might at a naughty child. Surah's gut clenched as she looked into his face and saw that his eyes were the exact same jade color as Charlie's. "Let's not be hasty," Black Heart said. He offered Surah a small bow. She seemed to be struck speechless.

The instinct to snap her fingers and teleport out of here came, but she cursed in her head when she realized she would need her Stone to do this. The next realization that came was even worse. Black Heart was blocking the door. The Black Stone, much larger than she expected, hung around his neck, pulsing that sickening dark power that seemed to fill the room even more fully than the awful smell of the Witch's home. She was trapped.

Charlie Redmine had set her up. Somehow, though she knew this was completely insane, this realization was the worst of all.

When a familiar voice spoke in her head, Surah's knees nearly went lax with relief. In all the shock she had forgotten about Samson, who was slinking around the house just outside the door.

Can I kill him, love?

Surah couldn't stop her eyes from flicking to Charlie, who had a very peculiar look on his face, as if he was as taken off guard by all this as she was. She wasn't fooled. Charlie Redmine was an extraordinary actor.

"Yes," she told Samson silently.

"You ought to tell that Beast of yours to back up," Black Heart said, his voice deep and gleeful. He wrapped his hand around the Black Stone, thick fingers barely covering the surface. "Unless you fancy yourself a dead tiger and a severed throat."

Hot, red anger welled up in Surah now, and her fists clenched at her sides, but she said nothing. She could tell by Black Heart's hard expression that he would do exactly as he promised if she made a false move, and it would be all too easy with the Black Stone in his hand. Even if she still had her small piece of the White Stone, she would be no match to the power that he had stolen. The fact that she wasn't dead already gave her a dash of hope, but it was just a dash. She told Samson silently to stand back, and the tiger retreated into the grasses a bit with barely contained rage.

Surah's heart was tripping, but she inclined her head, holding Black Heart's gaze with concealed effort. "If you wanted to kill me, you would have already done so," she said her soft voice clear and strong. "So what is it you want?"

Black Heart smiled. He had an ugly smile, nothing like his brother's, who hadn't said a word at this new arrival. Carolyn stood over by Charlie, just as silent, but with a very pleased look on her face. Surah didn't see what either of their expressions were though, because she thought that taking her gaze away from Black Heart for even a moment would be a very stupid idea. This was the first time she'd encountered the man other than when he'd busted his brother out of the holding cell, but she could see why he'd gained the reputation he had. Darkness seemed as part of him as shadows are part of the night.

"I do want to kill you, Princess," Black Heart said, and his pleasant tone did not at all match the words. "Just not quite yet. I want to kill both you and your father…How is he by the way?"

Now the anger Surah felt turned into fury, something that she could feel in her bones and taste in her mouth. Her next words came out her mouth quickly, and she made no effort to stop them. "Not concerning himself with the piddling of common cowards," she said.

Black Heart struck out so fast that even if Surah had known what was coming, she probably wouldn't have been able to avoid it. The hard knuckles on the back of his hand connected with the side of her cheek so hard that a few stars burst behind her eyes, and the cracking sound it made resounded like close thunder in the tiny room, drowning out the sounds of breathing and racing hearts. The pain that exploded on the left side of her face was immediate and harsh and terrible, making her eyes water and her back hot. Her head was whipped to the side, wrenching her neck.

Surah did not cry out. She didn't make a sound.

She reached up and touched her lip, seeing a spot of blood on her gloved finger, and met Black Heart's jade eyes with a death promise clear on the surface of her violet ones. Her face still hurt, was rippling with pain and heat, but her lips pulled up in a small smile.

She refused to look over at Charlie, so she didn't see the barely concealed fury on his own face. She just stared at Black Heart, thinking that if he had any brains at all, he would kill her now, because if she were going to live through this, she would see to it that he wouldn't.

Samson was coming now, she could practically feel the heat of his anger across the distance between them, and she told him very sternly to stand down. Black Heart could do any number of things with that Stone around his neck, and Surah would not be able to contain herself if something happened Sam. Attacking Black Heart right now was a sure way to get them both killed. The man obviously had no boundaries, and Surah could be a very patient person.

She pushed her chin out, ignoring the blood that spilled from her lip there, her voice strong and steady, royal. "Feel better?" she asked.

Black Heart laughed heartily, the Stone around his neck bouncing a little on his wide chest. He ran a hand through his hair, which was slicked back into a tight ponytail. He came forward and gripped Surah's shoulder, his touch rough and slightly painful. "Much better, Princess," he said, giving her that toothy smile. "Thank you for asking. Now if you've nothing left to add, let us be on our way. There is so much to be done."

He turned to the others. "Thank you for your help, Carolyn."

The Witch nodded, batting those black eyelashes and smiling that red smile. Black Heart looked at Charlie and jerked his head. "Come, little brother," he said, extending his free hand to him. "You've done well."

Charlie came over to them, his movements robotic, his heart sinking and dropping and hurting in his chest. He took his brother's hand, as he had done so many times when they were children, only now Charlie wished he didn't have to.

Surah finally looked at Charlie as he came to a stop in front of her, and though he'd kept hoping she would look at him earlier, he wished very much that she didn't now. Her face was smooth and expressionless, the spot where Michael had struck her blooming red and a bit of blood still marring her pretty lips, but the look behind her purple eyes, the eyes that Charlie had so often seen in his dreams, was almost too much to bear.

Surah pulled her eyes away a moment before Black Heart teleported them to wherever he had in mind, and her last thought was one that she would never—*if* she lived through this—ever forget. It was the thought that Charlie had seen in her eyes, the one that made his chest ache.

I gave you an inch, and you took way more than a mile.

PART II: SEALED WITH A KISS
CHAPTER THIRTY-ONE

The jump in location still gathered Charlie as if by a divine hand and tossed his across their world like a child's rejected plaything. His stomach lurched and dizziness surrounded his head. The scene in Carolyn's cottage disappeared, the sharp stink it carried disappearing with it. For a split second his feet felt no ground, his brain suspended as if in space. Then they landed, a silent impact that rode up through the heels of his boots, his confused senses slowly sharpening back to focus.

He dropped his brother's hand—more than glad to be free of his touch—and clutched his knees, holding back retches. After a moment—a slightly shorter moment than the previous trips, which meant he was getting used to it—he regained his composure, his stomach settling and senses unlocking. He straightened from his position, and the first thing he saw was the deep violet of the princess's eyes.

He thought, *if looks could kill...*

Charlie had to pull his eyes away. He couldn't stand it.

Black Heart still had hold of Surah's shoulder, and she yanked herself away from him and delicately smoothed out her cloak, returning his annoyed stare defiantly. He may have taken her captive, and he may be planning to kill her, but she did have her pride, and right now it was getting the best of her. Surprisingly, it was anger that was fueling her, rather the fear she certainly should be feeling. It took her a moment to realize she was angrier with Charlie Redmine than she was afraid of his brother.

At least, for the moment. That would change very shortly.

Surah jerked a little as her hands clasped in front of her without a signal from her brain, and smoky black handcuffs enclosed her wrists, making an immovable figure eight there. Black Heart released hold of the

Stone at his throat and smiled as Surah tested the strength of her dark magical bonds.

"I assure you they are quite solid, Princess," he said.

Surah returned his smirk, forcibly ignoring Charlie as if he weren't even there. "Of course," she said, her voice smooth and calm. Inside, her heart was threatening to rip through her ribcage.

They were in the jungle. Exactly *what* jungle, Surah hadn't a clue. The trees were thick and green, crawling with vines and bursting with colorful plants. She could hear the sound of a waterfall in the distance, the call of smaller birds and the rustling of smaller animals. The sunlight peeking through the lush canopy shifted down in glittering, golden streams, the thickness of the brush surely hiding much greater Beasts. They could be in any one of the eight jungles that bordered her father's kingdom. Some of them were more dangerous places than others, but all of them were dangerous places.

Black Heart leaned into her now, his neck craning down and his hot breath pushing into her face. He towered over her. Surah met his eyes and refused to flinch. Next to them, though the princess didn't see it, Charlie tensed.

"Don't be scared, Princess," Black Heart said, his voice pitched low and falsely gentle. He patted the Stone around his neck with his right hand. "The Beasts wouldn't dare attack while I have this. Come now." He gave her a rough push forward. "Let's get moving."

Surah didn't know this either, but Charlie thought he just might try to beat the shit out of his brother right now if Michael put his hands on her again. Black Stone be damned. Now wasn't the wisest time, but Mikey had an ass-beating coming, Charlie was sure of that.

Surah walked, her back straight and head high and heart low. She couldn't believe she was in this situation, couldn't believe she had been so stupid as to trust a man like Charlie Redmine, with his handsome face and calm manner and blunt, inappropriate way of talking. She should have killed him in her bedroom. Hell, she should have killed him as soon as she set eyes on him. Or let Theo kill him. Now, she was in the middle of some Wildland with a crazed Sorcerer and Samson wasn't here and her Stone was gone and her father was dying. All because she'd given an inch. If she lived through this, she was going to literally punch Sam in the nose for that terrible advice.

The two men walked behind her, their heavy shoes making the vegetation crunch underfoot. Surah kept ahead of them and concentrated on two things; keeping her calm, and making sure she lived long enough to see the two of them punished. It was a savage part of her that had been cultivated over the years, a strong survival instinct that had saved her on more than one occasion. The ability to shut out her emotions and be pragmatic was key right now.

Theo would be looking for her, as would her father, if he was even physically able. So would Samson. She just had to wait for her moment to escape, and seize it when it came. Easy.

She swallowed. She hated Charlie Redmine and his woman-hitting brother. She *hated* them.

They walked for a little ways through the trees, the sound of the waterfall in the distance growing closer and closer until at last they reached the source. The cliff from which the water poured over was small, only fifteen feet or so high. It spilled into a small river that shimmered in the sunlight, reflecting the images of the trees leaning out over it. The rushing of the water filled Surah's head, and she was glad when it drowned out the sound of the blood rushing in her ears.

When Surah came to a stop Black Heart reached out to push her forward again, but before he could Charlie snatched up his wrist in a hard grip and met his brother's eyes with a level stare. Black Heart smiled innocently and Charlie released his hold slowly, ignoring the urge to punch the smile right off his face. And then punch him twice more for good measure. And maybe again for good luck. If he'd had any doubt before it was gone now. Michael was not the man he once was.

Charlie had made a serious mistake in thinking he could fool him, that Michael wouldn't know exactly what Charlie would do, where he would go. He should have never taken the princess to Carolyn's. He hoped like hell he'd be able to fix it. Suddenly, he felt very unsure about whether or not Michael would actually kill him. They'd had their disagreements in the past, which was why they hadn't seen each other for over a century, but this was different. For the first time, Charlie thought the answer to that question might be yes, and he also felt somehow certain that it might just come to that.

He was also certain that his brother would not put his hands on the princess again. Charlie felt like he could kill him just for that back-handed slap. The hardly contained fury in his chest confirmed it.

Black Heart stepped around Surah, his movements heavy and stiff, and toward the edge of the waterfall, where large gray rocks jutted out over the lake. He hopped onto the nearest one, the mist of water clinging to his black cloak in tiny droplets, and extended his hand to Surah, smiling. "Come, Princess. Watch your step."

Surah, her hands still bound in front of her, leapt onto the rock gracefully, not at all tottering for balance, ignoring the offered assistance. Black Heart laughed again and clapped his hands. Charlie followed behind her, and Surah resisted the urge to shove him over the edge and into the river, where maybe he would drown.

The string of obscenities running through her head in that moment would have put her lost mother to shame.

Black Heart led them into a small cave behind the waterfall, which was dark and damp and cool. He cast a small Light Sphere, which illuminated the place just enough to see by. Then he turned and faced them. "Have a seat, Princess. Make yourself comfortable."

Surah felt her knees give way and was forced to the ground under an invisible weight. Black tendrils of smoke rose from the floor and looped around the dark cuffs encircling her wrists, chaining her to the earth and making a lump form in her throat. Now the fear came, and it was all she could do to keep the tears from forming in her eyes. She refused to let them see her cry. She raised her chin and straightened her back as much as she could with her wrists chained to the floor.

"Comfortable?" Black Heart asked.

Surah gave a small, sarcastic smile. "Very," she said.

Black Heart clasped his hands in front of him and settled down to the floor in front of her. Charlie stood off to the side, silent, bright red still ringing his vision. The princess wouldn't even look at him, and this made him hate his brother more than anything Michael had ever done.

"Wonderful," Black Heart said. "We wouldn't want our princess to be uncomfortable."

Surah just looked at him.

He ran a hand over the slicked-back ponytail on his head, arranged his cloak beneath him. "First," he said, "let me apologize for this." He reached up to touch Surah's face, which was starting to darken to a deep purple where he had struck her. Surah jerked her head away from his fingers. Black Heart sighed. "I don't believe in hitting women," he said.

Surah's small smile was still in place. "Yes, that much is clear."

Black Heart laughed. "You've got spunk," he said. "I'll give you that, but it would behoove you to cooperate with me, Princess."

Surah said nothing.

"I just have a few questions to ask you, and if you answer them, this will all be quick and painless. Time is of the essence, as I'm sure you're aware."

Silence.

"What happened to your brother?"

This question was not what Surah had been expecting, but she was sure to keep the surprise free of her face. She pressed her lips together, held her tongue.

"He was murdered by the King of Vampires and Wolves, was he not?"

Surah said nothing.

"And your father, did he seek revenge for Syris' death?"

Surah inclined her head a fraction, held his gaze, said nothing.

Black Heart sighed. "Alright. Okay. You're not in the talking mood."

He reached into his cloak and pulled out a silver pocket watch, flicked open the face, glanced down at it, looked back up at her. "Your father probably has all of thirty-six hours left to live." He stood, towering over Surah like a pillar of black stone. "Perhaps twenty hours here will loosen your tongue."

Surah looked up at him, said nothing.

Black Heart's returning smile made her teeth clench, and she had to ball her bound hands into fists to keep them from shaking. "I'll see you soon, Princess," he said, and turned on his heel. He looked at Charlie. "Come, brother, let us have a discussion." Then he stepped out of the cave and beneath the waterfall.

Charlie stood where he was a moment, and couldn't help but look over at Surah, who was pointedly avoiding his gaze. His voice was low and deep and sad when he spoke. There was so much he wanted to say, but was sure that none of it would even matter. She would never believe him now, and he couldn't even say he blamed her. He had tried to help her, and he had only managed to make matters worse.

"I'm sorry, Princess." It sounded as lame as it felt.

She looked at him now, her purple eyes so full of hatred that Charlie's breath literally caught in his throat. "No," she said. "Not yet, you aren't."

CHAPTER THIRTY-TWO

Charlie exited the cave and stepped out onto the rocks, spotting his brother by the side of the lake. He hopped off the rocks and landed on the grass with a light thump, the anger he had been feeling since seeing Michael hit Surah returning to him in full force. He strode over to where his brother stood.

Black Heart smiled and spread his hands. "Sorry about this, little bro—"

Charlie punched him hard in the face, cutting Michael off mid-sentence. His head rocked back. Blood spurted from his nose and dribbled down his chin, his eyes went wide with surprise, a grunt of pain escaping his mouth. He looked at Charlie now and smiled through bloody teeth. "Okay, I guess I deserved—"

Charlie punched him again. Twice, then a third time. Michael's head whipped from side to side, more scarlet flying from his face in thick droplets, more grunts of pain. He doubled over, his hands clutching at his midsection as he spat more blood onto the ground in thick globs. The Black Stone hanging around his neck pulsed hot and cold, and when he looked up at Charlie now, his eyes had changed.

Charlie stopped his next assault mid-throw. Black Heart was no longer smiling. "That's enough, little brother," he said, his voice nearly a growl, and Charlie thought again that his brother might just be capable of killing him. He supposed that made two of them.

"What the fuck, Michael?" he said, his voice raised in anger.

Black Heart stumbled back a little and sat down on the trunk of a large fallen tree, wiping at the blood on his face. "Sheesh Charlie Boy, I said I was sorry."

Charlie just looked at him, thinking about what the princess had just told him. *Not yet, you aren't.*

Black Heart smiled through bloody lips. "You still hit like a girl."

Charlie clenched his teeth, barely able to stop himself from hitting Michael again.

"There was no other way," Black Heart continued. "I told you, I need you on my side for what lies ahead. I'd hoped you understood that. You said you did. You should be apologizing to me. I gave you that piece of Black Stone so you could help me, not betray me by trying to help that little stubborn princess."

"You set me up."

"You set yourself up. Now I know you can't be trusted."

Charlie was silent a moment, listening to the way the darkness rode his brother's tone. He felt very certain that the unspoken words there were something along the lines of *now I'll have to kill you, too.* He couldn't see any way out of this. The princess surely hated him, the king was dying, and his brother was bat-shit crazy. He knew he had to choose his next words wisely. It seemed that the princess was not the only one who was trapped.

"You can trust me," he said, and it sounded true. Of course it did. Charlie wished it *was* true.

Black Heart stood. He came over to Charlie and placed both hands on his shoulders, his jade eyes deadly serious. "Is that so?" he asked.

Charlie nodded, consciously keeping the disgust and anger off his face.

"Alright. Prove it."

Charlie's throat tightened. "How?"

Black Heart was silent as he considered, his eyes locked on Charlie. "I have some things to do," he said, speaking slowly. "Now that we have King's Syrian's attention, I want to make sure he understands who holds the cards. I need you to stay with the princess while I complete the rest of my...tasks."

Charlie didn't know what to say to this. It seemed too easy, and that was probably because it was. It had to be a trick. Another test. "And what're those tasks?" he asked.

Black Heart smiled. Not the smile he used to give Charlie when they were younger, but the dark, malicious smile that matched the Stone hanging from his neck. The dark power that emanated from the thing was slowly poisoning his brother's soul. Charlie could see it in his eyes. Even if the princess weren't in need of saving, Michael obviously was. The only question was, could Charlie somehow manage to save them both?

"You think I would give you that information after what you just pulled?" Black Heart asked, his tone accusing. "I explained to you how important it was to remove the royals from their positions, told you that another Great War is coming, and what do you do? You go to the enemy and try to help her." He shook his head. "No, I'm afraid you'll have to prove yourself first, Charlie Boy."

Charlie wished he would stop calling him by that name. For whatever reason, it made his heart hurt. "You really think a war between the races is coming?"

Black Heart smiled and squeezed Charlie's shoulders gently. "No, little brother. I *know* a war is coming, and these royals have proved themselves to be inadequate at protecting our kind. I'm not the bad guy here, Charlie Boy. If you could look past your...infatuation, you would see that. You *will* see that. I promise."

Charlie nodded once. "Then tell me what you want me to do."

"It's simple, really. I need people I can trust. I want to trust you. All you have to do is watch the princess until I return, not that she can escape anyway. But just watch her. I will be back as soon as I can."

"How long?"

Black Heart's eyes narrowed. "Not very." He stepped back from Charlie and waved a hand in the air, which shimmered as something began to take shape. "And here, I brought you something to help you pass the time."

It was Charlie's guitar, the one that he thought had been left behind in the holding cell back in King Syrian's castle. Charlie took it by the neck, feeling a little better being able to hold something so familiar. But not much.

"Thanks," he said.

Black Heart nodded and smiled again, and this time, Charlie thought the look was genuine. "Of course." He raised his hands, preparing to teleport out of there, but lowered them and looked at Charlie one last time. "I don't have to remind you that this is your last chance, Charlie Boy, do I?"

Charlie shook his head. Black Heart patted his shoulder once more, and then he was gone.

Charlie thought, *I'm pretty sure I got that part, loud 'n clear.*

CHAPTER THIRTY-THREE

King Syrian was in bed when the message came. He had been bed-ridden for the past few hours, having told the servants to make sure no one bothered him. He didn't want anyone to see him in the state he was in, which was, to say the least, terrible.

He was running a fever and all the muscles in his body hurt. It was as if he could feel the poison spreading through him, entering his bloodstream and making him weak. His head pounded, the dim light in the room making even his eyes ache. In all his years he couldn't remember ever feeling so awful.

And it was just getting worse.

The clock was ticking. He could practically hear it counting down the seconds of his life in the silence of his bedroom. What was worse, Theo said that Surah was missing, and he hadn't heard from her in several hours. He cursed his weakness as he lie there, wishing he was strong enough to go out and look for Surah himself. He wasn't quite panicked yet. Surah was a smart girl, a great fighter and well-trained in the Magics. He took comfort in this, and knew she could probably look after herself. In fact, chances were that she was just out looking for a way to cure him, and he could just picture her raising her chin and giving him that sweet smile, so much like her mother's, when he told her how worried he'd been.

Then the message came, and the fear and panic and dread came with it.

His eyes were closed when it happened, but he opened them when the world beyond his lids shadowed, like a cloud passing over the sun on a bright day. He lifted his head, then pulled himself into a painful sitting position, staring at the black smoke that was swirling in front of him, the source of the darkness that had fallen over the room. His eyes narrowed down to slits as he realized what it was.

A message, sent with Black Magic.

The smoke swirled and danced and finally settled into a black rectangle, like the frame of a picture. Then in the center of the frame, Black Heart's face took stage. Syrian knew the message was recorded, and that Black Heart could not hear him, but he uttered a string of obscenities that burned his poor throat.

The face in the picture smiled. "King Syrian!" It began, the voice gleeful and menacing. "How are you, my King?" A deep laugh. "Not so well? Well, that's most unfortunate. But I am so pleased to finally have your attention. I suppose I should have just gone after your precious Highborn ladies years ago. You wouldn't have disregarded me then. But hey, that's all in the past, right? There are more important matters to consider now, and I think you will be a wonderful listener this time. That is, if your old ears are still up to hearing."

Another laugh. King Syrian tightened his hands into hard fists in his lap. It made his fingers ache.

The recorded message continued. "My demands are simple, and though I shouldn't have to explain them to you, I will, because I am well aware that you can be a…slow learner. First, you will renounce the throne to the kingdom and name me, Michael Redmine, king."

A pause. Now King Syrian laughed. It shook painfully in his chest.

"You will do these things for two reasons," it continued. "The first one is because it is the right thing to do. You are old and weak. Your rein has run its course, and our people are in need of a capable leader in the dark times ahead. I will be that leader. I will protect those who you would disregard, the same way you disregarded them a thousand years ago in the Great War. The common people will stand behind me, and embrace the new way of life, because they too know you are weak."

Another pause. King Syrian rolled his eyes a little. Black Heart had always been a fanatic, and he would get nothing. Except what all murderers and traitors to the kingdom got, and it certainly wasn't the throne.

"And the second reason, in case you are not thus far convinced, my brave King, is because you are going to die anyway. No matter if you meet my demands or not. You will die. The only thing you can hope to do now is save your precious daughter from the same fate. She's a lovely woman, by the way. Such manners!"

Now Syrian's heart raced, his already sweaty back and neck springing fresh salt water from the pores, the room going instantly hot. Some of the pain rushed away from his body and he sprung up from the bed, exhilaration taking its place. Then the strength left him again, sliding away as though it had never been, and he fell forward again and landed back on the bed.

The recording continued on, as if it had been allowing for just such reaction. "I have her, Syrian. I have your daughter stashed away nice and cozy, but she won't remain that way for long. You can waste what little time I am going to give you checking to see if I'm telling the truth, or you can just believe me and start contemplating your decision. As far as how much time she has…let's just say it is even less than you do, my King, and in my experience, demon poison can be quite expedient. Have a good day, my Liege. It is, after all, your last."

Then the smoke vanished, taking with it the face of the man who claimed to have his daughter. King Syrian was beside himself, unable to process what was happening. It was a terribly paralyzing moment, because he was usually such a self-controlled man. So much had happened over the years, so many that he loved gone, so much lost. He wasn't sure he could bear to lose his last child, not his little Surah, too. It was unthinkable. It made him almost long for the death that was slowly taking him.

He fell back on the bed and stared up at the ceiling, the pain of his condition coming back to him in full force. He couldn't breathe. He rubbed a hand over his eyes, brushing away a single hot tear. He felt very common in that moment, not kingly or royal or even worthy. Then the anger came to him, his longtime enemy and savior, and it rushed through his body in a welcome wave.

He straightened himself up in bed with agonizing effort, gritting his teeth against groans of pain. When he was upright, he smoothed a hand through his hair and down his silk robe, brushing the moisture from his head with the sleeve of his arm. He snapped his fingers, and the door to his room swung open. One of the Hunters standing guard stepped around the corner.

"Yes, my Liege?"

Syrian suppressed a cough, cleared his throat. "Summon Theodine Gray," he ordered, and rested his head back against the high headboard of the bed, swallowing to keep back more bloody coughs.

A few minutes later, the Head Hunter entered the room, sweeping in gracefully, his cloak flowing behind him. He bowed. "What can I do for you, my Liege?"

"My daughter, has she returned?"

Theo shook his head, gray eyes taking in Syrian's condition. "No, my Liege."

"How long has she been gone?"

Theo pulled up his sleeve a little and checked his watch. "Nearly three hours."

Syrian met his eyes, his voice sounding stronger than he felt. "And you've looked for her, I assume."

Theo nodded.

"Black Heart claims he has her."

Syrian watched as Theo absorbed this information, saw the tightening of his jaw and the clenching of his fists, glad to see that the Head Hunter cared for his daughter so much, since someone strong would be needed if they had a hope of finding her. He honestly couldn't understand Surah's hesitation over marrying Theodine Gray. He would make a good husband, a good king, which may be likely to be sooner than Syrian had planned for. And which was of no matter right now.

"He sent a message?" Theo asked, his tone low and angry.

Syrian nodded slowly, his neck aching, regarding Theo through blurry eyes. A cough racked his chest, a deep, nasty rattling that was unstoppable. He snatched a handkerchief from the bedside table, too weak to even use his Magic to summon one. It went to his mouth white and came away red.

When the fit passed, Syrian said, "You love my daughter, Hunter Gray, do you not?"

Theo's response was immediate. "I do, my Liege."

Syrian nodded once more. "Then find her." He coughed again, this one lasting longer, his entire body jerking with the force. "Find her and save her. Kill this man who has dared to take her prisoner and threatened the kingdom. Kill Black Heart and his brother and anyone else who would stand beside them." Syrian stared at him, and Theo couldn't ever remember seeing his king as desperate as he was now.

"Do this for me, Theo," he continued, "and you have my blessing to marry my daughter. I will make the announcement myself, assuming I am still able."

Theodine Gray bowed low to his king, concealing the small, crooked smile on his face. "With pleasure, my Liege."

CHAPTER THIRTY-FOUR

Surah crossed her legs beneath her, trying to find a way to sit that wouldn't pain her wrists so much. Each time she shifted in the slightest, the dark bonds encircling her wrists tightened, and they were so constricted now that they pulsed. Her fingers were beginning to go numb.

The sound of the water rushing over the rocks was loud and constant and irritating, but did nothing to drown out the rapid beating of her heart. The moisture in the small cave was as thick as a sauna. She wished she could have removed her cloak, because the temperature seemed to be rising and rising as the day wore on.

Or maybe it was just that her panic and fear were starting to overtake her. She had to calm herself and think.

She looked all around the dark cavern, grateful that at least Black Heart had left the little Light Sphere ablaze for her to see by. She had no idea what she was looking for, even though she knew she wouldn't find it. It's not like he would have left some magical key to the handcuffs lying around for her to find and slowly drag toward her with the heel of her boot. This thought made her laugh, but it sounded wrong and small and forced even to her own ears.

She didn't hear his return, was too busy staring down at her bound hands and trying to gain control over her racing thoughts, but when she looked up again, he was there, and she breathed a mental sigh of relief to see that it was Charlie and not Black Heart, then chastised herself for doing so. Charlie Redmine was just as dangerous as his brother, probably more so. She would not make the mistake of forgetting that.

She stared at him a moment because there was nothing else to be done and because she couldn't help it. He had his old guitar in his hand, holding it at his side by the neck. His handsome face was blank and guarded, but his jade eyes betrayed some inner roiling. Surah jerked her gaze away. *Lying eyes*, those were.

He said nothing as he entered the cave, just went over to the rock wall and leaned against it, sliding down to a seated position with his long legs sprawled out in front of him, gently positioning the guitar in his lap. Surah could feel his eyes on her, but she refused to look at him again. He didn't deserve her attention.

When his hands began to stroke the strings, soft soothing notes coming together to make a lulling rhythm, Surah did look up, and her anger came rushing back to her in a hot wave. "Stop that," she snapped.

Charlie's fingers halted at once and his eyes flicked up to meet hers. "Alright," he said.

This response seemed only to anger her more. "How long have you and your brother been planning this?"

Charlie just looked at her, knowing that no matter what he said she wouldn't believe him. Surah gritted her teeth, her usually sweet voice edged with anger. "So you're just going to ignore me? You don't think I deserve to at least know the answers to my questions before your brother murders me? Or is that what *you're* here for?"

She couldn't be sure, but she thought she saw Charlie flinch.

Silence hung for a moment. Then he said, "That's not gonna happen, Princess."

Surah laughed. "Is that so? You could've fooled me."

Charlie said nothing, just looked at her underneath dark lashes.

Surah tried to throw her hands up, and winced when the cuffs tightened again and realized she couldn't. "That's all you have to say?"

Charlie shrugged. "I try not to say anything when I know what I got to say won't be heard."

"You're a true gentleman, Mr. Redmine. You know that?"

Charlie set the guitar gently on the ground and folded him hands in his lap. "Alright," he said. "You got any ideas, then?"

Surah laughed again, and the harsh sound of it reminded her that she was losing her composure. She pulled it back to her with some effort. "Oh, I have plenty of ideas. I just don't think you or your crazy brother would go for them."

Charlie sighed and rubbed a hand over his jaw. "Try me."

Surah's brow furrowed. What in the world was going on with this man? His words didn't match his actions and his actions never matched the emotions hidden behind his eyes. For a moment, she couldn't think of anything to say.

"What are you talking about?" she asked.

Charlie gestured to the black chains around her wrists. "Got any ideas on how to break those?"

Surah looked down at the cuffs and back up at Charlie, her eyebrows still furrowed in confusion. "And why would you want to do that?"

Charlie pulled his knees up and rested his arms over them, rolling his neck slowly so that his dark hair fell into his face a little. Then he looked up at her, and Surah hated herself for again thinking how attractive he was. "Because whether you believe it or not, I didn't want any of this to happen. I had nothin to do with it."

Surah just looked at him, the disbelief evident on her face.

"And," he continued, his voice dropping a fraction, "I got no intention of lettin Michael hurt you again. I coulda killed him just for hittin you the first time."

"Really? Well, you'll forgive me for calling bullshit on that one."

Charlie shrugged, held up his hands, as if to say *see*.

"Why is that, Mr. Redmine? Because you are so loyal to the kingdom that you would betray your own brother?"

He was silent a moment. Then he shook his head. "Not to the kingdom."

It took Surah longer than it should have to recognize the implication there. When she did, she tried to force it away, knew that it would be foolish to believe it, but a little hope spiraled in her chest nonetheless. "Then why did you take me to that Witch's house?" she asked, not liking that her voice came out smaller than she intended.

Charlie shook his head, as if he wondered the same thing himself. "I shoulda known better," he said. "I'm sorry bout that. This is my fault."

"That's the first honest thing you've said since we met."

"No it ain't."

Surah tried to throw up her hands again. The cuffs tightened. She winced.

"Stop doing that."

"Then stop saying things to irritate me," she snapped.

Charlie rubbed a hand down his jaw again. "Look, we can sit here and argue until my brother gets back, or you can start tellin me how those chains can be broken. You've got to get a hold of your emotions and think, Surah, cuz I ain't got the slightest clue how to help you. All Magic can be broken, right? So…how?"

"Stop calling me that."

Charlie sighed.

Surah stared at him, her mind flying a mile a minute. She knew she couldn't trust him, but what choice did she have? No one was going to find her in time, and her father was as good as dead if she didn't find a way out of here. She was as good as dead, too. She bit her lip, tasting the blood there from when Black Heart had struck her, and tried to think.

He was right, all Magic could be broken, just like the demon poisoning could be cured with the Black Stone. So there had to be a way to break these bonds. She was sure she had read about just such a thing in her studies at some point, but how much was one really supposed to be able to retain in a thousand-year lifetime? Not enough, apparently.

But she knew someone who might know a way. It was a long shot, but it was all she had.

"Bassil," she said.

"What?"

"Bassil, the Shaman who works at my father's castle. Bassil might know a way."

Charlie straightened up and leaned forward, jade eyes intense. "How do I get to him?"

Surah's eyes flicked to him, and she hated that his very serious expression caused more hope to spiral in her. "Do you still have the piece of Black Stone your brother gave you?"

Charlie nodded. Then he reached into the pocket of his flannel shirt and pulled out two items. Surah gasped and her heart nearly stopped when she saw what they were. "How did you get those?"

Charlie smiled, that small quirk of his lips that made heat pulse in her midsection in spite of herself. "I took em from Carolyn's," he said. "Thought they might come in handy."

Surah stared at the Stone Vial and another one with a dark purple liquid inside, a Shading Spell. The Stone Vial could be used to capture power from the Black Stone, enough with which to save her father, and the Shading Spell was for invisibility. Surah was so relieved she thought she could kiss Charlie Redmine. Then she remembered how ridiculous that was and slapped the thought away.

"They could help," she said.

Charlie stood, his movements slow and graceful, and came over to Surah, kneeling down in front of her. She could smell the clean scent of him, which was like rain and pine and sunlight blown to her by a warm breeze. His handsome face was level with her own, his bright eyes standing out like gems in the darkness of the cave. "Tell me what to do, Princess," he said, the slow drawl of his voice somehow very intimate in the small space.

Surah found that she had to swallow before she could speak. Twice. Her voice came out low and husky, almost a whisper. "You have to go to the castle and find Bassil. Explain to him the situation. He will help you...if he believes you are telling the truth."

"No trouble there."

Surah found a small smile trying to touch her lips, but stopped it before it could make an appearance. "Of course not," she said.

One side of Charlie's mouth pulled up. "I'll be back as soon as I can," he said, and then, as if he just couldn't help himself, he reached up and brushed back a lavender curl that had fallen forward on her face, covering the purple bruise where Black Heart had struck her. His fingertips were calloused but gentle, running lightly over her soft skin, making her shiver in spite of herself. "This won't happen again," he said, voice low and deep, studying the bruise with what Surah thought was concealed anger and something else she didn't care to contemplate. "You have my word on that, Princess."

Surah's heart did a flip. There was nothing she could do to stop it. "Okay," she said.

Charlie's hand lingered by her face for a moment, then he stood to go. Surah called out to him before he slipped beneath the waterfall. "Charlie?" she said.

He turned back to face her.

Her voice was small and soft and completely unguarded when she spoke. She didn't hate it as much as she thought she would, as much as she probably *should*. It was almost liberating to speak so truly. "I really hope you're not lying."

Charlie smiled, and she hated that it was impossible to hate him when he smiled. "I ain't, Princess," he said. "I ain't."

CHAPTER THIRTY-FIVE

He was exhausted. Pain-in-his-side, panting-for-breath exhausted. He was not built to run very long distances, more so for short, quick bursts of speed, but he could not stop. No matter how tired and hungry and thirsty he was, he could not stop.

He was headed for the Wildland jungle to the northwest of the kingdom, and he still had a good distance to go. Time was his greatest enemy right now, because time was also hers. Who knew what that man could be doing to her? The thought made fury burn in his chest.

Samson held his head low as he crossed the grasslands, his powerful legs propelling him forward. The scents of the land assaulting his nose, pollen and pine and wild honeysuckle and so on. The sunlight beamed down on him harshly and made his eyes slit to half-mast. This was not the ideal way to spend an afternoon. He much preferred sleeping.

But Surah needed him. Now more than ever before, she needed him. He had no doubt in his mind about that the man who called himself Black Heart would kill her; *if* he hadn't done it already. How badly Samson had wanted to rip his throat out back in that Witch's rank cabin. How badly he'd wanted to kill them all. Black Heart and the Witch and Charlie Redmine, that deceitful bastard. He could practically taste the tang of their blood on his tongue now.

He couldn't believe he'd told Surah to give that man an inch. He couldn't believe his instincts were wrong about Charlie. He'd known upon first smell of that cottage that darkness lived inside. He could smell it on Black Heart as soon as he'd appeared, all the way from the field behind the cottage. But Charlie Redmine hadn't been like them. He'd been almost an exact opposite actually, all calm waters, where the other two were raging seas. Samson couldn't ever remember being so wrong about someone before.

Now he had to fix it. And he would. They would pay for every hair harmed on the princess's head in pounds of flesh and blood. As far as Samson was concerned, they were dead men walking.

He stopped only once because he had to, at a small river, about halfway to his destination. He not only drank the water, but waded into it, letting it cool his hot fur and soothe his parched throat. Then he was on his way again, racing under the sun with wide strides and a heaving chest.

When he came to the edge of the Northwestern jungle, he nearly collapsed into the shade of the thick green trees. His tongue felt like a very large, dry sponge in his mouth. His eyes were wind-burned and his jaws agape as he sucked in painful air. He knew he needed to hurry, but he also knew it would be a death wish to head any further into the jungle in such a weak state.

So he slept. Well, he napped. Only for twenty minutes or so. He just lay there, on the edge of the jungle, in the partial shade of the trees, his eyes closed and his troubled mind letting go for a moment. Then he was up again. Rested and ready to move to the next necessities. More water. And food.

And precious time was ticking away. But he couldn't very well help her if he was dead. Also, he was resourceful. He could probably kill two birds with one stone. But first, the water.

His head lifted as he tested the air, searching for the scent of moisture. He found one and followed its trail, his ears perked, amber eyes watchful as he passed beneath the trees. He could feel them out there, the other Beasts, watching him, their own heads surely cocking or tilting as his smell found them on the breeze. It made a rush of exhilaration fill him, his heart kicking up in speed. He was already fantasizing about the hunt ahead.

Nothing attacked him, and he made it to the source of the water, which was just more than a stream running over a bed of jagged rocks, one he could easily hop over. He lowered his head to the edge and drank for a long time, until his belly sloshed inside when he moved. When he was finished he looked all around, trying to figure the quickest route to complete his task. He had no factual basis with which to believe that Black Heart would have come to this particular jungle, only pure instinct. The Northwest jungle was the second smallest of the eight, just a patch on the map compared to most of the others, but if he was going to hold someone prisoner, this is where he would come. It was a good distance from the city, and also had the most hidden caverns and small caves. You could hide someone in one of those small spaces for an eternity and not have them found.

It just seemed right. And he really hoped it was. He didn't have time enough to travel to one of the other jungles. *She* didn't have time enough.

He would need to speak to the Beast King in this land, and if memory served correctly, the Beast King of the Northwest jungle was one volatile son of bitch. He was sure to be difficult to persuade.

Well, he had to find him first.

Samson lowered his head between his shoulders, his body slinking low to the ground. He found the trail of a female panther and followed it, his paws moving silently over the earth. High above him, great birds called out to the open skies, serpents wound around branches, and primates sat atop limbs. The canopy was a thick, impermeable green, only traces of sunlight forcing through. The ground was soft with moisture, the air free of the smells of men. Sometimes Samson longed roam free again, to prowl the jungles, stalking at night, hunting and eating and sleeping on low tree limbs during the day, letting the sunlight sink into his fur, letting his instincts rule him.

But he had given that all up, and would do so again, for her. She had given him a greater purpose in life, one he wouldn't have ever known existed. She had given him love. He simply could not fathom a life without her.

He stopped when he heard the female up ahead, only twenty feet or so southwest, downwind. She was a young one, by the smell of her, and in the middle of a hunt. He could smell the trail masked beneath her own, that of a buck. His eyes narrowed as he smiled inside, thinking of how right he was about two birds and one stone. This was almost too easy.

The female panther broke her cover, charging ahead. Samson followed and watched as she leapt into the air, the buck realizing she was there just a moment too late and trying to break into a run. The black panther landed on its back, square between the buck's shoulders, powerful jaws sinking into the meaty flesh of his neck, claws digging deeply into the hide for purchase. The buck reared, sharp antler's slashing the air as its eyes went wide with terror. It ran thirty feet or so and fell to the ground, blood seeping down its neck where the female was busy ripping and tearing, trying to get at the throat without being snagged by those deadly antlers.

Samson watched from the sidelines, his blood rushing in his ears, his heart racing like a prize horse. He watched and waited. Slowly, the buck ceased its fighting, one dead eye staring heavenward where it lay on its side. The female dismounted her kill, her midnight coat as black as oil. She delicately licked the blood from her face, then moved in to claim her prize.

Samson moved forward.

She was mid-bite when she saw him step through the trees, and a low growl issued from her throat, her eyes locked on his. She was smaller than Samson, of course, but not by too much, standing nearly twelve feet tall from head to paw. Her head lowered and her slim legs coiled, determined to keep her kill.

Samson couldn't help an internal chuckle. The female was no match for him, and they both knew it.

Her voice sounded in his head, a husky, deep growl riding the words. *Get your own, tiger.*

Samson took a few steps forward, amber eyes locked on hers. *I think not, panther.*

He rushed forward, jaws wide and snapping, slashing at her with his sharp claws. The female snapped and slashed as well, but she back-pedaled, nearly tripping over her prey in her escape. Samson stood over the buck, his head still low, daring her with his eyes to try and take the kill back from him. When she just stood there, her black chest heaving with anger, he bent down and tore at the flesh of the buck with his teeth, swallowing large chunks of raw, bloody meat.

The female stood watching him. *You fool,* she growled silently. *You have no idea who I am, do you?*

Samson continued eating, flicking her a look that said he couldn't care less.

The panther narrowed her silver eyes. *My father is king in these lands, and he will have you killed for this. I will taste your flesh by nightfall.*

Samson lifted his head, really looking at her for the first time. He saw now what he should have seen before. The silver of her eyes, the scar on her left flank, the arrogant tilt of her head. He wasn't sure how he'd missed it in her scent, but he could smell it now. His rough tongue ran out slowly over his lips as he tried to jumpstart what was suddenly his frozen thoughts. It had been over eight centuries since he'd last seen her, since that day when Surah had saved him from the serpent and claimed him for her own.

"Mila?"

The panther's head tilted, her eyes widening. *Who are you?* she asked.

He stepped back from the buck, who was a mess of entrails and torn flesh, his eyes on her. Her defensive posture relaxed as she raised her head to her full height. The angry growl was gone from her voice when she spoke again in his head.

Sam?

Samson lifted his head in a nod.

I thought you were dead.

"I almost was."

She was silent for a moment, as if she just couldn't believe it. *Where have you been all this time?* She asked, and Samson felt a little guilt spiral in him at the slight hurt in her tone.

He was almost ashamed to answer. "Living with a Sorceress."

She took a step forward. *You were captured?*

"No."

She took a step back. "What do you mean, no?"

Samson sighed internally. There was no way to explain this that she would understand. Beasts, as a rule, did not live among people. They certainly didn't leave the jungles to be with them. He didn't even have time to begin to explain Surah to Mila. Surah didn't have time.

"The day the serpent attacked us, when we were both cubs, you remember?"

Mila gave him a look that said that was a stupid question. Samson continued on. *"I tried to fight the thing, and sent you off to find help."*

I know, and when I got back with help, you were gone. I thought you were dead, digested by that snake and being shit out somewhere. You think I would have forgotten? What does that have to do with living with a Sorceress?

Samson could tell she was angry, and he couldn't blame her. He remembered now how vulgar she could be when she was angry, so different from Surah with her constant composure. It brought back many memories he didn't care to think of.

I would have been dead. But a Sorceress saved me. She subdued the serpent and took me to safety and I...stayed with her.

For a moment, Mila was silent. Then her voice took on that growl again in his head. *"You stayed with her? Everyone thought you were gone! We held a ceremony in your name! Your mother cried in front of both of our families! I cried!"*

Samson's gut twisted, but he ignored it. She had every right to feel this way, but it wasn't like he could do anything about it now. But he was going to need her help, and if he had learned anything about females from living with Surah for so long, it was that you caught a lot more bees if you used honey.

I'm sorry, Mila.

Mila let out a loud growl that reverberated between the trees. *"You're sorry? That's all you have to say? You're sorry?"* She turned around and began heading through the trees, her muscular shoulders stiff, her tail held still. *"You're sorry doesn't mean shit to me. Enjoy the buck, traitor."*

Samson sighed. Surah was lucky he loved her. He would not have come home to face this if he didn't. Then again, he never would have *left* home if not for her, either.

He left the downed buck and chased after Mila, catching up to her easily. She held her head forward and refused to look at him.

Mila, please, I need your help.

Mila huffed. *"Go ask your precious Sorceress for help."*

Samson came to a stop in front of her, blocking her path. *She can't. She's been captured, and I think she's here somewhere. The man who has her will kill her if I don't find her.*

"And why the hell should I care? I don't give a shit about Two Legs, and they don't give a shit about us. Let her die."

She went to move around him. He blocked her path again. *I can't do that, Mila. You don't understand.*

"You're right, I don't."

Samson had to suppress a growl. He didn't have time for this. Females could be so exhausting. He took a deep breath, completely unsure as to whether his next words would help his case, or hurt it. He said them anyway.

I love her, Mila.

Mila just stared at him, unblinking. She stared at him for so long that he felt sure she was going to refuse his request. Then something flashed behind her eyes that made his heart seem to stop in his chest, and the guilt he felt over leaving her and everyone else slammed into him as hard as it first had eight hundred years ago.

Finally, as if it hurt her to do so, she said, *"How much?"*

How much what?

Mila rolled her eyes, something Samson remembered her doing with annoying frequency when they were younger, an odd Two Leg quality for a feline. *"How much do you love her?"*

Samson's response was immediate, and though he knew it would hurt her, he also knew it was the right one.

More than the moon loves the night and the sun loves the day.

He was right, it did hurt her. He watched with an ache in his heart as the pain flashed behind her eyes. This was something only mates said about one another, something that, once upon a time, in a different world where different things might have happened, Mila and Samson were supposed to say to each other.

Her voice was a pitch lower in his head when she spoke, just hardly above a whisper. *"You'll have to prove it."*

I know.

Mila studied him, and Samson was very aware of the way her silver eyes ran over his body. *"Are you up for it?"* she asked.

Samson tilted his head, giving her a look that said that was a stupid question. Mila rolled her eyes again. Some things just never changed.

"Well," she continued, *"I suppose you'll have to be. I can't imagine what sort of test my father will give for you to gain his assistance. He won't be pleased with all of this."*

I know.

Mila huffed again and circled around Samson. He followed, thinking that maybe he wasn't up for this after all. He knew what the reaction would be to his arrival, knew his choices would be seen as traitorous, knew this would probably be one of the most difficult things he'd ever had to do, aside from leaving them all in the first place.

But what choice did he have? He'd meant what he said.

He really did love Surah more than the moon loves the night and the sun loves the day. Even if it was such a hopeless, reasonless love. Often times, the greatest of such is just so.

CHAPTER THIRTY-SIX

Theo's large, rough hand was tight around Jude Flyer's throat, not enough to cut off his air, not yet, but at a point where it seemed inevitable. The Head Hunter's face was inches away, his neck craning down so he could stare the smaller man in the eyes, his breath hot on his face.

Theodine Gray was very angry. Jude Flyer was literally shaking in his boots. He tried to swallow and was just able. "You don't understand, Sir Gray," Jude said, his voice trembling, "There are confidentiality issues. I-I took an oath."

Theo's hand tightened. Jude squealed once like a stuck pig. "I understand perfectly well," Theo said his voice much calmer than his eyes betrayed. "I understand your loyalty is to the king, or am I mistaken?"

Jude shook his head, jowls jiggling almost comically. "You are not mistaken, S-Sir, but I don't think I know anything that can help you." Tears rolled down his puffy cheeks, hot and embarrassing, and he decided in that moment that he *hated* Theodine Gray.

"Just tell me everything you know, Flyer. Spare no detail." Theo released his hold and stepped back, but only a little. He still had Jude pinned against the wall. Trapped.

Jude rubbed his chubby fingers over his throat, swiped the tears from his eyes, straightened his cloak. "Charlie Redmine told me he hadn't spoken to his brother in years, that he had nothing to do with the murders or the disappearance of the Black Stone."

The Head Hunter's eyes narrowed. "How did he know about the Stone? That information was not released to the public."

Jude shrugged. He almost said that the princess had told Charlie, because that's what Charlie had told him, but something inside him screamed to not share this information with the Head Hunter. So he lied.

He did it so suddenly it sounded true. "I don't know. Mr. Redmine just said the Black Stone was missing, explaining how a man like Brad Milner had a piece of it when he murdered Merin Nightborn. He said Black Heart could have something to do with it."

Theo stared at the fat little man, his gray eyes colder than a winter morning. Jude couldn't help but push back against the wall, and hated that he was cowering, hated Theo more for *making* him cower.

Theo's voice was flat and threatening when he spoke. "Anything else?" he asked.

Jude shook his head, ran a hand through his slick hair.

Theo turned on his heel and left, leaving Jude Flyer staring after him with a look of dark red behind his eyes.

CHAPTER THIRTY-SEVEN

He loved the reaction she gave every time she saw him. She looked over from the tree branch on which she was perched, her head cocking in that bird-like way. Her wide, slanted eyes glittering, the shimmering wings on her back fluttering. Bits of pink leaves floated down to the earth as she bounced up and down, shaking the branch, the claws on her feet digging into the bark.

"Michael!" she trilled. Her head cocked from side to side. "Michael is here! Wonderful! Michael is here, everyone!"

Black Heart came forward, ignoring the looks from the Fae Queen's guards as he stepped into her palace, which was ringed with a high stone wall and was composed of all earth and trees. The weather was always pleasant here, warm and moist, the sun filtering down gently through the multi-colored trees and creating rainbows where there should be shadows. Black Heart loved this place.

"My love," he said, coming to a stop beneath the tree in which she was perched, his neck tilted back to look at her.

She floated down from the tree gracefully, her long gown flowing and shifting in color from purple to blue to pink. Her wings fluttered once, and she landed lithely on her feet, clapping her hands and grinning widely to reveal sharp teeth.

"My love, my love!" she sang. "My love has returned!" She flicked her hands, shooing away the two Fae guards nearest them, and snatched up Black Heart's hand in hers the way a love struck child might do. She led him into her bedroom, which was just a close ring of trees that were so thick they served as walls. The sun shined down overhead. A bed with a silk canopy sat in the center. This is where she led him.

"What's new?" she asked. "Tell me everything! It must be so exciting!"

Black Heart smiled, sat down on the bed. She immediately climbed on top of him. Her strange, beautiful face inches from his. His heart quickened. "It is, my Lady," he said, running his hands down her waist. "It is, indeed. It's going even better than I expected."

Her wide, slanted eyes sparkled. She clapped her hands, bouncing him up and down on the bed. "You've killed the Sorcerer King!" She giggled. "The king is dead! The king is dead!"

Black Heart grabbed her wrists and moved her arms around his neck, leaning up to kiss her soft throat. She giggled again softly. "Not yet, my love," he whispered, "but soon. Very soon. I have his daughter, too."

She pulled back, the grin still wide on her face. "Surah Stormsong? You've captured her? Where is she? I want to meet her! Bring her to me! Bring her!"

Black Heart kissed her neck again. She shifted her hips, quieted. "I have no intention of doing that," he said. "I'm going to kill her."

She pulled back, her red mouth drawing down in a pout. She crossed her arms over her chest. "You have all the fun! Bring her here and I will kill her! A test! I'll give her a test she can't pass! It will be wonderful!"

Black Heart sighed and laid back on the bed, propping his hands behind his head. "Too dangerous, my love. I'm sorry, but no."

She bounced up and down again in anger, her legs tightening almost painfully around him. "I can make sure it gets done! You don't think I can! Shame on you, Michael! Shame on you!"

He stared up at her. "You didn't do so well with the Sun Warrior. You told me she would be hopelessly outmatched. What happened with that?"

Her eyes narrowed and her voice lowered, as it only did when she was truly mad. She spoke between sharp, clenched teeth. "She was," she said. "She *was* outmatched. I placed thirty of my best warriors against that girl, and she slaughtered them all like they were nothing more than annoying insects. You should have seen it! I underestimated Alexa. I won't make that mistake again. I will kill the Sorceress Princess myself! You're selfish! That's what it is! You are a selfish man!"

He pulled her down to him roughly, pressing their bodies together, kissing her neck. She tried not to, but she giggled. He spoke softly against her skin. "Because of that, the Vampire King is dead, and I have only rumors to base the claim that he killed Syris Stormsong. I'm sorry, love. I won't risk it."

She pulled back again, a slight flush on her cheeks, her chest heaving. "Where is she now? The princess? Who is watching her?"

Black Heart hesitated. She threw up her hands, crossed her arms over her chest. "You left him with that brother of yours! Fool! You are a fool! He has proven he can't be trusted! Michael is a fool!"

His teeth clenched. "Watch your tongue, my love."

Her head cocked, grin slowly returning. "Or what? You'll cut it out?" She leaned down. "You just try! Just try! Just try!"

Black Heart smiled. She was so lovely when she was angry. "Of course not, my love. Wouldn't dream of it."

Her eyes narrowed. He pulled her to him again, their chests flush against one another's. "He is my little brother, and he deserves one more chance to prove himself. I'm giving him that. Charlie loves me. I know he does."

She licked his throat, making him shiver. "But he also loves this princess," she mumbled against his skin. "You said he's loved her since he was a boy. Would *you* betray *me* for your Charlie Boy? Would you?"

Black Heart didn't know the answer to that question, but he knew what she wanted to hear. "Of course not, my love."

"Fool! You are a fool then!"

"There is no risk, so I am no fool. Even if he does try to help the princess, I won't give him time to break her restraints. I'm going back as soon as I leave here." He lifted her skirt and ran his hands up her thighs, knowing this would cut off any response. Her skin quivered under his fingers. He kissed her neck. "I thought you'd be pleased I made time to see you."

She sat up and began working at his belt. "Of course!" she sang. "Always happy to see Michael! We will be quick! Princesses to kill and kingdoms to steal!" She laughed. "Quick! Quick! Quick!"

Black Heart smiled. "Quick enough."

CHAPTER THIRTY-EIGHT

She was lucky she was a woman. Otherwise, Theo would be holding her by her throat the same way he had Jude Flyer. Instead he smiled and looked into her eyes. Of course, her cheeks lightened softly and she returned the gesture.

"I don't think you understand, Tyra," Theo said, voice as smooth as velvet. "Dark Magic was used to teleport into the castle by an...unsavory person. You were the person on watch over the Security Spells that are *supposed* to keep out just such people during the time of the breech." He tilted his head, regarding her with false gentleness. "Just explain to me how that can be. It is a matter of great importance."

Tyra's brow furrowed in thought, her cheeks still flushed from Theo's penetrating stare. He could tell just by her face that she was attracted to him, and he had no patience for idle talk just now. He could also tell she was hiding something.

He took a half step forward, leaning down to catch her eyes when they dropped to the floor. He placed his large hands gently on her shoulders. She looked up at him with wide eyes. "It's all right, my Lady," he said, his voice a low purr. "You can tell me what's on your mind."

Tyra looked down again. Then, all of a sudden, she burst into tears, her chocolate hair falling into her face and her hands coming up to cover it. Theo raised an eyebrow and suppressed a sigh. This was exactly why women shouldn't be able to run kingdoms. They were always crying for no apparent reason. No control over their emotions.

Well, Surah had control. It was one of the reasons he liked her. He suppressed an eye roll and patted Tyra's shoulders. "Tell me what troubles you," he said, his voice slightly less gentle.

She ran her sleeve underneath her nose, swiping at tears and snot.

Theo swallowed back disgust and made sure his smile was in place. Her voice trembled when she spoke. "I didn't have a choice, my Lord," she said.

More sobs racked her chest. Theo's eyes narrowed. "A choice in what?"

Her words came out so broken he could hardly understand her. "B-Black Heart…he…he had my *son!*" She was becoming hysterical. Theo just let her continue. "He-he said he'd kill Tony if I didn't cooperate. I was so sc-scared! You have to believe me!"

Theo's mouth was tight. "What did he ask you to do?"

She swiped at her nose again. "To l-lower the spells blocking teleportation inside the castle. I-I didn't know what to do. He had Tony! He had my son! He showed him to me through a Vision Spell, showed him bound and gagged and unconscious!" She grabbed his wrists. Theo resisted the urge to yank free of her touch. "What else could I have done?" she sobbed.

"Did he return your son?"

She nodded, her eyes hopeful. Theo turned to leave. "Then enjoy your time with him, my Lady, because I'm sure that King Syrian will want you brought forth on treason."

Tyra began to sob again, asking over and over what else she could have done. He opened the door of her chamber and turned back, his gray eyes cold and hard. "You could have been loyal to your kingdom," he said, and then he left. He could hear her sobs all the way down the hall.

He was angry. He basically had nothing to go on and time was running short. His could practically feel the heat of the situation on his neck. Everything he'd wanted for so long was just within reach. King Syrian had promised his daughters hand, and all Theo had to do was find her. It was proving to be easier said than done.

But he was not quite out of ideas yet. There were others who might know more about the princess and her whereabouts. The tiger was gone, having disappeared along with Surah, so he was out. Not that Theo would have relished trying to strike up a talk with that Beast. That left the Shaman and Surah's two personal guards, Lyonell and Noelani.

He decided Bassil would be his next stop, and the Shaman had better be forthcoming. Theodine Gray's patience was wearing terribly thin.

CHAPTER THIRTY-NINE

It was a good thing Charlie didn't have to teleport into the castle again, as the first time had nearly knocked the stomach out of him. He'd barely been able to slip the spells his brother had surely strong-armed someone to get access to, and he was sure that situation had been rectified by now anyway. But the Shaman's home was just outside the castle, which was too close to comfort for Charlie.

This whole mission was too close for comfort. It was borderline insane. But he couldn't just let her die.

He hoped he had the Invisibility Spell right. The princess had told him three times the words that would ignite the potion he'd taken from the Witch's cottage, but he wasn't used to using Magic. He lived a simple life. Well, he supposed, not anymore he didn't. Things had grown incredibly complicated.

He teleported into the field behind the Shaman's home, which was just a medium-sized hut with a thatched roof. Charlie recited the Invisibility Spell as soon as he appeared, and he watched in disbelief as his body faded and became imperceptible. He looked around, trying not to look at the looming gray castle only fifty yards to the south. It was quiet, the only sound that of the breeze shuffling through the long grass.

Charlie began to move forward, his heart beating out of his chest, hoping like hell that the Shaman was home, that he wouldn't have to lie in wait for him. The sooner he could get what he needed and get out of here the better. Not only was the princess running out of time, but the longer Charlie stayed here the bigger the chance that he get caught. And he had a feeling that a certain Head Hunter would love to have a…conversation or two with him. He was not at all interested in having any conversations with that man.

He moved quietly, trying not to disturb the ground with his steps, and snuck around to the front of the hut. Wind chimes hung from the roof here, but the breeze was not strong enough to make them sing. Sunlight reflected from their surfaces, glinting on the metal. The door was just a thick gray blanket hung over an opening. No light peeked out from its closed edges.

Charlie took a deep breath and pushed the blanket aside, stepping into the darkness. The first sense that struck him was the smell. It was a tangy, green smell that reminded him a little of the jungle. He jumped when a Light Sphere appeared, illuminating the darkness, and a deep voice spoke from somewhere off to his side.

"Make yourself known," the voice said.

Charlie's head whipped to the right, and there he saw the Shaman sitting on a small stool, his patchwork cloak around his shoulders. His skin was the color of dark chocolate, and he was bigger than Charlie expected, with large square shoulders and huge hands. For a moment, Charlie didn't know what to do.

The Shaman held his palm up, and a bit of blue fire appeared over his hand, licking up off his fingers. "Reveal yourself," the Shaman said, "or I will make you reveal yourself."

Charlie ran a hand down his jaw and said the words to break the Invisibility Spell. He held up his hands, regarding the Shaman carefully. "I don't mean no harm," Charlie said quickly.

He wasn't sure what kind of reaction he was expecting, but he didn't get it. Bassil just sat on his stool and stared at him, the hand that held the blue fire closing and going out. He placed it in his lap. "Then why have you come, Charlie Redmine?" he asked, eyeing the piece of Black Stone around Charlie's neck.

Charlie didn't ask how he knew who he was, wasn't sure he wanted to know. Besides, he was a man who liked to cut to the chase. "Because I need your help to save the princess," he said.

Bassil's dark eyebrows arched. "Is that so?"

Charlie nodded. "She said you would help me."

"Did she?"

Charlie kept the annoyance off his face with some effort. "I need to know how to break her restraints. She's bein held in place by Black Magic. Will you help?"

Bassil was silent for a moment, and Charlie felt the urge to thump him on the head. The clock was ticking. "Time is, uh, of an essence here," Charlie added.

Bassil nodded, his very white teeth shining out in his dark face. "Oh, indeed. Indeed it is. But you must know you are a wanted man. An enemy of the kingdom. Or has this news escaped you in your travels?"

Charlie was growing frustrated, but he knew he had to play this cool. Surah had told him that the Shaman was not someone he would want to piss off. "No," he said. "It hasn't escaped me. But I ain't no outlaw, and I'm here because the princess is goin to be killed if I don't help her. If *you* don't help her."

Bassil tilted his head. "I see," he said, and then he went silent again, staring at Charlie with dark eyes.

Charlie did his best not to shift his feet. He wanted this done with. The Shaman was stalling. "She said to tell you somethin."

"Oh? And what was that?"

Charlie licked his lips. "She said—and I quote—to not be a stubborn Wildman and help me out, or the next time she saw you she would show that she doesn't really throw like a princess."

Charlie had no idea what the Shaman's response to this would be, and a long half of a heartbeat passed before Bassil broke into deep, rumbling laughter. "You're telling the truth, Mr. Redmine," he said, his smile less threatening and more intrigued.

"Yes, I am. How do I break the bonds on Surah?"

"What do they look like?"

Charlie thought a moment. "Kinda like black smoke, but solid. They circle her wrists and anytime she moves them, they tighten. Her fingers already looked a little blue when I left her, and the chains seem to be rooted into the earth, so she can't even stand."

"What was used to cast the spell? The Black Stone, I would assume."

"You assume right. Can they be broken?"

Bassil smiled, but worry was creasing his brow now. "Of course, Mr. Redmine, all spells can be broken…though some things are irrevocable as well."

"What the hell does that mean?"

The Shaman's eyes had gone distant, almost casting a slight glaze over the irises. His gaze snapped back to Charlie, and now he couldn't help but shift on his feet. He had a gut feeling he didn't want to hear what the Shaman had to say.

"It means you can save her, Mr. Redmine." Bassil stood from the stool now, towering over Charlie by a good five inches even though Charlie was not a short man himself. He moved over to a shelf where books and vials holding multi-colored liquids and powders sat. He plucked one off the shelf that had a pure, silver color inside, like mercury. Charlie eyed the spell and swallowed.

"How?" he asked.

Bassil handed over the vial. Charlie took it. "Hate is what binds us, Mr. Redmine. It is what traps us in place and refuses to let us move forward. It's the driving power of dark Magic and troubled minds and bad deeds…Would you like to guess what sets us free?"

Charlie just looked at him, said nothing.

The Shaman's smile returned, and if Charlie hadn't known better, he would've thought he saw a little sympathy behind his dark eyes. "Alright, I'll tell you. Love, Mr. Redmine. Love sets us free."

Charlie's heart seemed to have stopped beating in his chest, and his mind couldn't quite process what it was being told. His voice came out a touch robotic. "What do I have to do?" he asked.

Bassil gestured to the vial. "Poor that on the bonds and then cast your spell."

"That's it?"

"Well…not precisely."

"Runnin outta time here."

Bassil nodded. "But it's tricky to explain. I've only ever performed such a spell once, and I was just barely able. The thing is, there are no specific words that you can say to get it to work, no text or chant written down anywhere that work for certain."

Charlie rubbed a hand over his jaw. "What's the trick, then? How can I perform a spell that there are no instructions to?"

"You just use love, Mr. Redmine. You use love to break it." He smiled again. "I've a feeling that won't be as difficult for you as it was for me."

Charlie's jaw fell open. "What the hell does that—?"

The Shaman held up a hand, cutting Charlie off mid-sentence. His dark eyes went to the front of the hut, and his voice came out in a deep whisper. "Someone's coming."

Now Charlie's heart was beating out of his chest. "But I don't understand yet," he whispered, his eyes glued to the dark gray blanket serving as the door of the hut. "What do I do? How'd you get the spell to work?"

The look the Shaman gave him then made Charlie's gut twist. "I recited a nursery rhyme my mother used to sing to me before bed," Bassil said, speaking quietly and quickly. "And I think you understand better than you would let on, Mr. Redmine. Either way, you must go now."

Charlie didn't give himself time to contemplate what in the world the Shaman meant by that. "Thank you," he said, and wrapped his fingers around the piece of Black Stone hanging from his neck.

He disappeared from the room just a split second before the blanket covering the entrance to the hut was pulled back, streaming sunlight into the dark place. Bassil was not at all surprised to see Theodine Gray standing there.

"Knock, knock," the Head Hunter said, stepping into the hut and looking all around with curiosity. He clucked his tongue and grinned. "Come now, Shaman. I'm sure we pay you better than this."

Bassil moved slowly over to his stool in the corner, folding his big body down to sit. He looked up at Theo with calm disinterest. "*You* don't pay me anything, Hunter Gray. King Syrian does, and he provides everything I require."

"I know common people who live better than this," Theo replied.

Bassil's voice was low and smooth. "Did you come here just to insult me, Hunter Gray, or is there a matter with which you need my assistance?"

Theo's jaw tightened as he turned to face him. "As a matter of fact, there is." His head tilted. "See, the princess is still missing, and you happen to be the last person who saw her."

No he wasn't. Charlie Redmine was. Bassil smiled and nodded, spread his large hands. "I suppose that's so," he said.

Theo took a step forward. "Did she say anything to you about leaving? Did she mention anything that might be of use to me in finding her?"

Bassil pretended to think. Then he shook his head. "She told me just what I told you. That she wanted to leave at first light for the location the eagle's blood led us to. I suppose she could have gone there. The princess is not one for patience."

This was a lie, but Bassil was sure it sounded true.

Theo shook his head. "She is not there. I'm sure of it."

"How?"

"That is none of your concern, Shaman."

Bassil stood now, the top of his head nearly reaching the roof of the hut. He stared down at the Head Hunter. Theo stared back.

"I believe it *is* my concern, Hunter Gray. You are not the only one who cares for the princess. I've been her instructor since she was a child. If memory serves, you are also a former student of mine."

Theo smiled amicably, but Bassil could see the malice behind his gray eyes. "This is true," Theo said, spreading his hands in front of him. "I have reason to believe the princess has been taken prisoner by Black Heart and his younger brother, a man named Charlie Redmine."

Bassil could tell just by the way Theo said his name that he hated Charlie. It made him wonder just what he had set in motion by assisting Redmine, and he had a feeling it would not be a pretty thing. But Bassil didn't like the Head Hunter, had never liked him, not even when he was a little boy, and Bassil liked all children. Theodine Gray was the same as he was then. Cold-hearted. Only he was much more dangerous now because he had become a man. A man who held a powerful position. A man with an agenda.

And he *did* like Charlie Redmine. Maybe it was foolish, but he liked Charlie after only having just met him. He also had a gut feeling the princess was fond of him, too. This didn't make the decision of what to say next easy, but it made the decision.

Bassil looked the Head Hunter in the eyes, his face stone and grave. "Then I suppose we shall have to hope the princess is resourceful," he said, "because I'm afraid there is nothing useful I can tell you."

CHAPTER FORTY

Samson followed Mila through the jungle. She didn't say a word. He wished he could explain himself to her in a way that wouldn't hurt her feelings, in a way she could understand, but he knew there was no use even trying. The ways of the jungle were too reinforced in her—too reinforced in all of them—that loving a Sorceress would sound like an insanity.

Samson supposed it sort of was, but his instincts pushed him onward. He had a gut feeling that he if didn't reach Surah in time, it would mean her death. And that, as insane as it may be, could not be allowed to happen.

He knew he would have to face his kind at one point or another, now was as good a time as any.

The two of them slinked through the undergrowth, the ground soft and moist beneath his paws. He kept tilting his head up to test the air, taking in the clean, untouched smell of it. There were many things he missed about his home, and the smell was one of them. You didn't get air like this where there were people. You didn't get plants this green or silence this deep or sunlight as soft as this, either.

Mila kept moving onward, no doubt leading him to her father. She didn't look back even once to see if he was still following, didn't slow down to make sure he wouldn't lose her. She navigated her way over downed trees and swam across cool rivers and slipped between the plants easily. Samson, though he was nervous about the task ahead, liked watching her move. She was so at home here, her powerful muscles shifting under her dark fur, silver eyes flicking back and forth. Her head and tail were held low, her progression silent. Mila had grown into a fine female while he'd been away. An alpha.

This made him think of Surah, as most of his thoughts led him to. People didn't label themselves alphas, but if they did, the princess would certainly be one of them. He wondered what she was doing just now, knew she was probably scared but calm, trying to figure her way out of whatever situation she'd found herself in. He supposed that made two of them.

Mila came to a stop in front of him, and Samson was so absorbed in his thoughts that he had to lock his forelegs so as not to run into her. Her head swiveled as she looked back at him. *You sure you want to do this?* She asked him silently.

Samson's tongue flicked out, running over the blue and black fur around his mouth. *"Yes,"* he said.

She stared at him a moment, her round, silver eyes pinned to his. She looked like she didn't want to say what she said next. *You'll probably be fighting Reno.*

Samson looked at her a moment, then laughed internally. *"Reno? You think I should be worried about fighting Reno?"*

She didn't seem to share in his amusement. *He's not the same as he was when you left. He's no longer a cub. He's grown strong. Fighting him is no laughing matter.*

Samson went to move around her. *"I'm sure he has. Don't worry. I'll be fine."*

Mila blocked his path, her head held low between her muscular shoulders. *I'm not worried,* she snapped. *What have I to worry about? I accepted your death a long time ago. It's you who should be worried. Reno has lived life here, among the Beasts, while you have laid atop fluffy pillows on the bedroom floor of a Sorcerer princess. You would be a fool to underestimate him.*

Samson raised his head, the fur on his back standing a little on end. He decided it would be best not to respond to that. It might just come out in a growl.

She whipped her head back around and began to move forward again. *Fine. Have it your way.*

Mila led him into darker, thicker vegetation, and at a few points, Samson had to crouch low to pass under thick tree branches that scratched at his back in a sort of pleasant way. The sunlight was muted to a dim glow in these places, where the green above was so thick and heavy it seemed as though you could walk on it. Samson's heart kicked up in pace with each step he took. But Mila didn't know what she was talking about. Reno may have grown up in the jungle, but just in the past week Samson had battled demons and a Great Eagle for his Sorceress. Living with Surah, protecting her and loving her, were not easy things. Over the years he had faced things more terrifying than even the jungles could offer. And his mind was sharp. Dealing for so long with people had made it so. Beasts were fearsome creatures, with sharp fangs and claws and deadly strength; what you saw was what you got. But people plotted and deceived and cheated and covered it all with smiling masks. People were far more dangerous. The true

Kings of the Jungle.

Samson could handle this.

At last, the vegetation thinned, and Samson stepped into a large clearing where the sunlight managed to reach the earth. The ground was a deep, healthy green, spotted with the most vibrant red and purple flowers in all the lands. Straight ahead, relaxing in the daylight, was a pride of twenty large felines, whose heads perked up as Samson stepped forward. Above them all, staring down from a large rock that sat near the stream that ran through the center of the open place, sat Drake, Mila's father. The cat who called himself king of this land. The one who had offered his daughter's hand in marriage to Samson's father so long ago.

Samson lifted his head, amber eyes watching both the king and his followers, thinking he would be lucky if he got through this with only having to face Reno in battle. If Drake had his lot attack, Samson wouldn't make it out of here alive.

Mila led him forward, silver eyes also watching her father, who was now standing atop the rock, his ears perked forward, nose testing the air, sampling the scent of the newcomer. The sunlight caught in his dark fur and revealed hints of midnight blue amongst the black. His eyes were round and silver, like his daughter's, and by the time Mila came to a stop only fifteen feet from the rock on which her father stood, Samson could tell that Drake knew exactly who he was.

He hadn't heard the voice in nearly a thousand years, but as soon as Samson heard the king speak in his head, the memories came flooding back to him. Drake's voice was a deep, rumbling, almost chocolaty sound. He said one word.

Samson.

Samson lowered his head respectively. *"Yes, my King."*

Drake's eyes flipped to his daughter. *What is this, Mila?*

Mila's tail swished low, back and forth, and Samson could tell she was nervous, despite her having said she didn't care what happened to him. But her voice sounded clear and strong when she spoke. *He has come for our help, father,* she said.

Drake looked back at Samson. *Really. How is it that a dead cat can need help?*

Samson spoke now for the first time. *"As you can see, my King. I am not dead."*

Drake's eyes narrowed to slits. *Then I am not your king. You have not been living among us.*

Samson raised his head, bringing himself to his full height. To show weakness here would be a death sentence. *"No, I have not. But I come willing to prove myself worthy of your assistance."*

What is it you want?

"I believe there may be a Sorceress held prisoner in your land. If I'm correct, I'm sure you know about it. I just want to know where she is."

The king was silent for a moment, silver eyes just staring down at Samson, who held his gaze steadily. Then Drake laid back down atop his rock again, lowering his head between his paws. Samson held his breath.

So be it, Drake said finally, his eyes flicking to the group of huge cats that were watching with keen interest to the left.

He called out Reno's name, just as Mila had predicted, and Samson had to admit he was impressed with how much his old friend had grown. He was no longer a scrawny cub, but had become a large alpha, matching Samson in weight and size. Reno moved toward the rock where they were standing, his wide chest out, dark head held high.

Samson met his stare. Reno's voice was edged with a growl when he spoke in his head. *We thought you were dead.*

Samson sighed internally. *"I'm not."*

Enough, Drake said. *Move out into the clearing and get on with it before I get bored and decide to kill you both.*

Mila went to stand beside her father, flicking a nervous look between Samson and Reno, who were walking side-by-side toward the open place that served as the arena for just such a competition. Reno's head tilted as he looked over at Samson.

So where have you been? he asked.

Samson didn't want to answer, but he did anyway. He didn't see any point in lying now. *"Living with a Sorceress."*

The one you're looking for?

"Yes. Is she here?"

You haven't earned that information yet...A Sorceress, huh? You always were a big dumb cat.

"And your talk was always bigger than your bite."

Not anymore, my old friend.

"Let us see, shall we?"

Certainly.

The two cats separated and moved to face each other, powerful muscles bunched and heads held low between their shoulders. Samson saw his own excitement reflected in Reno's black eyes. Without signal, Reno pounced forward, sharp claws extended, deadly teeth bared. Samson leapt to the side, his paw lashing out and scraping Reno's side as he sailed by him. Reno growled, low and deep and rumbling, and it was answered with growls from the other cats on the sidelines, filling the quiet clearing with their roars.

Samson was already charging forward, and he caught Reno in side, the two of them crashing to the earth and rolling in a terrible display of teeth and claws. Blood and chunks of fur flew as fangs found purchase again and again. Samson disentangled himself and charged again, his amber eyes wide and glittering. His ears were flat on his head, his heart racing and thumping in his chest, blood pumping hot and fast.

Reno's paw lashed out and caught him across the face, and Samson returned the blow with one of his own, shaking his head at the stars bursting behind his eyes. Mila had been right. Reno had learned a thing or two in Samson's absence. He needed to end this, and quickly.

He stepped back and roared, calculating his next attack the way people calculated theirs. It was a thing that had taken Samson years to master, being able to step out of his animal instincts in the heat of battle and use his mind. Surah had taught him to do it.

Reno was doing no such thing, he pounced forward again, and Samson crouched low and leapt upward, locking his powerful jaws around the underside of Reno's thick neck. Reno growled and snapped, trying to knock Samson free with all four paws as the two of them tumbled to the ground again. Samson tightened his hold, locking his jaws just short of crushing capacity around the other cat's throat, his huge claws digging into his thick fur for even more purchase.

He held Reno trapped beneath him. Reno went still. Samson had him in a death hold and they both knew it.

When Reno growled enraged surrender, Samson released him slowly, back-pedaling and not taking his eyes off his opponent. His head was still low, his mouth bloody and his body scratched and battered and bleeding in various places. Reno looked even worse off, but he found his feet, his head and tail lowered in defeat.

Samson watched him closely, knowing that some Beasts had a way of not accepting loss. But after a moment of hard staring Reno turned and limped his way back to the other cats, licking at his wounds. Samson felt like doing the same, but this was not over yet, and there was simply no time for weakness.

He slowly approached the rock on which Drake was still perched, his chest pushed out and head high, tongued flicking out and tasting the blood still ringing his mouth. He bowed again to the king, his massive head coming down between his shoulders.

Drake's deep voice sounded in his head. *Still as fearsome as ever, I see.*

Samson said nothing, only watched the king with wary eyes.

I will make a deal with you, Samson, and if you agree, I will provide the information you have asked for.

Samson's heart sunk. He had been expecting something like this. "What deal?" he asked. "I want only to know where the Sorceress is, and then I will leave your land and not return."

Mila shook her head once, but Samson didn't look at her.

Drake stood now and hopped down from his place on the rock,

155

approaching Samson boldly. Drake was the biggest cat Samson had ever known, and the most people-minded of the bunch as well. Samson supposed he had to be to rule over the Beasts of the Northwest jungle for so long, but it also meant that Samson was probably about to be faced with an unfavorable decision.

Drake held his head above Samson, looking down at him with sharp eyes. *I will tell you where the Two-Leg Sorceress is if you agree to the arrangement that your father agreed to nearly nine-hundred years ago.* His head swiveled as he looked back at where Reno was still nursing his wounds. *You are stronger than my strongest, as you have just proven, and that makes you the only proper suitor for my daughter. The only cat fit to rule this land following my demise.*

Samson's eyes flicked to Mila, who looked slightly horrified, which was comical on her feline face. But there was absolutely nothing comical about this situation.

Samson didn't like to do it, but there was another thing he had learned from living with people for so long, and that was how to lie.

"You have a deal, my King," he said.

Mila looked at him now, her silver eyes round and shimmering. He could tell just by the look there that she knew he was lying, that she was thinking of what he had told her to get her to bring him here.

How much do you love her? she'd asked.

More than the moon loves the night and the sun loves the day.

Yes, Mila knew he was lying, and for a moment he feared she would share this information with her father, but she didn't. She just tore her gaze away. The hurt look behind her eyes made Samson's chest ache, but he was beyond grateful for her silence.

Drake didn't even consider the possibility that he was being fooled. Why would he? One did not lie to a King of Beasts.

A man wearing all black led your Sorceress through the jungle early this morning, Drake said, accepting the matter as done. *He had a dark power radiating from him, so the Beasts let him be. He stashed her on the far edge of the land, where the sun rises in the morning, in a small space behind a wall of water. I have been told you can follow the trail once in the area, but have not been out to check myself. Two-legs yielding dark power are dangerous creatures.*

"Thank you, my King." Samson said, and turned to leave, anxious to get to where he was going now that he had a location. He knew this land, and he would find his princess. He just hoped he wouldn't be too late. The eastern side of this jungle was at least an hour's travel from here. More running. He wondered if he would ever just get to nap today.

I expect you to uphold your end of this deal, Samson, Drake, the Beast King, called after him.

Samson turned his head and looked back, but his eyes found Mila's and held them. He did not feel at all good about his next words. *"And so I shall, my King."*

Then he left, racing eastward to save the person who his allegiance was truly to, feeling damned if he did and damned if he didn't. Tired and hurting and worried and just damned.

CHAPTER FORTY-ONE

Her hands hurt. They throbbed and pulsed and felt ten degrees warmer than the rest of her body, which was covered in sweat. Her fingertips were blue and her mouth felt dry. The left side of her face hurt where the back of Black Heart's hand had struck her. She stared into the waterfall, listening to the sound of the rushing liquid and wondering how much time had passed.

Too much. That's how much.

Surah shoved the thought away, careful not to move her throbbing wrists. Her back was beginning to ache from the slumped position, and she rolled her neck slowly, trying to work out muscle there. It wasn't really helping. She was starting to really think about the possibility that she may not escape. She could perform simple magic without her piece of the White Stone, but none of it would be of use here.

She let out a long breath and looked up at the ceiling of the little cave. It wasn't so much the thought of dying that pained her—though it scared her, admittedly—but rather the people she loved and how she might not get to see them again. It was the probability that if she died, her father would die too. It was that she may never get to run her fingers through Samson's thick fur again, or see his wide, amber eyes staring at her in that open way, a way he only had with her, and she only with him. It was Lyonell and Noelani, how she knew they would blame themselves for whatever happened. Even Theo would be sad, she knew.

No, it wasn't so much death that pained her. It was the way they would all grieve. She knew the feeling well, the empty, aching feeling it would bring them. She didn't want them to feel that. She didn't want to die.

A single tear sprang from her eye and rolled down her cheek, hot and wet. She'd been restraining them for the past twenty minutes or so. She wished so badly she could reach up and wipe it away, because she didn't want it to leave a trail there that would be visible to her captors. They could kill her, but they would not see her cry. They didn't deserve to.

Surah tilted her head to the side, trying to brush the tear off on her shoulder without raising it so the cuffs wouldn't tighten any further. It was a more difficult task than one might think. Her wrists shifted. She bit back a cry of pain. It came out in a sort of grunt.

"Got an itch?"

Her head snapped up at the voice, her heart jumping into her throat. The urge to wipe at her face to make sure it was clear of salt water struck her. She resisted. Barely. Her mouth fell open, and she tried to quiet her suddenly heaving chest. "Yes, actually, Mr. Redmine," she said finding her composure very quickly under the circumstances. She was proud of herself. "I've got an itch. I've had several of them in the past ninety minutes or so I've been chained here. Thanks for asking."

Charlie was silent for a moment, green eyes staring at her. "Just looked like you was tryin to rub your face is all." He said, and paused. "And it's only been bout seventy-five minutes."

Surah raised her chin, clenching her teeth so it wouldn't tremble. "It felt like seventy-five hours."

Charlie's mouth pulled up a bit in that small smile, making a dimple appear on his right cheek. "I missed you too, honey," he said.

Surah felt her anger come rushing back. "Did you see Bassil?" she snapped, ignoring his inappropriate address. "Did he know a way to break these restraints?"

Charlie nodded slowly. "Well…yeah, I guess."

"What the hell does that mean?"

"You ain't gonna like it, and you're already mad."

Surah looked indignant. "Ridiculous. I'm not mad. You haven't seen me mad."

His head tilted as he looked at her. "Never heard you curse before. You must be pretty mad."

Her eyes narrowed. "You're wasting time, Mr. Redmine."

"I know."

She almost threw her hands up, but remembered just in time that she couldn't. Her teeth ground together instead. "What is this?" she asked. "What have you to gain from tricking me this way? You already have me captive. Do you get some sick pleasure out of this, Mr. Redmine?"

Charlie sighed, running a hand over his short dark beard. "'Course I don't," he said, as if that were the silliest accusation in the world. He pulled out the vial of silver liquid the Shaman had given him and held it up so she could see it."

Her lovely face lit up, and Charlie felt a twist in his stomach.

"Bassil gave that to you," she said. "I recognize the vial." Her violet eyes flicked up to his. "You really did go see him, then. He knew a spell that would break these." She smiled, pink lips turning up at the corners. "Of course he did. Bassil knows more spells than anyone I know."

Charlie knew these last comments were not really meant for him, that the princess was just thinking out loud, but he didn't want to get her hopes way up when he knew it wasn't quite so simple.

"Yeah," he said, and paused. "Somethin like that."

Surah looked up at him, face wary again instantly. Charlie held up his hand before she could say anything. "Let me explain," he said. "Yes, Bassil knew a spell he thought could work…but he didn't exactly explain very well *how* to get it to work."

Surah laughed shortly, her shoulders relaxing when she hadn't known they'd been tight. Charlie thought her laugh was a pretty sound, like soft bells, even if it was edged with anxiety. She gave him a droll look. "I can perform the spell, Mr. Redmine. I have trained in all Magics since I was a child. Just pour the potion over my wrists and tell me the words I need to know."

Charlie moved toward Surah and took a seat in front of her, folding his large body to the ground. He was close enough that she could hear his slow, steady breaths, could smell the clean scent of him. His handsome face was as unreadable as ever, but Surah thought it was more carefully so than usual. She tried not to let the green of his eyes capture her as he faced her, but it seemed somehow inevitable when he was so near.

She fumbled for words, surprised anew every time he made her do so. "I don't understand," she said. "There must be words to the spell. Tell me what Bassil told you, word for word if you can."

Charlie did. Surah listened with growing horror.

When he was done, Charlie just looked at her. Surah pulled her gaze away from him so she could think for a moment, staring down at her hurting hands. When she looked up again, there was hope in her violet eyes. "Did you get a chance to ask him how he got it to work? What words he used when he performed the spell?"

Charlie nodded. "Yeah. A nursery rhyme."

"A what?"

"A nursery rhyme. You know, like the ones that mothers—"

"I know what a nursery rhyme is."

"Okay."

A string of expletives ran through Surah's head. Her mind was trying to fly a mile a minute and instead seemed to be stuck at a rest stop. A spell that came with no definite language. She concentrated, running back over every bit of her training she could remember. She had learned something about such Magic, she was sure of it. She just had to find the memory in a whole ocean of memories.

She looked at him again, this handsome, mysterious man who she still didn't know if she could trust. She seemed to be changing her mind about him around every corner. Right now he seemed like the only hope she had. Some of her memories came back at this thought, and a small smile found her face.

"What is it then?" she asked. "What did he tell you was the driving force of the spell? If there is no definite language, then the words used must have a specific meaning."

Charlie rubbed his hand over his jaw. Then he looked the princess in the eyes, his glittering like jewels in the dark closeness of the cave. "Love," he told her. "The words must speak the language of love."

CHAPTER FORTY-TWO

Surah's eyebrows shot up. *Love,* she thought. Of course. Now she remembered. It all came back to her in a rush. Bassil had taught her this after the Great War, in which she'd lost her mother and her sister. She had been in a bad place, angry at the world and filled with grief and hate. She remembered what he'd said to her now, word for word.

Do not allow yourself to be full of hate, Princess. Hate is a heavy thing. It weighs us down, chaining us in a dark place. You focus on your love, if you want to be free of this heavy darkness you feel, focus on love. Love is a chariot with a skeleton key to the chains which hate can wrap around you. To love is to be free.

She was pretty sure she'd rolled her eyes when he'd told her this. She wasn't rolling her eyes now. She was thinking. Thinking very hard.

A nursery rhyme, like the ones mothers sing to their children. What did she know of Bassil's mother? Not much, except that he'd lost her when he'd been very young. He rarely spoke of his mother, or about anything in his past, actually, but Surah was sure there had been hints about it in all the years that she'd known the Shaman. He was her instructor after all, and the best of all she'd ever had. To teach that well, one taught with heart and soul, with experience and learned lessons. Now she just had to prove a worthy student and put the pieces together.

And she needed to do it quickly.

Bassil loved his mother, she knew that, but Surah thought that he hadn't known his mother very well, because she had died when he'd been so young. She knew he probably wished he'd had a chance to know her, bet he wondered how his life would have been different had she lived on. This was all speculation of course, but it was based on an overall impression she had of the Shaman, and at least it was a start.

So he'd used a nursery rhyme to perform a spell that could break the chains of Dark Magic. Could the nursery rhyme be one of the only memories Bassil had of his mother? She couldn't be sure, but she thought this was right. Her gut said it was right, because words that meant so much to someone could create powerful Magic indeed.

Charlie was silent as she worked through all this, and now she wasn't sure who would be a better choice to perform the spell. She was trying hard to think of something her mother used to say to her, but other than simple I love you's, most of the things she remembered her mother telling her were about how to be a proper princess. She thought of her sister, but it had been so long since she'd lost Syra that the memories were a distant thing, something she'd probably blocked out long ago so she could get on with her life, and now it pained her to think that she'd done so. Her brother and father were not men who often spoke words of love, they more so showed their care through their actions. She couldn't think of a nursery rhyme, or a lullaby, or even a simple sentence that meant so much to her.

It was such a heavy, defeating thought.

"What're we gonna do, Princess?" Charlie asked.

Surah bit her lip, her eyebrows furrowed now with worry. "I don't know, Mr. Redmine," she said. "I seem to be drawing a blank."

"You must know something, some memory that, I don't know, can fuel this thing."

She stared at him a moment, at the strong line of his jaw. She shook her head slowly. "If I do, it won't come to me right now. I have to think. I don't suppose you have anything that can do it?"

Charlie was silent for a long time, his jade eyes going deep in thought.

"You do?" she asked, her heart leaping with hope.

His shoulders lifted once in a small shrug. "I have to think."

"We don't have much time."

"I know."

Surah sighed and swallowed, wishing she could run her arm across her damp forehead. "Alright," she said. "We may as well get started, because Gods know how long this is going to take. Pour the powder on my wrists and then place your hands on mine. We'll both just have to concentrate. Say whatever words that come to you that you associate with love. I'll do the same." She glanced at the softening daylight beyond the waterfall. "Maybe we'll get lucky."

He did as she asked, popping the cork out of the vial and sprinkling the silver substance over her wrists, where it caught and hung in the black smoke that was holding her in place, like stars dusted over a dark sky. His large, warm hand closed over her numb fingers, which had gone from pulsing heat to terribly cold. His touch soothed her some, even through her thick gloves, and she found herself catching her breath.

"Ready?" she asked.

"Sure."

She took a deep breath and closed her eyes. After a moment of staring at her beautiful face, he did the same, his heart racing in his chest, his body practically humming with tension. This was never going to work in time.

They tried. And tried and tried. He said things that he remembered his mother telling him, sweet things that he still cherished after all these years. He thought of his brother, of the times Michael had saved him from something when they were younger, but thoughts of Michael were ironically unhelpful. She reached back in her mind and recalled the brunches she used to have with Syra and her mother, of the times they'd shared tea and secrets. She thought of Samson, of how he would always call her "love" or "honey" or "sweetheart" when they were alone, of how he would lick her wounds when she was injured.

But nothing worked. The chains remained as immovable as ever. She wouldn't have thought such a task would be so hard, but then she supposed that it really would be for most anyone. Who, when faced with this situation, with the clock practically ticking between thier ears, could think of words that meant so much to them that they could set them free? It was a lot harder than one would think.

Twenty minutes passed. There were both sweating heavily now. Then thirty minutes. Surah was starting to get a headache behind her closed eyes. Charlie's hands were growing moist. Then forty minutes, and at last, Surah opened her eyes, releasing a heavy breath.

"It's useless," she said, and didn't even care that her voice sounded uncharacteristically small.

Charlie's eyes opened and he looked at her. She was looking down at her hands, her face blank of any expression at all. Before he could stop himself, he reached a hand up and placed it under her chin, gently tilting her face up to look at him. She offered no protest.

"No," he said. "It ain't. We just gotta keep tryin. It'll work. It has to."

She shook her head, fighting back more tears. "No, it doesn't."

"Yes, it does."

She cleared her throat. "Why is that?"

"It just does."

Surah looked down at her hands again, clearly not believing him. Charlie sighed at looked around, not sure what he was searching for. His eyes fell on his old wood guitar, where it rested against the wall. His mind leapt with realization at the same time that his heart sunk with it. He stood up slowly, ignoring the princess's raised eyebrows, and went over to where the guitar sat, picking it up and adjusting the strap around his neck. He knew what he had to do, and he had a gut feeling it would work, too. But he wished there was another way. He wished like hell there was another way. If he did this there would be no more hiding, the mask would have to fall free. His soul would have to be bared.

She stared at him. He stared back. Then he settled back down in front of her, the guitar across his lap. He would do it. He had to. She needed him to.

She watched him as his fingers settled over the strings, his hands moving the guitar into position. "You have an idea?" she asked.

He nodded, swallowed. "Yep."

"A song?" she asked, and smiled, that hope flooding back into her violet eyes. "You know a song that speaks about love? What song is it?"

"You've never heard it before."

"I know a lot of songs."

"Not this one."

"How do you know?"

He hesitated, and when his eyes met hers, she saw something there that she couldn't quite pin down. "Because," he said, "I wrote it and I've never played it for anyone before."

Her smile grew. This might actually work. "What's it called?"

Again, he hesitated. "It doesn't have a name," he said.

For some reason, Surah thought this was a lie, and that was because it was. The song did have a name, but Charlie had never spoken it out loud, and he never would, not that it would matter after he played it. After he played it, she would know.

Surah waited silently. Charlie pulled his eyes away, looking down at the instrument in his lap. He'd played the song countless times before, on long nights in his cabin when sleep wouldn't find him. He knew the chords and words perfectly, and riding the rhythm was as easy as breathing to him, but this time was different. This time, his fingers felt stiff over the strings and his voice felt tight in his throat.

"Just play it," she said gently. "It's worth a shot."

Charlie nodded, still staring at the strings. Then he took a deep breath and began to play. His fingers began to strum the strings slowly, releasing a gentle melody. Then they moved a little faster, not much, but a little, the chords taking on a soft rhythm that made goose bumps pop up along her arms. Before he even began to sing the words, Surah could tell this was love song. Just the soft, sweet notes said it was.

Then Charlie began to sing, his deep voice a perfect pitch that accompanied the melody. More goose bumps worked their way across her neck, and she found herself watching his lips move as he sang the words. She listened. She had a feeling that when Charlie Redmine picked up his guitar and played a song, anyone within hearing distance stopped and listened. But it was just the two of them in the small, slowly darkening cave. Just them and the music and his deep, country voice. A humble, beautiful drawl.

The words were simple, lovely. Perfect.

I can imagine
What my father would say
He's been gone a long time
But he never went away
He wasn't the kind of man
Who minced words or spared hearts
He would prob'ly tell me
Our paths are too apart
That it's a cruel world
Not to love that girl
He'd say, son, you might as well shoot at the stars
Cuz the thing you aim to hit is just too far
And there's no way that you can't see
That there's no way this can be
And saying this to you is really hard
But boy, you may as well be shooting at the stars

The world seemed to have fallen away. Surah could no longer feel the pain in her wrists, the ache in her back. She could no longer hear the clock ticking between her ears. All she could hear was Charlie. His deep voice and sweet song and the beating of her heart. He continued to play, filling up the cave with the soft music, filling up the world with it.

And though a fool I may be
That girl could never be in love with me
I can't seem to get her off my heart
Lovin' her was written in the stars.

The tempo picked up again here, his fingers strumming the strings with rapid movements, dancing over them. Surah felt her own pulse quicken, her throat go tight, a taut little knot forming in the pit of her stomach. Then the music slowed again, coming to an end, and Charlie's voice was so quiet as he sang the final words that she had to strain to hear. She didn't realize it, but she was leaning forward.

But there's no way that I can't see
That there's no way this can be
And though on nights like this it's really hard…
…Lovin' her was written in the stars.

Surah's hammering heart stopped and seemed to stay stopped. Her breath halted in her throat. Charlie's fingers stroked the strings slowly, then settled. The last chord hung in the air for a bit, as if she could reach out her hand and touch it, and then silence fell around them. She stared at Charlie and was surprised to find that he was not looking up at her. His eyes were downcast, a direct opposite to his usual direct stare, and she wondered if his cheeks were slightly red under his dark facial hair. There was no way to know.

No way to know, but she did, didn't she? She could feel it. She could hear it whispered on the notes that had faded away and yet seemed to still be lingering in her ears. She could see it on his face, in the jade of his eyes that would no longer meet her own. Perhaps it was presumptuous of her, perhaps she was completely off the mark, but she didn't think so. She thought the song just might belong to her, despite the fact that she had no real reason to believe this. Just a feeling.

She had no idea just how right she was.

She wanted to ask him, but found she didn't have the nerve. How arrogant would that sound? She couldn't just say, hey, you wrote that for me, didn't you? No, she couldn't say that. She wouldn't say that. She opened her mouth to say it.

For whatever reason, she had to know.

But she didn't get the chance, because in front of her, Charlie's eyes widened, and she followed his gaze to see what had made them do so. While listening to his song she had completely forgotten about the restraints around her wrists. She had forgotten about everything, the whole situation, and now that the music had stopped, it all came back with crushing clarity.

And she also couldn't believe what she was seeing.

The black smoke holding her in place was loosening. The relief was instant, though pain still coursed through her fingers. She watched as the Black Magic receded and folded into itself, then disappeared altogether. She wiggled her fingers. It took more effort than it should have. There were angry, red rings around her wrists, like bloody bracelets. She could feel the blood slowly beginning to course back through her fingers, and it felt wonderful and awful at the same time.

She was free.

Without thinking, she threw her arms around Charlie's neck and pulled him into a tight hug, breathing in the fresh scent of him, absorbing his heat. Slowly, his strong arms came up and held her even tighter, their bodies pressed close together, his chest warm and solid against hers.

"Thank you," she whispered against his neck, thinking she should pull away. Lingering.

He was silent for a moment. Then he said, "Anytime."

"Well, isn't this just precious?" said a voice beside them.

Charlie and Surah broke apart instantly, hearts leaping in their chests, eyes going wide like children who have just been caught doing something naughty. They saw him at the same time, saw the Black Stone weighing heavily around his neck, saw the murderous glint in his jade eyes.

Black Heart had returned.

The heels of his boots clicked as he stepped forward, his dark cloak rippling like something alive as he moved. His pale hands came up and slipped the hood back from his head, revealing his dark, slicked-back hair. He was smiling, but there was only malice behind it, making it an oddly terrifying gesture. The antithesis of a smile.

Black Heart clucked his tongue, cold eyes flicking back and forth between Charlie and Surah, who were now on their feet, postures stiff. His eyes settled on Charlie and he shook his head. "I'm disappointed in you, Charlie Boy," he said. "*Extremely* disappointed."

CHAPTER FORTY-THREE

Silence hung between them for what seemed to Surah to be an incredibly long moment. It was as though time itself had paused, as if everything in the universe hung suspended in space. Waiting.

Then, Charlie said, "I guess that makes two of us, brother."

Surah's head jerked toward Charlie, her mind momentarily unable to process coherent thoughts. Charlie Redmine was staring levelly at his brother.

Black Heart shook his head again, his hand coming up and rubbing his jaw. Surah realized this must be a habit for both men, except it was somehow attractive when Charlie did it. "What am I supposed to do with you now, Charlie Boy? You haven't left me many choices."

Charlie's voice answered smooth and calm. "There are plenty of choices."

Surah stood perfectly still, saying nothing. Black Heart looked at her, and she tilted her chin up and held his gaze. He laughed. "Still so proud, are we?" he asked, taking a step toward her.

Surah held her ground, but to her surprise, Charlie moved between her and his brother. His voice sounded more serious than she'd ever heard it when he spoke. "Leave her alone, Michael," he said.

The anger that flashed behind Black Heart's eyes was so intense that Charlie thought he could feel it burning his skin, but he didn't step back. He'd made a promise to the princess. He had no intention of letting Michael hurt her again. But the Black Stone, which seemed to be pulsing a dark, squirming energy into the air, was going to make that promise hard to keep.

Black Heart's eyes fixed on Surah over Charlie's shoulder. His lips were tight when he spoke. "Move aside, little brother."

Charlie folded his arms over his chest. "I'm 'fraid I can't do that."

Black Heart's eyes flicked back to him. "Fine, have it your way."

His hand whipped to the side, and Charlie was lifted from his feet and slammed into the rock wall of the cavern, as if one of the Gods had reached down and slapped him aside. Black Heart's hand was raised, holding Charlie in place without even touching him.

Surah was already in motion.

She moved so fast that Black Heart's one moment of forgetting her was enough. She rushed forward, the sais that had been tucked under her cloak already clutched in her hands, which were still in pain from the restraints. She dropped to the ground and swept her leg around, knocking Black Heart hard in the legs and sending him down to his knees. She raised her weapons, preparing to send them through his neck. She thrust them forward.

But Black Heart was no longer distracted, and before the sharp points of the sais could hit their mark, she was tossed into the air in the same way Charlie had been, scooped up and thrown aside by dark Magic, her body becoming weightless. Then she slammed into the stone wall hard on her left side, knocking her head against it and seeing stars. Pain shot down her body in a hot rush. Black Heart held her pinned to the wall, almost crushing her with the force of the Black Stone's power.

She couldn't move, could hardly breathe. This was it then, she was going to die. The thought made a terribly silent terror boil inside her.

Black Heart was sweating, the Stone around his neck heavy and pulsing heat. The thing was fueled by hate and anger, and Black Heart had plenty of that to spare. But it still was not easy using so much power. He was getting better at it, and soon he would be unstoppable.

He held them both to the walls, like flies caught in a spider's web. His boots clicked as he approached Surah. "I know what to do, little brother," he said, the smile returning to his face as he looked over his shoulder at Charlie. The look in his eyes made Charlie's heart go cold in his chest.

It hurt to talk, took great effort, the force under which he was being held was so cumbersome. But Charlie said, "Let her go, Michael."

Black Heart laughed, and Surah could do nothing but stare at the dark Sorcerer in terror. "Oh, I think not, Charlie Boy," he said. His head tilted as his eyes fell back on Surah. "I think I will make you watch her die. Cure you of this…unhealthy obsession once and for all."

Charlie tried to yell, but Black Heart flicked his wrist and Charlie felt an invisible hand slap over his mouth, cutting off his words. Black Heart moved to stand in front of Surah. Smiling. "I'll give your regards to your father," he said. "Perhaps you two will meet in the heavens."

Surah shook her head. "No, we won't," she said.

Black Heart's head tilted again, his eyes dark and amused and murderous. "Why is that, Princess?"

Surah met his stare, held it. "Because I'll be waiting for you in hell."

Black Heart laughed, deep and bellowing, his wide shoulders shaking. Then his laughter cut off abruptly, as if by a switch, and his hand came up and clenched into a fist. Surah felt a crushing weight drop on her throat, cutting off her air completely. Her eyes bugged out of her sockets, and her vision went black for a second before returning in a blurry haze. Her muscles jerked, but remained plastered to the wall. Her brain began screaming for oxygen. Didn't find any.

Black Heart leaned in close, the look on his face pure joy. "In death you will finally learn how to hold your tongue," he said, and tightened his fist further still. Now the world outside Surah's eyes went black and stayed black, and she knew she was only moments from slipping away, no matter how hard she tried to cling to the surface.

It was almost a relief.

CHAPTER FORTY-FOUR

Samson came to a stop when he reached the water. He lowered his head and lapped at it with his dry tongue, watching all around him, scanning the ground, the trees. She was near, he could feel her, could smell her, and this was where the trail ended. After taking some water he lifted his head and scanned the surroundings again, spotting a waterfall some twenty yards upstream. Behind a wall of water, Drake had said. Samson's gut told him that she was there. He made his way back to the trees and began his cautious approach.

Now that he was here, he knew he would need to move silently, carefully. It was no wonder that the Beasts had steered clear of this area. The dark energy in the air grew thicker as he approached the waterfall. He could almost taste the Sorcerer in the air, the one who had hurt and captured his beloved Surah, and his killer instinct was set ablaze by the scent. But Black Heart had the Black Stone, so Samson would need to wait for the perfect moment to strike, and if the foul energy exuding from the hidden cavern that was behind the waterfall was any indication, that moment was near.

He held his body low to the ground, creeping closer and closer. Now he could hear voices from inside the cave, made indistinguishable by the sound of the rushing water. His ears swiveled and perked, trying to make out what was being said. He needed to get closer.

He reached the waterfall and hopped over onto the rocks that were on its edge, his paws landing silently and lithely. He listened again before moving forward, but the voices had stopped. They were no longer talking. Samson moved forward, the waterfall concealing him, and peeked his head into the dimly lit space. What he saw made a red hot fury burn through his chest.

Surah hung on the wall like some macabre portrait, her limbs limp, eyes closed, pretty face a disturbing blue color. Charlie hung on the opposite wall, his face twisted with silent agony as his eyes stared widely at Surah. Black Heart stood in front of the princess, his back to Samson, his attention focused on killing her and making his brother watch. Samson decided right then that he did not want to kill this man, he *had* to. If it was the last thing he ever did, he had to.

He leaped forward into the air, his ascent soundless, his huge claws extended and large teeth bared. Black Heart's head turned just in time to see the tiger's terrifying face flying at him before Samson landed on his back and sent him crashing to the ground. Black Heart tried to move his throat away, but Samson snagged the necklace holding the Black Stone around his neck between his teeth and snapped the chain, ripping it free. His head whipped to the side and the necklace flew over to the wall, the Black Stone making a sound like rock crashing into rock when it hit the wall. Then it clunked to the ground.

Charlie and Surah fell to the ground in the same moment.

Black Heart still had Surah's piece of White Stone, and he used it to teleport out from underneath the tiger. He removed the sword from beneath his cloak, aiming it at Samson, who was standing over the Black Stone, his head low, amber eyes glowing, teeth bared.

Black Heart moved cautiously forward, his hair standing out around his head, his jade eyes angrier than ever. He held his sword up and spoke between clenched teeth. "I will kill you for that, you stupid beast."

Samson growled, the sound rebounding off the close walls of the cave, like caged thunder. Black Heart teleported to the spot above Samson's back, planning to send his blade through the neck of the tiger, but Samson anticipated this move, and he leapt to the side, swiping at the Black Stone and sending it skidding over near Charlie, who was just finding his feet.

And Surah was finding hers.

She felt like lying down, like closing her eyes and letting sleep take her. Her throat burned and throbbed, her wrists were on fire, and the whole left side of her body was a network of pain. But there could be no resting, not now, and the warrior in her refused to let her do so.

She rushed forward with her sais. Black Heart turned just in time to block her strike with his sword, the weapons clinking together with the sound of metal on metal. Samson sprang forward, and Black Heart spun around, slicing the air with his blade and sending the tiger skidding back out of the way.

Surah struck again. Black Heart evaded. He was faster than she would of thought, which was not at all a good thing. Samson kept trying to get at him, but Black Heart teleported out of the way again and again, doing a disappearing and reappearing dance all around them.

Meanwhile, Charlie Redmine was bending down to pick up the Black Stone. He took a deep breath as his fingers wound around it. He held it tight and said one word.

"Stop."

All three of them, Samson, Surah and Black Heart halted in their movements, their bodies freezing in place. Charlie suppressed a gag as the dark power ran through him, making his head go light and his vision swirl. He was overwhelmed with a feeling of blackness, a feeling that sucked the light out of the world along with all the laughter. It was no wonder his brother had gone insane. The power was potent, noxious.

"Let me go, Charlie Boy," Black Heart said, watching his brother the way a lion will watch a pack of hyenas.

"Kill him, Charlie," Surah said.

Samson just stared.

Charlie kept his fingers firmly locked around the Black Stone, his mind racing with options. He went over to where his brother was frozen in place and put a hand on his shoulder, looking into his eyes. "I'm sorry, Mikey," he said.

Then he moved over to Surah and Samson, taking her by the hand and placing his other on Samson's large back. Black Heart's voice was an angry growl. "She's right, Charlie Boy. If you do this, you're better off just killing me now."

Charlie stared at Michael, knowing that his words were no bluff. If he did this, the line would be drawn, the decision irreversible. If he didn't, that same line would still be crossed, only he would be on the other side. He was stuck firmly between a rock and a hard place.

Surah's eyes flicked to Charlie, her hand warm in his, her fate heavy on his shoulders. She wasn't sure when it had happened, perhaps it was a combination of things, but she trusted Charlie Redmine, and though she wouldn't admit it, not even to herself, she more than trusted him. She *owed* him. Though his face was that smooth, unreadable mask that seemed to be his default expression, she could tell by the look in his jade-colored eyes that this decision was not easy for him, that his heart was split clean down the middle, and he was faced with choosing which side to try and salvage.

She honestly did not know what his answer would be, though looking back she supposed it should have been clear, and they all stood in silence, the only sound that of the rushing water and the thumping of their hearts, and Charlie made up his mind. For better or worse, and everything that would follow, he made up his mind.

He looked at his brother with too many emotions roiling inside of him to make sense of any of them. He supposed there would be time for that later. He had no idea how right he was.

"I can't," Charlie said. "I can't kill you, Mikey. But I can't let you kill her, either."

And then he closed his eyes and teleported himself and the princess and her tiger out of there, the Black Magic from the Stone engulfing them and tossing them across space and time. The last thing he heard before leaving the jungle was Black Heart's howl of anger.

It sounded oddly like a nail being pounded into a coffin.

CHAPTER FORTY-FIVE

They landed in Surah's bedroom in her father's castle, stumbling over their feet and falling to the ground in a heap. Charlie was not so great at teleporting yet, and controlling the Magic using the Black Stone was quite a task. They laid sprawled out on the ground for several moments, trying to catch their breaths and slow their racing hearts. All of them were either injured or exhausted or both. Samson had travelled much further today than his body was built for, and his stomach heaved as he lay on his side panting, his long tongue lolling out of his mouth.

Surah was hurting all over. It would be easier to count the places on her body that were not in pain rather than the other way around. Her wrists were bleeding, her face was swollen, her head pounded and the left side of her body was screaming sorely. Charlie was very close to heaving up the meager contents of his stomach, so nauseated he was from the trip. He couldn't seemed to catch his breath.

So they all just laid there. Surah climbed to her feet first, moving over to Charlie. Her lavender hair was a wavy mess around her face, which was pinched with worry. "Are you okay?" she asked.

Charlie waved a hand, not even trying to make a move to stand. "Be fine," he said. "I should ask you the same."

Surah shrugged. "I'll live."

Charlie gave that small smile of his, still staring up at the ornate ceiling. "That's good."

Well, I'm fine, too, love. Thanks for asking, Samson said in her head.

She moved over to him and crouched down, running her hands through his thick fur. Samson closed his amber eyes and chuffed a little at her touch. *"Thank you, Sam,"* she told him silently. *"You saved my life."*

Samson gave her a toothy smile, his eyes still closed. *What else is new?*

All of a sudden she remembered her father, who was dying from demon poison as they sat here taking stock of each other's injuries. She prayed to the Gods that it was not too late, that the poison could still be reversed. She glanced at the grandfather clock that stood in the corner of the large room, a family heirloom that had been passed down to her from her mother. The hour read six-thirty, and Surah looked over to the arched windows to see the sunlight had nearly bled completely out of the sky.

Charlie had an arm draped over his face, but he lifted it and looked at her. As if he had read her thoughts, he held the Black Stone out for her. "Here," he said. "Take it. Go save your father."

She didn't hesitate, just stepped forward and wrapped her fingers around the cold Stone, her hand brushing against Charlie's warm skin. "Thank you," she said. "I am in your debt, Mr. Redmine."

Charlie draped his arm back over his face and waved his hand again. "Don't worry about it, Princess," he said. "Just go save the king."

Surah nodded. "What are you going to do?"

Charlie peeked out at her beneath his arm. "Lie here for a second, if that's alright."

I second that, Samson said.

"Okay," she said, "but be quiet. If anyone finds you here…it won't be good."

Both Samson and Charlie gave small grunts.

Surah turned toward the door, moving quickly, but when she got there, she turned back. "And Charlie?"

Charlie lifted his head, his eyebrows raised over deep jade eyes. Surah smiled at him. Not her princess smile, but her real one, and it felt right being there. Charlie returned it, thinking of how beautiful she was when she truly smiled. "Yes, Princess?"

Surah opened the door, peering out into the long hallway to find it empty. Thank the Gods. She looked back at him once more. "Call me Surah," she said.

Then she shut the door to the room and raced down the hall in the direction of her father's chambers, hoping beyond hope that she wasn't too late. She was in such a hurry that she did not see Theodine Gray as she rushed by the doorway he was standing in. His eyes narrowed as she ran passed.

Theo stepped out into the hallway after she was gone, his eyes locked on the wood of her chamber doors, wondering what surprises waited behind it. He was sure it would be something. He'd heard her talking to someone, telling someone to call her by her first name, an invitation she had never offered him in all the years he'd known her.

He strode over to the doors and pulled his sword free on his cloak, clutching it in his right hand. Then he flicked his wrist and the double doors to her bedroom swung open.

Theo heard the voice before he saw the man, but he knew just by the slow drawl of the words who it was. His fingers tightened around his sword and a nasty smile appeared on his face.

"You forget somethin?" Charlie asked. He removed his arm from his face and lifted his head to see the tip of the Head Hunter's sword only inches from his nose. Cold gray eyes stared down at him.

Samson was on his feet in less than a heartbeat. A low growl rumbled in his throat. Theo's head twisted to look at the tiger, surprise evident on his face. "Stand down, Beast," Theo told him. "This matter is none of your concern."

Samson made no move to do as he was told. He stood staring at the Head Hunter, his head lowered between his large shoulders and his muscles bunched and ready. Charlie was touched when he realized the tiger was defending him, but Samson had done enough, and killing Theo would do no good for any of them.

At least, that's what he thought. In hindsight, he supposed it may have worked out better if Samson had just ripped out the Head Hunter's throat right then and there. Maybe some of the things that followed could have been avoided. Maybe.

But Charlie Redmine, despite what the kingdom thought of him, was not his brother. He did not murder people. He was just a simple country man, and thus far in his life he'd made tremendous effort to do things the right way, to follow a moral code that the best of Gods could approve of.

Charlie pulled himself to a sitting position, holding his hands up and moving slowly, watching the blade of the Head Hunter's sword that was still trained on him. He gave a small nod to Samson, and to both men's surprise the tiger relaxed his stance and moved over to the arched window, plopping down to the floor. He set his huge head on his paws and watched them, his amber eyes closing and his breathing going back to normal. He was seriously beyond exhausted, and if the fool didn't want any help, the fool wasn't going to get any. His Surah was safe, and that was really all that mattered.

Theo's smile wide and white, his gray eyes full of triumph. "I would kill you now," Theo said, "but I'm afraid there is a whole kingdom who would like to watch you die, and I am not selfish enough to deny them the pleasure."

Charlie, his hands still held up in surrender, pulled himself to his feet. He said nothing at all to this.

Theo gestured to the door with the tip of his sword, his grin wide and eyes shining. "Get walking, dead man. You've got yourself a date with the devil and I'm going to make sure you keep it."

Charlie allowed himself to be led out, cursing himself for resting on

Surah's floor when he would have been better off climbing out the window and trying to scale down the tower which held her bedroom. At least then he would have a chance at escape, and if he fell and died, at least his death would be quick.

It was clear just by the Head Hunter's face that he could expect no such mercy from him. If Charlie was a betting man, he would have bet all his marbles that Theo was going to enjoy this. He rubbed his hand down his jaw and thought, *well, damn.*

CHAPTER FORTY-SIX

"Why isn't it working?"

Bassil lifted his hand and placed his palm on her father's forehead. "It is working, Princess," he said. "His fever is already breaking. You just have to be patient. The demon poison has been in his system for too long. It could take several weeks for him to fully recover."

Surah's mouth fell open, and she snapped it shut and clenched her teeth, fighting back tears. It was hard to look at her father this way. She had never seen him look so bad before. His skin was a startling ashy white, like old chalk, and his usually perfectly combed hair sat in thin tangles atop his head. She could see his chest rising and falling with thin, inadequate breaths, his eyes closed as if they would remain that way forever. He looked like a dying man.

All the emotions she had been bottling came rushing over her in a harsh wave, and her knees buckled. Bassil grabbed her elbows gently, supporting some of her weight, his dark face drawn with concern.

"Perhaps you should be resting, Princess," he said. "You don't look well."

Surah shook her head and locked her knees, smoothing her cloak out with shaking hands. "I'll be fine," she said.

Bassil gave her a dubious look but offered no protest.

Surah moved a chair over by her father's bed and took a seat, staring at the Black Stone sitting atop her father's chest. She could see the Black Magic at work inside the Stone, which seemed to slither and writhe, sucking out the poison that was running rampant in her father's body.

"I just want to stay with him for a while," she said. "I will rest as soon as I am able."

Bassil quirked an eyebrow. "You mean when you can no longer stand on your own two feet?"

Surah gave no answer, just sat watching her father, wishing he would open his eyes and smile at her. She knew Bassil was right. She was in more pain than she cared to admit at the moment, and the thought of crawling under her covers and falling into a deep sleep sounded like pure heaven. But she would do no such thing. She would just sleep in this chair if she had to. She wanted to be there when her father woke up. She had to, because despite what Bassil said, some panicked part of her feared that Syrian might not wake up at all. After all the events of the past two days, the thought of leaving him was just beyond her.

Bassil released a slow sigh. Then he bent at the waist and placed a small kiss on her forehead. "All right, Princess," he said. "Do as you please. I will be back in soon to check on you. I'll bring you some soup. I bet you don't even remember the last time you ate." His nose wrinkled. "And you may want to consider taking a shower. You don't smell good."

Surah gave a short laugh, but there was no humor in it. "Anything else, Shaman? I suppose you also want to tell me that I'm having a bad hair day?"

Bassil smiled. "As a matter of fact…"

Surah rolled her eyes. "Oh, just be gone with you," she said.

Bassil chuckled as he stepped out into the hall and shut the door behind him. He turned around to find himself face to face with Theodine Gray. The Head Hunter gave him an annoyed look. "Get out of my way, Shaman," he said.

"The king is resting, Hunter Gray."

Theo nudged Bassil aside. "I have no intention of waking him," he said, opening the door to the king's bedroom and shutting it in Bassil's face before the Shaman could protest.

Surah's head turned as he entered. She said nothing, just sighed internally and turned back to her father.

Theo took a few steps toward her. "I'm glad to see you've returned safely, Princess," he said, and his eyes fell on the Black Stone resting on Syrian's chest. "And you've brought back the Black Stone as well. Impressive."

Surah's hand came up and she rubbed at her forehead. "Thank you, Hunter Gray," she said.

Theo spied the red ring around her wrist that peeked out of her cloak sleeve, and he stepped around the bed, anger spiraling in his belly as he took in the black and purple bruise on the left side of her face. "Who did that to you?" he asked.

Surah's voice sounded robotic when she spoke. She considered lying, but saw no point in it. "Black Heart," she said.

"So he did have you captive, then?"

Surah nodded, her eyes still glued to her father.

"And how did you escape?"

Surah looked up now. "If you don't mind, Sir Gray," she said, using great effort not to speak between clenched teeth, "I would like some time to rest. I'm sure you will get all the details from my father, after I speak with him, but for now, I'm tired. It's been an extremely long day. I believe some silence is in order."

Theo gave a low bow, and Surah watched him closely as he did so, unable to tell how he was taking this command. She didn't even really care if he was offended. She was too tired and hurt and worried to care.

Theo moved toward the door again, flicking his wrist so that it swung open. He stopped when he got there and looked back at her. She was still facing the bed. "Of course, my Princess," he said. "I've other things to attend to anyhow."

Surah said nothing, and Theo's anger grew as he stared at the back of her lavender head, the curve of her fine neck.

In a light voice, he said, "I've got a prisoner to question and a very probable execution to arrange, pending trial, of course."

Theo saw her shoulders tighten a fraction. He smiled.

Surah's head turned to the side, looking at him over her shoulder, her violet eyes narrowed. "What are you talking about?"

"I don't want to scare you," he said. "But Charlie Redmine was found lying in wait in your chambers about an hour ago." He paused. Surah's teeth clenched at the dramatic effect. "Don't worry, Princess. You're safe now. The traitor is locked away in the dungeons, and you have my word that it will be the last place he ever sees on this earth."

Then Theo shut the door behind him, leaving Surah alone with her unconscious father, her heart jackhammering in her chest. She rubbed her forehead with her fingers and thought, *well, damn.*

CHAPTER FORTY-SEVEN

Two days had passed and her father had yet to gain full consciousness. He awoke only a handful of times, and even then his eyes stayed just below half-mast, his voice coming out in nonsensical mumbles. Surah was present for every awakening, leaning over his bedside and smiling down at him with unshed tears in her eyes. He was getting better. She could see that, but Bassil had been right about the king's recovery taking some time, which seemed to be the one thing she'd been running short on lately.

She stayed by her father as many hours of the day as she could spare, which was not as many as she would have liked. She had been a busy girl these past two days, tending to royal matters in her father's stead, making comforting speeches to the people, most of whom were completely unaware of how close they'd come to losing their king.

On top of that, she'd been trying to figure out how to clear Charlie Redmine's name. To put it truthfully, she'd been trying to find a way to save his life.

It wasn't as easy a task as one might think it should be.

The royals were angry, and understandably so, but that didn't make their refusal to see reason any less aggravating. They were calling for blood in the names of their lost ones. She had spoken to several of them privately, including the parents of Merin Nightborn and Cynthian Lancer, to try and explain that Charlie Redmine was not like his brother, that he had assisted in her escape, that he had nothing to do with the murders of their children.

Lady Nightborn responded with a threat to take the matter to the public. Lord Lancer accused Surah of having a soft heart, of incapable of ruling because she was a woman, and even used the word coward.

To say the least, the talks had gone less than well.

And to make matters worse, Theo seemed determined to keep his promise. Surah wasn't sure why Theo wanted Charlie dead, except that she suspected he knew more than he was letting on. She told herself that was silly, that there was no way Theo could know about the…relationship between her and Charlie, if you could even call it that.

She'd visited him in the dungeons, but only once, and for less than five minutes, just long enough to tell him she was trying to clear his name, to assure him she hadn't forgotten about him, and that everything would be all right.

But everything was not all right. Everything was about as far from all right as it could get.

Her father couldn't help her, not in his condition, and she knew the royals would not wait long enough for him to recover. Theodine Gray wouldn't wait, either. They wanted answers, an open and shut trial, and yes, an execution. On top of that, Black Heart was still on the loose, probably plotting his crazy revenge.

The only fortunate thing so far was that Jude Flyer had been surprisingly eager to help when she'd come to him, asking him to defend Charlie. The pudgy little man's face had lit up, and he'd listened to Surah's story—with the understanding that it was completely confidential—with excited attentiveness. She'd told him the truth, leaving out the parts that didn't seem to require adding, like the song Charlie had sung her to set her free, like the embrace they'd shared that had made her insides twist and her chest go warm. Those things had nothing at all to do with the matter.

Or so she kept telling herself.

But even with Jude Flyer's help, the odds of getting Charlie clear of the charges were not looking good, and Jude had told her this flat out. Charlie—Jude referred to him as Chuck, but Surah only thought of him as Charlie—was the only witness to the murder of Merin Nightborn and Brad Milner. The place they died was his establishment. He was the brother of a feared criminal, kin to a known outlaw. These things may all have been circumstantial, but all he had in his favor was the word of the princess, and grieving people could be relentless in their efforts for revenge.

They had a bird in the hand and they wanted its bones crushed under their fingers.

Surah sat in her chambers now, having sought a few moments of peace away from her father's room, which she had come to think of as the Sick Room. She sat up in the wide window sill beside Samson, her knees drawn up and tucked under her cloak. She stared out at the kingdom below, at the ornate houses and tall towers, at the glittering lights and purple pathways and red rooftops. People moved around down there, going about their lives as if nothing was wrong, completely unaware of the turmoil going on inside the castle. This was why she envied them sometimes. It seemed like such a dream to be able to live life so simply, a thing she could only see but never touch.

She was not fit to rule a kingdom. She'd suspected so before, but she knew now. Her respect for her father had grown greatly. It was a terrible thing to be under this kind of pressure, to have people depending on her to do what was right and fix things, as if the things that were broken could even be fixed.

A knock sounded on her door, and she climbed down from the window and stood, smoothing out her cloak as she did so. With a flick of her wrist, the door swung open, and Bassil stood there. The grave look on his face sent a shiver down her spine.

The Shaman entered the room and shut the door behind him, his patchwork coat flipping with his rushed movements. Surah stepped forward, her pulse racing. "What's going on?" she asked.

The big man said nothing, just took her by the hands and pulled her to a seat on the bed. Surah was surprised by this, but offered no protest. She was too busy just breathing.

"I'm afraid I have bad news, Princess," Bassil said.

Surah's heart dropped. She'd suspected as much, but hearing him say it was worse. Her face was carefully void of expression, her voice painfully light. "And what news is that?"

Bassil's dark brown eyes held hers for a long moment. Then he said, "Charlie Redmine will not live to see the morning."

CHAPTER FORTY-EIGHT

Surah couldn't think of a single thing to say. She just sat there, staring at him, her face smooth and blank. After several minutes Bassil cleared his throat. "Those who are angry have arranged his death, my Lady. They have no plans to let him see trial."

Surah let out a slow breath. "How did you come by this knowledge?"

"In the way that I come by all knowledge, my Lady. I am a Watcher, as you well know. I believe it is the real reason your father has kept me around for so long. I see most all that goes on within the castle and city." He gave her a knowing smile, and Surah looked away.

Bassil's deep voice was just a whisper now. "You know I speak truth, Princess."

"Who is behind it, Bassil? Who has given the word?"

"There are several, and I bet you could guess most of them, but that's not really what's important right now." The Shaman reached into his cloak and removed his pocket watch. He flipped the face open, looked at it, and flipped it shut again. His dark face was deadly serious when he looked back up at her. "How did your Charlie put it? Time is...of an essence."

Surah stood from the bed and paced over to the window, where Samson still sat, his head raised, ears perked. "Why do you call him 'my Charlie'?" she asked. "That man is not mine."

Bassil's head tilted, and his white teeth flashed in a small smile. "No?"

Surah threw her hands up, all the frustration and anxiety that had been building up the past two days snatching away her composure. "Enough of this, Bassil. If you've got something to say, speak plainly. I am not in the mood for games. What is it you think, that I'm in love with the man?"

"I never said that, Princess."

Surah placed a gloved hand on her hip, trying to keep the pink out of her cheeks. "Then what are you saying?"

Bassil sighed and stood. He went over to Surah and placed his large hands on her shoulders. "What I am saying, Princess, is just what I said. I make no suggestions or accusations. What you do with the information is your decision. Forgive me, but I thought it would be of your interest. I may be wrong, but the point is, Charlie Redmine will not live to see the sunrise on this day if he remains where he is."

Surah looked over at Samson, and the tiger could see plainly the horror in her lovely violet eyes. He had been mostly silent over the past couple days, as if brooding over something he hadn't bothered to tell her, and of course, he was. But he could see she wanted his council, his help. Her eyes begged him to tell her what to do, to make the decision for her, as if there was a choice here at all. As if there ever was a choice.

What he said was: *More than the moon loves the night and the sun loves the day.*

Surah did not know what to say to this, so she said nothing.

CHAPTER FORTY-NINE

Charlie sat in the corner of his cell on the cold, hard ground. The dungeons were nothing like the cozy hotel room where they'd held him the first time. The dungeons were exactly what they sounded like, dark and damp and unpleasant. There wasn't even anything to sit on, just three stone walls and a barred forth. They'd placed a bucket in the corner of the cell for him to do his business, and brought by three bland meals a day that only left Charlie hungrier than before. It was quiet down here in the bowels of the castle, so quiet that he could hear the rats scurrying around and the drips of water trickling down the walls. The place smelled too, like mold and body odor and feces.

He wondered why he never suspected that a place like this existed in the kingdom, but then again, why would he? Most common folk wouldn't. He had subscribed to the belief that the legal system was a flawed, but mostly fair system, but he could see how foolish that was now. Of course they had places like this, of course they had secrets.

It didn't so much make him angry as it made him sad. He had to admit that his brother had a point, if this was how the royals did business behind the walls of the castle. He hadn't even had a trial yet, and already he felt like the noose was being strung around his neck.

The worst part of it was, even if he could go back, he wouldn't have done anything differently, except maybe he would have hidden when Theodine Gray had found him in the princess's room, but even then he'd still be a wanted man. It all seemed terribly inevitable, as if it had been written in stone long ago.

He knew they would come for him. They were like a bunch of Beasts who had scented blood, and they would come for him. If the feeling in his gut was correct, they would come for him soon. He could only imagine the look on Theodine Gray's face when he carried out the deed, because his other gut feeling was that the Head Hunter would be the one to do it. The man had even promised to do so. Rather plainly.

When the princess popped into his cell at about quarter passed midnight, Charlie damn near jumped out of his boots with surprise. He found his feet and stood facing her, making sure it was really her, even though he knew, as it was hard to see clearly in the dim light.

But even in darkness he would know her. There could be no mistaking.

His voice came out in a deep whisper. "Surah."

She came forward and took his hands, surprising him, making his heart leap. "Charlie," she breathed, releasing a long breath, as if she had been worried he wouldn't be here.

Charlie bent his neck down to look her in the eyes. "You okay?" he asked.

She gave a quiet laugh, but it was ringed with anxiety. Her high cheekbones were flushed, and her violet eyes kept darting around the cell. "Oh, I've been better," she said.

Charlie just looked at her, his shoulders relaxed, face calm. "What's going on?"

Surah spoke lowly and quickly, deciding to get on with it before she lost her nerve and changed her mind. "That song you sang to break the spell, to free me," she said. "What was the name of it?"

Charlie's throat tightened, and for a second his mind could form no words. He looked down at his hands, which were still clutched in hers, the rich fabric of her gloves soft against his skin. He spoke his answer in a whisper, with more hesitancy in his voice than she had ever heard from him before, as if it pained him to speak it.

"Surah's Song," he said. "It's called Surah's Song."

And what he did next took even him by surprise, but especially her. His strong arms encircled her waist, sliding under her cloak and pulling her to him, pressing their bodies close together. His hand came up and lifted her chin. Then he brought his face down and kissed her on the lips.

Surah's mind raged at her to pull away, but her body leaned into him, her own hands coming up and her fingers holding his face to hers. His arms tightened around her waist, and she was glad for this because her knees were feeling less than sturdy. Her heart was thumping in her chest, her blood racing and rushing through her veins, and no matter how much she told herself she should stop this, she was powerless to do so. She didn't want to pull away. She didn't want the moment to end. She didn't want his lips to ever leave hers. Not ever.

And it would have gone on longer. It would have lasted a lifetime, and in a way, she supposed it would, but then a voice spoke from the shadows outside the cell, and the moment was broken like so much shattered glass. She could almost hear the crack.

The voice said only one word, but the cold, hard way it was spoken was enough for both Charlie and Surah to know the speaker instantly, and they looked over to see the gray eyes of the Head Hunter staring at them from the shadows beyond the cell.

Theodine Gray said, "Traitor."

And there was murderous anger laced in his tone.

Surah did not allow herself time to think. She just took Charlie Redmine's hand and wrapped her other around her sister's Stone that hung around her neck, a temporary replacement for the one she planned to get back from Charlie's brother.

Because she was sure she would be seeing Black Heart again. It was not over between them. No, she had a feeling it had only just begun.

She took a single deep breath and teleported Charlie out of there, the imprint of Theo's angry gray eyes stuck behind her lids like a flash of light. Surah held his hand tightly as they flew over space and time, wondering what in the world she was doing. It felt so much like the closing of an envelope and the opening of a door.

She understood the words of Charlie's song now, *her* song. It really was as if it all had been written in the stars.

Like fate, sealed with a kiss.

The End...For now.

Look for book two of The Surah Stormsong Novels, Falling Stars, coming in September 2013.

ACKNOWLEDGEMENTS

As always, thank you to my mother, who gets me through the ups and downs that accompany being an author. I'm pretty sure I wouldn't be able to do this without you. I love you.

To my father, for encouraging this dream when so many others told me it was futile. I showed them, huh pop? I love you.

To my family, for being there for me when it matters most.

To Regina Wamba, thank you for bringing this cover to life. I never doubted you.

To all the readers and bloggers out there who have been so welcoming and supportive. I am honored to be a part of the warm community. I love you all.

Finally, to my daughters, Soraya and Akira, for just being. You know every bit of this is for you. I love you more than life.

ABOUT THE AUTHOR

H.D. Gordon is the bestselling author of The Alexa Montgomery Saga, the Surah Stormsong novels, and a paranormal thriller entitled *Joe*. She is a lifelong reader and writer, a true lover of words. When she is not reading or writing, she is raising her two daughters, playing a little guitar and spending time with her family. She is twenty-four years old and lives in the northeastern United States.

Connect with H.D. Gordon:

Website: http://hdgordon.com/
Twitter: https://twitter.com/#!/hd_gordon
Facebook: https://www.facebook.com/HDGordonauthor
Goodreads:http://www.goodreads.com/author/show/5189455.H_D_Gor
don

Made in the USA
Charleston, SC
06 June 2013